I MARRIED A BIRDMAN

Prime Mating Agency

REGINE ABEL

COVER BY
Regine Abel

Copyright © 2021

CONTENTS

I MARRIED A BIRDMAN

Her sacrifice could save her people.

Luana's colony is under threat of an impending attack. As the sole child of their grievously wounded leader, she seeks aid from the only other native species on the planet. Consenting to a marriage of convenience with one of the Zelconians, a peaceful bird-like race, would secure the protection her village desperately needs. As much as that prospect terrifies her, Luana cannot deny being intrigued by the hybrid she is to marry, with his strange eyes full of stars, his majestic wings, and his hypnotic voice.

Dakas is shocked when his soul clamors for Luana the moment she enters their Council chamber. Who would have thought the brewing war would have finally allowed him to find his soulmate? Her delicate and demure appearance cannot fool his empathic abilities. Dakas senses the fire and strength burning within Luana. He's more than eager to take the human as his mate to serve both of their peoples' best interests. But he wants more than to protect her village; he wants to conquer her heart.

Can Luana embrace their union despite the circumstances, or will the war destroy any chances they had of a future together?

DEDICATION

To all those who faced tragedies, dealt with terrible hardships, or lived in fear and refused to let it break you. Once you've reached the bottom of despair, the one path remaining is up. Whatever challenges are thrown at you, the only guarantee of defeat is giving up.

CHAPTER 1
LUANA

I checked on my grievously wounded father once more, then exited the medical clinic with a heavy heart. Outside, the villagers of Kastan—the human colony on Cibbos—had gathered near the stables to see me off.

I hated being in this position. I was only twenty-six and a physician, not a diplomat, and certainly not a leader. But apparently, being our leader's *daughter* meant, the minute things went belly up, it became my job to pick up the pieces and clean up the mess.

I'd warned my father not to go out on that scouting mission to spy on our belligerent neighbors, the Yurus. They were one of two native sentient species on the planet Cibbos. With an average height of seven feet and a weight of over three hundred pounds—of pure muscle—the Yurus looked like the offspring of a furry minotaur and an orc. They had only three passions in life: fighting, fucking, and feeding … in that order. It was a miracle—an unfortunate one—that they hadn't wiped themselves out from within. They usually resolved their constant conflicts with bloody, and often deadly, duels.

And now they'd set their sights on our colony. We'd butted

heads countless times over the decades since we'd settled on this planet. Normally, a bribe in food—a portion of our harvest, herd, and processed goods—sufficed to appease them. Not this time. They appeared hellbent on slaughtering those who could laughably be described as our defenders and enslaving the rest of us.

Our only hope—a flimsy one at best—rested in the feathered hands of our neighbors. The Zelconians lived high in their mountainous realm to the west, the sky city of Synsara. We'd never had much contact with them, as they had not welcomed our illegal arrival on Cibbos. However, so long as we didn't interfere with their lives, they'd been content to let us be.

Martin led my zeebis, Goro—a native species resembling a winged ibex—out of the stables. I would have preferred he hadn't. Martin always tried too hard and refused to see the writing on the wall. Aside from the fact that I had zero interest in his increasingly less-than-subtle advances, my mount didn't like him either. Now Goro would be agitated, which made him more challenging to fly.

I took the reins from him with a stiff nod while he flashed me his signature 'I-am-the-sexiest-man-in-this-godforsaken-colony' smile that always gave me the creeps. Technically, he was indeed the most attractive man in the colony. At twenty-eight, Martin had most women in Kastan drooling over his tall frame, muscular body, golden-blond hair, hazelnut eyes, and pouty lips, which he loved to purse at them in a way he thought sexy. I just thought it gave him a duck face. Being the village's carpenter and mason kept him fit. To the ladies' delight, and my utter annoyance, he never missed an opportunity to strut about shirtless, flexing his abs.

I wished he would let himself be caught by one of the women who were more than willing to put that ball and chain around his ankle. But no. He wanted me. Not for my beauty, brain, or sunny disposition, but because I was the colony leader's daughter. Martin saw me as his ticket to becoming Dad's heir, which was dumb since Dad had been *chosen* by the colony when our previous leader passed away. The next one would be elected in a similar fashion.

Goro bumped his snout against my arm in greeting. I rubbed his forehead and patted his long, recurved, ridged horns. The zeebis rams, like my Goro, made amazing flying mounts. Their protective instincts towards their owners also made them great defenders in a sticky situation. Our colony bred and trained them with the hope of establishing a profitable trade market with other member planets of the United Planets Organization. However, we were considered an illegal colony for having settled, without the blessing of the UPO, on a planet designated as "primitive." And we had a long way to go to get back into their good graces.

Goro lowered his wings to allow me to hop onto his back. Hope gleamed in the eyes of all assembled. A silly hope that I, too, was foolishly clinging to.

"Are you sure you don't want me to accompany you?" Martin asked.

I shook my head, fighting the urge to roll my eyes at that bullshit offer. He didn't want to go anywhere near the Zelconians —even less than I did. A part of me wanted to call his bluff. The malicious side of me would have derived great pleasure at his dismay. He wanted the prestige of being a leader but not the headaches that came along with it. He also lacked the diplomatic skills required to handle this situation. I couldn't risk him sabotaging what little chance we had of receiving help from above— quite literally.

In response to my vocal command, Goro took flight amid the cheers and encouragements of the villagers. Normally, I flew my zeebis to enjoy a moment of freedom and relaxation. I loved feeling the wind blow through my hair while I gazed upon the untamed beauty of this world—the only home I had ever known. But not today. Eyes locked to the high, distant mountains of Synsara, I replayed each of the arguments I would present to the

Zelconian Council in the desperate hope of securing an alliance with them.

As I closed in on my destination, I noticed majestic silhouettes flying around the different entrances carved into the mountain face of the multi-level city. Numerous large terraces could be seen with some even larger ones in the immense town square between two peaks. As I understood it, this was only one of three plazas—the other two were protected within the mountain.

Our village reflected the simple life my ancestors had desired and which led them to this planet. Synsara similarly reflected the Zelconians' aspirations to beauty, technological advancement, and power. Each entrance was exquisitely carved and highly adorned with a variety of luminous crystals.

I didn't know much about those crystals, only that the Zelconians grew them and had a way of imbuing them with unique powers. And I didn't doubt for a second that, as pretty as they looked, many of those crystals could turn my mount and me into charred husks if they believed us to be a threat.

A pair of Zelconians, probably guards, flanked us. Their demeanor was courteous as they expected my presence. The one on the left gestured with his head for me to follow. Saying I was intimidated would be the understatement of the century. These guys were just as tall and muscular as the Yurus, but beautiful feathers covered their otherwise naked humanoid bodies. Their uncanny faces had a wide beak, and a stunning crown of feathers that vaguely reminded me of a handheld fan, topped their heads. Their gigantic wings flapped powerfully as they cast sideways glances back at me. And those eyes ... Good heavens! They looked like they had trapped a constellation of stars within.

My escorts landed on one of the largest balconies, and I settled Goro next to them. There were no obvious stables around, not like they would need any.

"Does your mount need to be tied, or will he stay?" one of the two males asked.

"Goro will stay," I said in a nervous voice.

"Very well," he replied with a nod, his deep yet musical voice strangely soothing. "This way, please."

The two massive doors leading into what appeared to be their gathering hall or Council chamber lay wide open. I felt tiny and exposed as I entered the circular room. At least two dozen Zelconian males and females—all of their starry eyes locked on me—sat on high stools in a half circle at the back of the room. Intimidated didn't begin to describe how I felt. And yet, I couldn't help being relieved that the entire population of the Zelconians' capital city wasn't crammed into the room, bearing witness to my making a fool of myself as I groveled for assistance.

I didn't know any of the other Zelconians in the room, but I didn't need to be told that the extremely imposing male in the middle—with the blue crest on his head that matched the down feathers on his chest—was their leader, Graith. He exuded an incredible aura of authority. He gestured to the single chair and small table in front of the council. I made my way there and sat down.

I tried not to be obvious as I observed my "hosts." Most of them had black, dark-brown, or midnight-blue feathers covering their wings and body, with skin tone to match. They had brighter feathers on their crest and chest.

A single male among them held my attention. Unlike the others, he didn't possess a beak, but a very sexy pair of human lips. He also had stunning midnight-blue feathers on his shoulders. They quickly tapered off to reveal impressive biceps and muscular human arms. A golden crest on his head somewhat matched the color of the down feathers on his chest. The latter also tapered off, giving me an enticing glimpse of the type of sexy chiseled abs that would have Martin eating his heart out.

Although I couldn't see any clothes on him—or on any of the other Zelconians for that matter—this one appeared to have the same kind of down feathers around his private area to hide the goods. Due to his sitting position, I couldn't say if he could also to retract his genitals into his body. But his bare legs were definitely human, aside from the smattering of blue scales—a slightly darker shade than his skin—around his calves, ankles, and feet. While his bare feet and toes looked generally human, something was definitely off about them.

It was common knowledge that the first humans to have visited Cibbos had mingled with the Zelconians. But I'd never heard about them fraternizing, let alone having offspring. However, this specific male appeared to be of an age with me or maybe a few years older. There was no way anyone from our colony could have been his parent. Were our winged neighbors entertaining closer ties with off-worlders—human ones at that—than we had realized?

And above all, would that play in our favor?

Some amused chuckles made me realize I had been rudely examining the hybrid in my stunned fascination. My face burned with embarrassment, and my head jerked towards Graith. I could only hope that my gawking hadn't offended or sunk my chances. To my relief—but confusion—all the faces around me had the same knowing smile.

"Greetings, Luana, daughter of Colony Leader Mateo Torres," their leader said in a booming voice. "I am Graith Devago, Exarch of the Zelconians. You have requested an audience."

"Greetings, Graith Devago, Exarch of the Zelconian people," I said, proud that my voice sounded firm despite my wobbly knees. "Thank you and your Council for agreeing to see me on such short notice."

I nervously tucked a strand of hair behind my ear while gathering my thoughts. From what little we knew of the Zelconians, they were rumored to possess some psychic abilities. Therefore, the intensity with which they were looking at me was beyond unnerving. I only prayed they weren't mind readers.

"As you can probably guess, something serious has occurred that has prompted me, instead of my father, to disturb you in your city. Although the conditions under which my ancestors settled on Cibbos may have been questionable, our humble colony of Kastan has tried to be a peaceful neighbor to both the Zelconians and Yurus."

My heart soared when most of them slowly nodded in agreement.

"However, things have always been a little tense with the Yurus," I added.

Graith snorted as if I'd stated the obvious. "They are warmongers. The only peace to be had with the Yurus is by not mingling with them *at all.*"

"We are in agreement on that," I replied. "However, *they* are not leaving *us* alone. They keep launching the occasional small-scale raids on our village and randomly attacking our foragers in the woods, not to kill but to wound or harass—essentially, bullying tactics. Lately, things have escalated quickly in both violence and frequency. A week ago, Chieftain Vyrax informed us that Kastan and our surrounding territory would be annexed to their capital city, Mutarak. We must either submit to his rule or leave. Those who resist will be executed."

Graith and a few other of the Councilors cocked their heads to the side in that way birds often did, their uncanny eyes narrowing. I couldn't read their expressions.

"Leaving isn't an option," I continued. "All of our colonists were born here. Cibbos is the only home we know. But even if we wanted to leave, where would we go? And with what technology? Our ancestors came here specifically to go back to a simple life, mostly devoid of the trappings of technology. We no longer have a vessel capable of space travel."

I shifted on my seat, hating both how helpless I felt and how pathetic our colony sounded. But there would be no hiding our sad reality from the Zelconians. I could only hope they would take pity on our plight and aid us.

"Fighting the Yurus isn't a viable option," I continued. "We're not warriors. Earlier today, my father led most of our able-bodied men on a reconnaissance mission to assess the imminence of an attack. We lost two men, and all of the others returned severely injured. My father is still in a fairly critical state, but I am confident he will recover."

"I am sorry to hear about the hardships you are facing," Graith said in a detached voice that immediately ignited a sense of dread within me. "In truth, I am amazed the Yurus allowed you to remain in relative peace for so long. Then again, I shouldn't be surprised. After all, you have done all the work of developing thriving farms and orchards, healthy livestock to feed their people, and a nice village for their overpopulated capital city to expand into. The question is: how is that our concern?"

My heart sank. It took every ounce of my willpower not to show how much his words devastated me. I'd hoped for a different response, despite knowing this would likely be the one I received. Why indeed would they care when we'd hardly exchanged two words in decades? Whether humans were wiped out on Cibbos or not would make zero difference to their lives.

"Because once they are done with us, they will come after you," I said with conviction.

Graith smirked. "Like humans, they are land bound. Synsara is much too high and out of their reach."

"But we breed zeebises in Kastan," I countered. "Once they've wiped us out, they will have an entire stable of the finest flying mounts to come after you."

"It sounds to me like you're saying we should slaughter your herd of zeebises before the Yurus get to you in order to protect our city," said another Zelconian with a dark red crest and chest feathers who sat right next to Graith.

Graith chuckled. "Although he put it in a brutal fashion, Skieth has a point."

"No, that is not what I'm saying," I replied stiffly, glaring at the male named Skieth before turning back to Graith. "Whether with our zeebises or otherwise, the Yurus *will* come after you. They have also acquired an insane amount of technology over the past few months, increasing exponentially in recent days. They are too undisciplined to be developing it themselves, so I can only surmise that they are trading."

By the way Graith's expression, already difficult to read, went totally neutral, I guessed he'd been aware of this for a while but hadn't wanted to show his hand.

"If we joined forces, we might have a chance of defeating them," I continued.

"Assuming they truly are in a technological armament race, why would we split our forces protecting humans who are essentially helpless?" Graith asked in a conversational tone.

The absence of contempt or aura of superiority from him almost made it hurt more. He wasn't being cruel or dismissive, merely logical and factual. The worst part was, in his shoes—although he wore none—I'd ask the same questions. Why indeed would they spread themselves thin for us who were as weak as newborn babes?

"If the Yurus come after us, the wisest course of action for Zelconians is to preserve our forces," Graith continued in a gentle voice. "I sympathize with your situation, but you have nothing to offer us."

"I disagree," I said, lifting my chin defiantly. "I'm a doctor. Healers are always greatly needed during a war. I may not know much about Zelconian anatomy right now, but I learn quickly. As for the other members of the colony, we have farmers and crafters who can provide food, weapons, armor, and whatever else is needed to support those who will go to the front."

"All practical things," Graith conceded. "But they are too

little compared to the strain it would put on us to protect your people. I suggest you contact the United Planets Organization."

Each of his words struck me like a searing blade stabbing me in the heart.

"I've already reached out to the UPO," I replied stiffly.

"And? What was their response?" the hybrid asked with undisguised curiosity. His voice, deep but incredibly soft, caused goosebumps to erupt all over my skin.

"They said they would study our case. Which means they will then look into what refugee planet they can dump us on. You may not have welcomed us to Cibbos, but this is our home!"

I hated the pleading edge that had seeped into my voice. For a split second, I thought maybe my words had gotten through to the hybrid. He was half-human. Surely, he would want to support us? But he merely nodded, his face taking on the same neutral expression the others were displaying.

"Maybe they will surprise you with a different outcome." Graith's gentle but firm tone made it clear this audience had run its course. "Although we cannot help you at this point in time, we would appreciate it if you kept us informed of your final plans based on whatever your UPO offers you."

I clenched my teeth, fighting back the tears pricking my eyes. I'd known coming here had been a long shot, and yet, I felt crushed. My tongue burned with the urge to tell him to go suck on a rotten egg.

"Whatever you may think, Exarch Graith, you need us far more than you realize," I said proudly. "You cannot be strong without someone weaker lifting you up."

My gaze roamed over the twelve Zelconians in attendance, lingering a second on the hybrid. Although it was unfair of me to expect him to side with me simply because of his genetics, I still felt betrayed by his stoicism.

"Thank you for your time and for listening to my request," I continued in a clipped tone. "You will know soon enough what is to become of us."

With a curt nod, I turned and marched out of the room. Chin high, back straight, I exited onto the balcony where Goro awaited me. Not until my faithful companion took flight did I allow the crushing waves of despair to take over.

What the heck was I going to tell the villagers?

CHAPTER 2
DAKAS

I couldn't decide if guilt, relief, or a sense of loss dominated within me as Luana left the chamber. A part of me wanted to chase after her and reassure her that all would be well. But as a member of the Council, my personal feelings had to take a backseat to my duties to the people.

As soon as her zeebis took flight, every head turned towards me. Stunned at first, my face heated seconds later as I realized the cause.

"You've never broadcast your emotions so strongly, Dakas," Graith said pensively. "Initially, I was going to tease you for how you had caught the female's attention, but your reaction gives me pause."

"She has stirred my mating glands," I said matter-of-factly. "I failed to shield my emotions because I was fighting my soul's attempts to bond with hers."

A collective gasp rose in the room, shock quickly giving way to congratulations. Finding one's soulmate was the greatest blessing anyone could hope for. Why did mine have to occur under such unpleasant circumstances?

Graith stretched his wings, his face taking on a serious expression. "Does that mean you want us to assist her colony?"

I pursed my lips and took a moment to reflect on my answer. As the main strategist of our people, my opinion held great weight when it came to political and war-related decisions. Now more than ever, I needed to remain objective. But the image of Luana, which was burned in my brain, made it hard to focus on her words. Concentrating on the issue at hand had required all of my willpower.

I always believed I would mate with a Zelconian female. While Luana having no feathers or wings was unfortunate, the rest of her made my mouth water. She was beautiful, with big brown eyes that looked innocent even when they burned with anger. I longed to kiss her plush lips—something I never thought I could do with a Zelconian because of the beaks. And that lovely tan skin ... I couldn't tell if it came from her Latin ancestry or time spent under the warm sun of Cibbos. Either way, I wanted to lick every centimeter of it. My fingers still twitched with the urge to release her long, curly mane, which she had in a messy bun. Her hair would look glorious flowing behind her while she flew through the sky.

I cleared my throat and forced myself to concentrate on my answer.

"From a selfish point of view, yes, I want to assist them," I replied. "The Yurus will slaughter most of their males and enslave their females ... in every way. While I obviously plan to rescue my mate, she would never forgive me for not assisting the rest of her people."

The others nodded.

"As my father informed us before his final departure from Cibbos, the United Planets Organization does not recognize the colony of Kastan. They will *not* send troops or weapons to aid them. The Peacekeepers would already be here, otherwise. The UPO will relocate those willing to leave to another planet and abandon the others. I do not particularly care about the colony, but I cannot allow my soulmate to go with them."

I shifted on my seat and stretched my wings to relieve some of the tension building in my back.

"With that in mind, what do I think *we* should do? From a purely tactical standpoint, and although your response was a little cold, I concur with your assessment," I continued. "The humans have certain things to offer that could benefit us, but it is too little."

"Like what?" my cousin Minkus asked.

"They have large farms," I replied. "With this local food supply, we wouldn't have to migrate in a couple of months. Migrating during a war would split our forces and severely weaken us. Whatever the outcome with the colony, we need to fill our granaries to face whatever may happen in the future."

"Fair point," Graith said. "We will coordinate right after this meeting."

I nodded before continuing. "But as beneficial as their food and experienced crafters would be to us, protecting them would likely cost us too many lives with our current technology versus what the Yurus have been acquiring."

"So, you concur that we should let them fend for themselves?" Skieth asked.

"I'm merely saying we should wait and see what the UPO offers them. I also think we should reach out to the UPO ourselves," I replied. "They want our crystals. We want their technology. If Luana is right, and there's no reason to doubt her, the Yurus will come for our crystals. The UPO will not want to deal with the Yurus for them."

"Therefore, they will offer us a sweet deal to make sure they continue negotiating with us and not with Vyrax," Graith concluded.

"Exactly," I replied.

"Then it's a good thing their representative will be here in a matter of hours," our Exarch said smugly.

My eyes widened, the shock I felt reflected on every other face.

"I received a message shortly before Luana's arrival. They wish to discuss the situation of the colony," Graith continued.

"Then things must be even more serious than the human female let on," Skieth reflected. "The UPO has never moved so fast before."

"Let's wait and see," I replied with a grin.

I watched with fascination as the UPO's shuttle hovered a short distance from the city, its doors opening moments before a Temern flew out. I had often heard of that species, but never met one of our distant cousins in the flesh. They, too, possessed psychic abilities. However, while their great empathic powers gave the impression they could read minds and even see people's souls, they didn't have our telepathic abilities. Mind-speak was a game changer.

Like the rest of my pureblood people, the Temern possessed a short beak, but no crest adorned his head. His maroon wings had a slightly shorter span than ours. Golden down feathers covered his chest, and a long white tail trailed behind him.

I repressed a smile as I admired his majestic flight towards the balcony where we awaited him. Synsara possessed a landing pad on the plateau where his shuttle could have landed. But I believed this display had been a deliberate reminder that we were distant kin. Did he hope that would facilitate the negotiations?

The Temern landed gracefully. A thick psychic wall surrounded his emotions, making it impossible to read him. It was deemed common courtesy to rein in our emotions among empaths so as not to overwhelm those who weren't as strong at blocking out others and those who were too psychically exhausted to do so. However, depending on the circumstances, hiding one's emotions too hermetically could hint at deception. In the Temern's case, while I didn't suspect any malicious intent, I didn't doubt for a minute that it was in order to hide his hand. We, too, doubled our psychic walls, although I didn't know how much it would block an empath as powerful as this specific male.

His gaze slipped over us, lingering for half a second on me before returning to Graith. Although I could perceive no emotions from him, I knew in my gut that discovering the presence of a hybrid had surprised him.

As he approached our leader, the Temern expressed his pleasure of meeting him by pinning his eyes—a common gesture for birds—his silver irises enlarging while his pupils rapidly shrank. Our starry eyes didn't allow us to reciprocate this. He then clicked his beak in salutation at Graith, who responded in kind. The UPO often used Temerns as moderators and diplomatic representatives because of their empathic abilities. But in our case, I believed our kinship weighed heavily in their decision to send him instead of a human or any other species.

"Greetings, Exarch Graith Devago. I am Kayog Voln, envoy of the United Planets Organization," the Temern said. "Thank you, for receiving me on such short notice."

"Welcome to Synsara, Master Kayog Voln," Graith said with an unusual warmth towards a stranger. But the Temern did feel like extended family. "It is good to see our distant kin thriving. This is my Council. You will have time to meet them at your leisure after we've discussed the matter of your visit. Please, come in."

Kayog nodded at us in a general greeting then followed Graith in as we entered the Council chamber. His gaze flicked around the room, taking in the exquisite carvings on the wall depicting the three Founding Laws of the Zelconians. The bas-relief had been filled with colorful power crystals, giving the illusion of stained glass.

We resumed our seats in the half circle around the room, and Kayog settled in the chair my Luana had vacated earlier at the table in front of us.

"I will get straight to the point," Kayog said in a serious voice. "As you are probably aware by now, the human colony of Kastan is in peril. Their leader's daughter, Luana Torres, has reached out to us for aid. Unfortunately, beyond the fact that the Kastan village isn't recognized as a legitimate colony, the UPO cannot intervene in local wars. Each planet is deemed sovereign. Unless a clear genocide is taking place—and even then—quarrels among native species are for themselves to resolve, even if it means the extermination of one of them. It is survival of the fittest."

I cast a sideways glance at Graith, who cocked his head to the side, his emotions completely closed off.

"You've traveled far only to come tell us you cannot help the humans," Graith said nonchalantly. "I suspect there is more."

"There is," Kayog said with a nod. "We know that the Yurus have been trading with off-worlders to acquire advanced warfare technology. They will use the humans as slave labor to build an impressive arsenal then wipe you out. But again, this is a local fight, and the UPO cannot interfere ... unless the Yurus become a threat to other worlds."

"And yet, you still came here," I interjected. "Why?"

"Because we believe that once the Yurus take control of your crystals, they will wreck the global markets," Kayog explained. "You see, yours are even more powerful than the sidinium crystals our spaceships use. Why do you think we are so eager to secure a steady trade with the Zelconians under the umbrella of the UPO? The people Vyrax trades with engage in all sorts of illegal activities, from slavery and piracy to illegal arms trades. If they start developing vessels using your crystals, we will be unable to keep them in check."

"So, you cannot interfere in this brewing war, you cannot assist the humans, and in accordance with the Galactic Edict concerning 'primitive' planets, you are not allowed to sell or trade advanced weapons or technology with us to help fight the Yurus," Graith summarized in a factual fashion. "Are you telling us we should also start dealing with questionable traders to even the playing field?"

Kayog shifted on his chair, the subtle twitching of his wings indicating the first sign of nervousness or uncertainty since his arrival.

"No. We certainly do not wish you to engage with those people. Should that happen, it would make it nearly impossible for the UPO to perform any deal with the Zelconians as you'd also be considered rogues," the Temern explained. "However, there is a workaround to all the restrictions you have so accurately listed. I normally do not handle cases like this one as I am the Senior Agent of the Prime Mating Agency."

"A marriage counselor?" Skieth exclaimed, his shock reflecting the one coursing through all of my brethren. "With all due respect, Master Kayog, why would they send you to handle a matter of impending war?"

"Because the UPO wants to reach an agreeable trade agreement with the Zelconians, but it cannot be an excuse for us to meddle in a local planetary war," Kayog replied. "A marriage between a member of the UPO and a native of a 'primitive' planet *is* the solution."

I snorted, wondering what kind of nonsense this was. "What does marriage have to do with anything?" I challenged. "There will still be a local war brewing that you cannot get involved in."

Despite the stiffness of his beak constraining his facial expression, a smug smile stretched it, seriously piquing my curiosity.

"We still wouldn't be able to interfere," he conceded. "However, should a Zelconian choose a human spouse through the services of the Prime Mating Agency, that human would officially become a legal citizen of Cibbos and be recognized as such by the UPO. For each marriage I arrange, I am granted a discretionary budget so the bride may relocate to her new home and as a dowry to help her start her new life."

My back stiffened in sudden understanding. I narrowed my eyes at Kayog. "And what would be included in such a dowry?" I asked.

His smile broadened. "Anything beneficial to the welfare of said bride," he deadpanned. "You see, the UPO cannot trade with the Zelconians any weapons and technology you do not yet have the ability or knowledge to create on your own. But humans have already discovered all the things you would need to hold your own against the Yurus. A human bride from Kastan would want a dowry of technological blueprints—offensive and defensive—that their own crafters could build, and their allies could put to good use. And should a native species decide officially to commit to protect that colony, the UPO would consider such a colony as legitimate, thus lifting all restrictions imposed upon it."

I snorted, and a slow chuckle rose from Graith's throat. Skieth, his right hand, shook his head in disbelief while the rest of the Council eyed the Temern with undisguised admiration.

"A deviously clever way to work around the laws," Graith conceded.

"We do what we must to protect everyone we can," Kayog replied. "Naturally, this is all assuming a human female from the colony will consent to such a union, and should you also be agreeable to it." His eyes flicked towards me, and he held my gaze with an apologetic look in his. "I do not mean to put you on the spot, but asking a human to marry a hybrid might be easier than trying to convince one to mate with a pureblood."

I smiled. "You do not put me on the spot, Kayog Voln. I concur with your assessment. But you will be pleased to hear that their leader's daughter, Luana Torres, is my bond mate. She called to my soul when she stood before the Council this morning."

This time, the Temern made no effort to hide his shock, followed by a beaming smile. "This is wondrous news! I had feared condemning one of you to a life sentence with a mate not meant for you. But you have erased any doubt in my mind that this is the correct course of action."

"Luana still needs to consent," I cautioned.

"She will," Kayog said with certainty. "Her people are desperate, and you are her soulmate. As long as an agreement is reached with the Zelconians, I will make sure Luana gets onboard."

"Then, let us discuss the details," Graith said to Kayog, after grinning at me.

CHAPTER 3
LUANA

I stared at the Temern in complete shock and disbelief. When my com had beeped, a little over half an hour ago, informing me that the UPO's representative was on his way with a proposition, my heart soared. I'd believed my prayers were being answered. But this?

"I can feel your distress, Luana," Kayog said in a gentle tone, "but this is the best possible solution. Kastan becomes a legitimate colony for the UPO. You get powerful protectors that will allow your colony to continue to live here on Cibbos instead of being relocated to some struggling refugee colony. The Zelconians get access to the technology they need to maintain control of their crystals. And the UPO gets to resume talks of a possible fair-trade agreement with the Zelconians."

"Yes, the best solution for everyone but me and the poor Zelconian who will be stuck with me," I muttered. "This is a life sentence!"

Instead of the sympathetic—maybe even guilty—look I had expected from the Temern, Kayog smiled as if I'd said something silly.

"Actually, Luana, it is the best solution, especially for the two of you," he countered. "When I came to negotiate with the Zelconians, I expected it to be a hard sale, since their species mate for life. The bond is sacred to them. A marriage of convenience would be almost like blasphemy. However, it turns out that you, my dear, are the soulmate one of them has been looking for. And here you were, but a short flight away."

"Seriously?"

The agent chuckled at my dubious tone and disbelieving expression.

"Seriously," he repeated with a nod. "Like us, Temerns, the Zelconians are empaths. Unlike us, when they meet the one, they soul-bind. It is both a physical and spiritual reaction that can only occur with a single person in the entire universe. The moment you stepped into the room, Dakas felt the call of your soul and spent the meeting fighting the urge to bond with you."

I shifted in my seat, unsure how I felt about this. Obviously, I was still freaked out about having to marry a complete stranger to save the colony. That I would accept wasn't even up for debate—I'd do anything for my people, to preserve our way of life, and to stay on the only planet we'd ever known. But the possibility that this could truly be a happy marriage instead of a prison gave me hope. Temerns didn't lie, and their ability to predict a successful union was legendary.

"And you agree with his assessment that we are a match?" I asked.

"Absolutely! When I met him earlier, I felt the sincerity of his belief that you were his soulmate. But after meeting you and having empathically assessed your personality, I can confirm that you are a perfect match." He grinned and stretched his wings behind him. "Obviously, there will be awkward moments. You are different species with very different cultures. The bond doesn't mean instant-love either. Your feelings for each other will grow over time like with any other couple. But as long as you keep an open mind, I guarantee that things will work out wonderfully."

I frowned as I weighed his words. Kastan was a decent-sized colony, but not huge. I'd already made my peace with the fact that I'd likely remain a spinster, as I hadn't met anyone I could picture myself marrying. Worse case, I would have settled for someone tolerable to fulfill my duty of helping grow the population. Finding out I'd end up with my 'Prince Charming' should be thrilling ... but a prince with a beak?

"Well, I guess there's no point beating my chest over the inevitable," I said with a heavy sigh. "At least I know we're compatible since there was a human-Zelconian hybrid in their Council chamber."

"That hybrid *is* your soulmate," Kayog intervened.

"He is?!"

He nodded with that odd grin made stiff by his beak. "Are you pleased by this news?"

I didn't know how to respond without sounding crass. I squirmed uneasily in my seat while looking for the right words.

"To be honest, yes, I am. I guess him being half-human makes him more... relatable?" I said sheepishly.

"And you won't have to worry about him pecking you with his beak," Kayog deadpanned.

I squinted at him, wondering if he was serious. "You guys don't do that, do you?"

He laughed but didn't answer, making me even more curious.

"If we are in agreement, I will inform Dakas so he can come here for the human ceremony," Kayog continued. "Time is of the essence. The Yurus could attack any day. Dakas will stay here until your village is secure. Then you'll be expected to move in with him in Synsara, where you will perform the Zelconian binding ritual. But remember ... this is *for life*. The Prime Mating Agency usually grants a six-month trial period to the

couples. It does not apply here. Once you soul-bind, it is permanent until one of you dies."

A cold shiver ran down my spine. He was merely making
sure I knew what I was committing to, but it still freaked me out.

"I understand. And yes, we are in agreement."

"Excellent! I am sending the message to Dakas now," Kayog
said.

"I need to go tell the others before the ceremony takes
place," I said, rising to my feet, my knees wobbling.

"Of course," he replied with a nod.

I exited the house to find everyone crowded outside, the
same tension visible on every face.

"I have good news," I shouted to be heard by a majority.
"But let's go to the Great Hall to discuss it."

Excited shouts and relieved expressions greeted my words,
some faces even tearing up. In that instant, I realized that, happy
marriage or not, I'd made the right decision to save my people.
They followed me into the Great Hall, every seat filling rapidly,
the rest of the colony standing at the back along the walls of the
oval building.

As I gave them the abbreviated version of the agreement,
shock and dismay quickly gave way to excitement at the legiti-
macy and protection my arranged marriage would provide them.
My chest constricted as I realized that none of them seemed
overly distraught over my being offered as a sacrificial lamb. No
one commiserated or expressed concern for my feelings. They
only cared about how my change in status would affect them.

"You are the colony's medical doctor," Moira said. "Who
will treat us if you go live up there? And what of all our men
—and your father—currently wounded?"

"Synsara is only a twenty-minute flight on a zeebis. I'll still
be able to come down and take care of you. Tilda is also a qualified nurse, more than capable of handling most of your everyday
minor injuries," I replied. "And as I stated at the beginning, my

Zelconian husband will stay here with us until the village is safe. I have faith my father will be up and running by then. If not, we can re-assess."

"Are they going to become our rulers?" Alban asked. This stirred a great deal of worried mumbling from the audience.

"No, they are not. We are merely becoming allies. Each of our people will continue to self-govern as we've always done. They're only going to help us fight the Yurus," I said.

They showered me with countless questions, some completely inane. Through it all, Martin's resentful glare drilled into me. He seemed to think I'd found myself an alien husband just to deny him what he'd always considered rightfully his.

"They're approaching!" a voice shouted at the back of the hall.

Who would have thought the arrival of my soon-to-be-husband, whom I'd only met this morning and hardly talked to, would make me so happy? I was also beyond done with these questions. I pushed my way through the throng rushing outside to bear witness.

As soon as I exited the building, my eyes lifted to the skies where the dark silhouettes of three Zelconians grew more distinct. I wiggled through the crowd and stood by Kayog and Counselor Allan near the entrance of the temple.

The three males looked majestic under the early afternoon sun, their wings flapping almost in perfect sync as they began their descent.

"The dark wings of the angels of death."

Martin's voice uttering those words with contempt startled me. I'd been too fascinated by the arrival of my future husband, flanked by his buddies, to notice his approach. I bit back the sharp retort burning my tongue and chose to ignore him instead.

Dakas landed gracefully a couple of meters in front of us, his two friends touching down just as quietly and effortlessly. As soon as he straightened, Dakas folded his magnificent midnight-blue wings and deployed his fan-shaped crest like a peacock would his tail. He had closed it into a narrow bunch during flight, probably to make himself more aerodynamic.

Although their constellation-filled eyes made it difficult to know specifically where a Zelconian was looking, I knew Dakas had locked his gaze on me. I didn't know what I expected his reaction to be when we met again, but not for him to display this gentle, almost awed expression. I found myself instinctively smiling. His face softened further and a sweet, almost shy smile stretched his very sexy human lips. It was odd that the word *'shy'* should have entered my mind, as *intimidating* would better describe this mountain of a male.

Like the pureblood Zelconians, he wore no clothing. Unlike them, he had a lot of exposed human skin on his face, arms, abs, and legs. Only his shoulders, chest, and neck were covered in different types of feathers. At first, I'd believed he had none around his crotch, but I could now see very thin feathers hugging the skin of his pelvic area, the same light-blue color as his skin. The complete absence of bulge there seemed to confirm my presumption that, like the pureblood, his reproductive organs retracted inside the body. To my shock, what I'd assumed to be locks of straight blue hair at the back of his head were, in fact, long feathers.

Now that my earlier panicked anxiety over the fate of the colony no longer distracted me, I could better appreciate that, in spite of his otherness, my Dakas was rather easy on the eyes.

"Luana," Dakas said, bowing his head slightly in greeting. "It is a pleasure to see you again, this time under more auspicious circumstances."

My skin erupted in goosebumps at the sound of his deep, melodic voice saying my name. Describing it as akin to a phys- ical caress didn't begin to do it justice. It was soft, warm, and buttery, yet sinfully decadent like fresh strawberries dipped in melted dark chocolate.

A knowing smile stretched his lips, and my face heated as I realized his empathic abilities had snitched on how deeply the mere sound of his voice affected me.

"This is my brother Renok and my cousin Minkus," Dakas said, waving in turn at the two Zelconians by his side.

They bowed their heads politely in greeting.

"Welcome to our village, Dakas, Renok, and Minkus," I said while nervously tucking a strand of my curly hair behind my ear. I then gestured at the two males on my right. "You already know Kayog Voln. And this is Allan Stuart, our Spiritual Counselor."

Dakas smiled at Kayog then stared at Allan for a second before nodding his head at him in greeting.

"Counselor Allan is authorized to perform human weddings that are recognized by the UPO," Kayog said. "He has agreed to preside over the abbreviated ceremony between Luana and you."

"What's the rush?" Martin asked, his voice loud enough to be heard by the crowd eyeing us with undisguised curiosity. "An agreement has been reached with the Zelconians. That's great, but we should be working on defenses, not ramming through a wedding without proper preparation."

"Martin!" I exclaimed, staring at him in disbelief.

"Don't *Martin* me!" he retorted as if my behavior was scandalous. "Your father has waited his entire life to walk you down the aisle, and you want to rush through an expedited ceremony behind his back, with a complete stranger … and while he's fighting for his life?"

"You do not care about the state of Luana's father or his inability to be here," Dakas said in an icy voice, his mysterious eyes boring into Martin. "You want to block this binding out of spite because the woman you covet, but who has never wanted you back, is about to slip through your fingers and marry another."

Martin paled before his face turned crimson with humiliation as a few shocked gasps, snorts, and chuckles erupted from the crowd.

"You don't know what the fuck you're talking about!" he hissed. "But hey, you want to rush in and disrespect your father, knock yourself out. It'll be your funeral."

Mouth gaping, I watched him spin around and march away, shoving out of his way the people who had the misfortune to be standing in his path.

"He will become a problem," Dakas said pensively.

That snapped me out of my daze. "Martin is harmless. He just has a huge ego and hates losing. He'll get over it," I said dismissively.

Dakas stared at me quietly. I could see that I hadn't even come even close to convincing him. Had his empathic abilities revealed an even darker side to my pesky former suitor?

"Indeed, he will get over it," Counselor Allan said with a certain stiffness as he glared at Martin's receding back. "There will be plenty of time to perform a formal wedding ceremony or a renewal of your vows once Mateo is fully recovered and the safety of our colony is secured."

Approving mumbles from the crowd greeted his words.

"Agreed," Kayog said. "We should proceed."

He gestured at the entrance of the temple, and we filed inside quietly.

CHAPTER 4
DAKAS

I reined in the anger the human named Martin had stirred within me even before I landed in Kastan. Rising above the awed and hopeful emotions the other villagers had projected as they witnessed our approach, the spiritual energy oozing out of him had felt slimy.

I didn't resent him for coveting Luana. How could he not? Aside from her harmonious features, her aura was delicious. Anyone would want to bask in it. But that male was too self-absorbed to even appreciate it. He broadcast no love or affection for her, just a possessiveness enshrined in a sense of entitlement. He wanted to use my Luana for his own means. That alone made me itch with the need to beat him to a pulp.

However, his remark about rushing into the wedding infuriated me the most. Although he had known this to be a lost cause, he had spoken the words to hurt my mate's feelings and make her feel guilty for not waiting for her sire. He'd sought to ruin proceedings that were already challenging for Luana. Sooner or later, I would make him pay for that. Calling him out in public had only been the first salvo. No one messed with my female in all impunity.

We entered the wooden building they called a temple. Like everything else in the village, it was of simple—if not boringly humble—design. A wide aisle leading to a short dais at the front of the large rectangular room separated rows of cushioned benches. A pulpit occupied the left corner of the dais, and a long but narrow table sat in the center, no doubt serving as an altar. No lighting system illuminated the space thanks to the natural light flooding in through the massive windows lining both side walls. Two small doors indicated private rooms off of each side of the dais.

Counselor Allan led us straight to the altar, taking position in front of it. I frowned, realizing he was about to initiate the abbreviated ceremony Kayog had mentioned.

"I wish to have a word in private with Luana before you perform this ritual," I said.

My mate stiffened, and a wave of worry poured out of her. Did she think I was reconsidering?

"Of course," Kayog said, sensing my true intentions. He turned to the Counselor and gestured at one of the two doors on the side. "Could they use one of these rooms?"

The Counselor nodded with a slight hesitation, a concerned look also descending on his wizened features. "Yes. They can use my office. It is unlocked," he said, pointing at the door to our right.

"Thank you," I said before gently smiling at my mate.

She returned my smile, hers laced with uncertainty and a smidge of confusion, then we headed towards the office under the heavy stares of Kayog, the Counselor, and the villagers who were still pouring into the building. I opened the door and waved Luana in. She nodded in gratitude and scurried past me. As soon as I closed the door behind me, she clasped her hands in front of her and leveled on me her beautiful dark-brown eyes, filled with worry.

"Peace, Luana," I said in a soothing voice. "There is no need for alarm. All is well. We are about to bind our lives to each other forever, but have barely exchanged a few words. I would like to reassure you of my intentions before we proceed."

Her shoulders slouched as tension drained out of them, and she breathed out with relief. "Right. We haven't really had a chance to talk, have we?" she said with a nervous smile.

"We haven't," I echoed gently. "There isn't much time right now, so I will be brief. We will have a lifetime to make up for it."

I shifted my wings to loosen some of my own tension building in my back, while carefully choosing my words.

"Our respective peoples and the UPO see our union as a beneficial transaction for all parties involved," I continued. "You are entering into it out of duty to your people. But *I* am entering it because it will make me whole. *You* will make me whole."

Her lips parted in shock, and her eyes widened upon hearing my words.

"The minute you walked into the Council chamber this morning, you called to me. You are the other half of my soul. The situation with the Yurus and the promises of the UPO play no part in my consenting to this union. With or without this situation, now that I've found you, I would have come here to court you," I said fervently. "Vyrax's ambitions only rushed the process. But for me, it would have always been you."

Luana unclasped her hands to press one palm to her chest, looking at me like she didn't know how to handle the words coming out of my mouth.

"Whatever you may feel about this situation, and although we are strangers, know that I come into this union with a happy heart. The strong pull of the mating call I feel in your presence confirms that, in time, as you and I get to know each other, we *will* deeply fall in love. I have no expectations or demands of you at this early stage of our bond. I only ask that you keep an open mind and give our relationship a chance."

"I… I can do that," Luana said with a timid smile.

"Good," I said in a soft tone. "My number one duty is ensuring your happiness. After all, I am an empath. Your emotions are my emotions. The more joy I give you, the happier I will be."

"Happy wife, happy life," Luana whispered with something akin to self-derision.

I cocked my head to the side, sensing there was a greater meaning to the unfamiliar—yet accurate—expression.

"Indeed," I replied.

She examined my features for a few seconds, a slew of emotions flitting over her beautiful face.

"Thank you for this," she said at last. "Until now, I didn't realize how badly I needed this talk. I am feeling a little over-whelmed by this situation. I don't know you, and binding my life to a complete stranger until the day I die is a terrifying prospect. But Kayog also said you are my perfect match, and everyone knows the Temerns have a flawless record on that front. For what it's worth, you seem like a very nice guy … er male. And I really want this to work."

"Then let's make it work together," I said, extending a hand towards her.

Luana smiled and placed hers in mine. The wave of hope and tentative excitement radiating from my mate wrapped around me in a gentle caress that made me want to coo. I swallowed hard to rein in this instinctive response. I gave her hand a gentle squeeze and held on as I led her back into the main room of the temple.

Under different circumstances, the stunned expressions of the villagers upon seeing Luana and I walking out hand in hand would have made me laugh. However, their presence irritated me to no end. The binding of two souls was not a spectacle for a crowd to gawk at. It was a sacred and solemn moment to be shared in private by the two spirits becoming one. Although Kayog had explained that, for humans, it was a moment of celebration to be shared with friends and family coming to support the couple, it still chafed.

I fought the urge to invoke a nightmare that would have them all stampeding out of the room and focused on Luana's positive emotions. This was her people's custom. I would honor it. Kayog's amused expression made me want to throw something at him. The older male knew exactly what feelings were coursing through me. But his almost paternal approval at seeing my mate and me holding hands—and especially the aura of peace my talk with Luana had given her—dimmed my irritation.

The sincerity with which the Temern wished for my female and me to have a blissful union touched me deeply.

We returned to the Counselor, who still stood in front of the altar.

"We are ready to proceed," I said to him.

"Very well," Counselor Allan replied. "Please face each other and hold both of each other's hands."

Luana and I complied. Her nervousness washed over me like a swarm of butterfly wings brushing against my skin. Thankfully, it was now devoid of the almost panicked fear choking her earlier.

"Luana Torres, daughter of Mateo Torres and Emilia Garcia, do you freely take this Zelconian male, Dakas Wakaro, as your lawfully wedded husband?" he asked.

"I do," Luana replied.

"Dakas Wakaro, son of William Wakaro and Ireia Anteis, do you freely take this human female, Luana Torres, as your lawfully wedded wife?" Counselor Allan then asked me.

"I do," I replied.

"Kayog Voln, do you bear witness that this female, Luana Torres, and this male, Dakas Wakaro, freely commit and desire to be legally married to each other in accordance with both human and galactic laws?"

"Yes, I confirm it," Kayog said.

"By the power vested in me by the Clerical College of Earth and the United Planets Organization, I declare you husband and wife," the Counselor said. "Dakas Wakaro, you may kiss your bride."

I had always fantasized about kissing, thinking I never would until this morning when my Luana came into my life. But now that I would finally get to do it, the morbid curiosity of the crowd had me once again itching with the desire to wreck their minds for defiling what should be a sacred time between my soulmate and me.

Although I couldn't read their actual thoughts, their emotions were strong enough for me to get an image. To some, seeing me kiss Luana was akin to watching a freak show. To others, it felt like watching a sacrificial lamb about to be slaughtered. What did they expect? That I'd suddenly go feral and bite half of her face off? Then, there were those who felt disgust mixed with outrage that one of their finest would be 'ruined' by a thing like me, half-man, half-beast. And finally, there was the handful who just wanted these proceedings done so we could start working towards making them safe.

As much as their unwelcomed presence pissed me off, I would not let them ruin my first kiss. But seconds before I closed myself off from their emotions, I felt a wave of peace radiate from Kayog and settle over me. I didn't know whether to smile in gratitude or be annoyed with myself for how little I seemed able to control my emotions since meeting my mate.

But the expectant, and slightly timid look in my female's eyes worked as the most potent shield. Our surroundings faded away as I sank into the depths of her dark brown eyes. My skin tingled with the waves of anticipation flowing out of Luana as I lowered my face and pressed my mouth to hers.

Ancestors!

Her lips were so soft, so warm … The tiny speck of arousal sparking inside Luana ignited an inferno inside of me. It took every bit of my willpower not to release her hands and draw her body against mine. I reluctantly broke the kiss but couldn't pull my gaze away from hers. The most delightful mixture of hope, joy, and awe was blossoming inside my Luana. She couldn't read my emotions yet, but she could feel the chemistry between us.

Despite the doubts and uncertainty, which would linger in her mind for a while, my mate was beginning to believe in us as a couple.

The sound of the Counselor clearing his throat snapped Luana and me out of the entranced daze we'd fallen into. Our heads snapped towards him. Luana's tan skin turned a lovely red, while my own blue skin took on a darker shade, my embarrassment enhanced by hers.

Kayog hid a chuckle behind a cough while the crowd reminded me of its obnoxious presence by clapping and congratulating us. The villagers slowly filed out of the building, and the Counselor made Luana and me sign the wedding certificates by pressing our thumbs in specific locations on a datapad.

"Normally, you would be expected to perform the Zelconian bonding ritual today for this agreement to be fully valid," Kayog said after the Counselor had taken his leave. "But under the circumstances, and as the Zelconian customs require privacy and a specific setting, we have granted you a one-week extension so you can focus on securing the colony first. We trust you will act in good faith and honor the agreement."

"I will," Luana said in a firm voice filled with sincerity.

"As will I," I said.

"Good! I will now take my leave," Kayog said. "Over the next couple of hours, some blueprints will be forwarded to your com, Luana, and a few shuttles will deliver materials and equipment given to you both as your dowry."

"A *few* shuttles?" Luana asked, surprised. "Just how much stuff are you sending?"

Kayog's mischievous smile told me we would receive far more than expected.

"The right amount," the Temern replied mysteriously. "I wish you two the very best. Should you need anything, do not hesitate to reach out to me."

After exchanging our goodbyes, we watched Kayog leave the temple.

"The humans are getting restless, brother," Renok said in an apologetic tone.

I nodded. "Yes, I can feel them." I turned to Luana. "Although it is not ideal, we must delay getting to know each other better, my mate. For now, I would like you to give us an overview of the village's current defenses."

"Of course." Luana's aura of hope shifted from personal aspirations to excitement for the general welfare of her people. "This way, please."

The people's contentment at seeing us finally exiting the temple was almost palpable. They followed us at a respectable distance as Luana led us around the perimeter of the village.

"There are no predatory beasts nearby, so we never really bothered with a defensive wall before," Luana said apologetically, embarrassment building inside her as the extent of their lack of defenses became increasingly obvious. "But Martin and his team have been actively working to erect one since things went sour with the Yurus. You can see the main pillars going up all around. We also have some motion sensors, and our hunters are setting up traps."

My brother, cousin, and I felt the same dismay. What they were building was completely useless and just as inadequate, if not worse, than their previous lack of preparation. Although I tried to keep a neutral expression and refrained from broadcasting my emotions on a psychic level, Luana could see I wasn't impressed.

"Is it really that bad?" she asked sheepishly.

"I'm afraid your efforts are completely useless, my mate," I said in a gentle tone. "All this work you're doing will be trampled over in seconds by the Yurus. Here, let me show you."

I walked to one of the large wooden poles they had stuck into the ground and which would serve as support for the wall. I splayed my fingers as my vicious talons extruded. Luana stared in shock as I swiped both hands at the pole, one after the other, cutting deep into the bark. I immediately followed up with a solid kick with the flat of my foot right above the weakened spot. I'd expected the upper part of the pole to bend and topple over. Instead, the entire upper half tore right off and went flying a few meters away.

A general gasp rose behind me from the onlookers.

"No way!" Luana whispered in disbelief.

"I am a hybrid, which makes me a little weaker than the pureblood Zelconians, who are themselves generally weaker than the Yurus," I said factually. "If I managed to destroy one of your protective wall's main support beams *this* easily, imagine what an army of Yurus would do."

"Hey! What the fuck are you doing?!" Martin's despicable voice exclaimed in the distance.

I turned to see him pushing through the crowd, a look of outrage on his face.

"I thought the whole point of this *marriage* was so you could help us strengthen our defense. But you tear them down instead?" he added, putting as much contempt as he could into the word 'marriage' in order to get a rise out of me. Before either Luana or I could respond, he faced her to continue spewing his venom. "And you stand there gaping like a fish out of water while he does this instead of intervening? What the hell kind of leader are you?"

This time, my hackles raised. Attack me all you want, but don't you dare attack my mate. Snarling, I took a step towards him.

To my shock, Luana grabbed my forearm and thrust herself in front of me. Her beautiful eyes, leveled on Martin, threw daggers.

"First of all, I am *not* your leader. I am your leader's daughter. But the minute things got heated, everyone wimped out and dumped this mess on my lap to deal with," Luana snapped with a ferocity I had not expected from her. "Second, if I'm gaping like a damn fish, it's because I'm floored to see how pathetically flimsy these so-called defenses *you* have been building for us actually are. Dakas merely bitch-slapped that pole, and it keeled over. And this was supposed to keep the hundreds of souls in this village safe? Instead of making a nuisance of yourself, you should shut the fuck up—for once—and try to learn a thing or two from the people who actually know what they're doing and who are trying to fix what you failed to accomplish."

Renok and Minkus emitted the typical Zelconian cooing sound, which would be the equivalent of a human snorting. They made no effort to hide their amusement at my mate putting the wretch in his place. I didn't suppress the malicious grin blossoming on my face, although I still itched to give him a proper trouncing. This reaction from my Luana greatly pleased me. She had seemed so timid since my arrival in Kastan, I'd wondered what had happened to the inner flame I'd gotten a glimpse of when she'd stormed out of our Council chamber earlier.

As the crowd chuckled, Martin's face turned such a deep shade of red, I began to wonder if he was choking. But as much as I wanted to rub it in his face, the situation of the colony was far more dire than I had expected. Now wasn't the time to settle grievances or show which male was the strongest—not that this was even open for debate.

"Currently, your village is essentially defenseless," I said in a stern tone. "All the things you have set up will easily be bypassed, and even more quickly destroyed by just a handful of Yurus. Whatever your discontent, there is no time for your quarreling and bickering. The Yurus could attack any moment. If we do not erect proper defenses quickly, there will be no village left to save."

Approving murmurs rose from the villagers.

"It is a good thing you are not too advanced with what you'd planned on building," I continued. "This will spare us precious time that would have otherwise been wasted tearing everything down. We can use many of the poles already planted. We will reinforce them, and they will serve to support the relays that will connect the energy fields we will build instead."

"Energy fields?" said an elder female in the crowd, sounding both shocked and stunned, as if I'd said something offensive. "That sounds rather high tech. We came to Cibbos because we chose to reject technology."

Luana rolled her eyes before casting a disbelieving look at the woman. "Jenna, seriously?"

"They're here to protect us," the older female named Jenna argued, her face taking on a stubborn expression, "not to change our way of life."

"And how do you propose we protect you?" I asked in a factual tone. "By throwing sticks and stones at people who will come at us with blasters and laser beams?"

Jenna's face heated, and she shrunk in embarrassment. The emotions pouring out of her were interesting. Beyond her humiliation at the obvious response, she still didn't want her lifestyle upended. I took no pleasure in shaming her, but their entire colony needed to open their eyes and face reality.

"For what it's worth, my people and I do not care how you run your daily lives within your village. You can be—and remain —as primitive as you wish," I continued in a softer voice. "But when it comes to defending it, it is my people and I who will be putting our lives on the line. We will do so using tools that actually have a chance of defeating the enemy and keeping everyone on our side safe. So yes, advanced technology will be installed all around the perimeter of your village, and a few in the center at strategic locations."

While a few still appeared uncomfortable with this, all seemed to give their approval.

"Now, if we are done discussing, I will call my people so we can get to work," I said, projecting loudly enough so all could hear me. "Those of you willing and able to help with the construction work, please gather by the damaged pole." I turned to my brother and cousin, who both approached me. "I would like you two to go scout the area for any impending threat or weakness we need to address immediately."

They nodded and took flight, each heading in a different direction. My eyes went out of focus as my mind sought Graith's. Within seconds, our minds connected. I quickly briefed him on the situation and on how many people and resources would be required.

"Understood. We will be there shortly," Graith mentally replied.

"Thank you, Exarch," I said respectfully before disconnecting from his mind.

The concerned look on Luana's face as I refocused on my surroundings drew a guilty smile out of me.

"Apologies, my mate. I was communicating telepathically with our leader to request he send our people down," I explained. "When you see me suddenly go still that way, I'm usually communicating mentally with someone."

"Oh, okay. Thanks for clarifying. You went so still, it was freaking me out," she said with that nervous chuckle that gave the impression she was a timid little thing.

I smiled and resisted the urge to caress her cheek before turning to address the nearly fifty people—mostly males with a handful of young females—who had gathered around the broken beam. After giving some instructions, I picked up a few of the 2x2 wooden poles piled up nearby and broke them into short spikes that I planted in the ground at specific intervals to indicate where the large beams were to be moved or erected along the periphery of the village.

While it required little effort for me to stab one of the spikes solidly into the ground with a single movement, the feeling of awe it elicited in my female made me want to puff out my chest. To my embarrassment, I found myself making a show of it. I enjoyed basking in her admiration.

The arrival of my people had me reining myself in. Still, pride filled my heart as I watched the sky darken with a large flock of Zelconians. They looked impressive as they flew in disciplined formations, their wide wings flapping in perfect sync. Each unit surrounded a large hover crate containing—among other things—the precious crystals that would make the village safe.

Intimidated, the crowd moved back as my people landed. Considering how we towered over them by a good head, I could see why they would feel skittish.

"You haven't bound the female to you," Graith mentally said to me the minute his taloned-feet touched the ground a couple of meters from me. *"Why?"*

"I want it done properly, in private. And especially, I want her to be fully informed of what that will mean for her moving forward. I will not have my mate blindsided in this," I replied telepathically with firm resolve.

"When?" Graith insisted.

"Once this village is secured."

"What if she backs out once she's received what she wanted?" he asked.

The question was factual, devoid of actual distrust.

"Luana will honor her word. We are already bound through

the human ritual. Once the basic security is up and running here, I will bond with her," I reassured him.

"Very well."

With these last words, our leader disconnected from my mind and came to stand in front of my mate.

"We meet again, Luana Torres, mate of Dakas Wakaro," Graith said to her.

CHAPTER 5
LUANA

Graith intimidated the heck out of me. I couldn't tell if he disliked me or humans in general. Then again, maybe he didn't dislike us at all but simply had a strange way of interacting with people. The constellations in his eyes made his emotions impossible for me to read. But I constantly had the impression he was fighting the urge to kick me just for shits and giggles.

"Hello again, Exarch Graith. Welcome to Kastan," I said politely. "And thank you for coming with so many of your people to help secure our village."

"Zelconians only have one word," Graith replied, his odd gaze boring into mine.

"Excuse me," Dakas said distractedly before hurrying off towards some of his people who were opening the large crates they had flown in with.

My gaze lingered on him as he departed with determined steps. For the first time, I got a good look at his tail. It wasn't long or flowy like Kayog's, but the straight midnight blue feathers fell to the back of his knees, hiding his otherwise naked butt.

"Your mate is a fine male," Graith said in a serious tone, startling me. "He embodies the best of both our species. We are taking a huge leap of faith, doing all of this for your people."

I recoiled, wondering what he meant, but then it struck me. "Because Dakas didn't bind me yet?"

It was Graith's turn to be surprised. "You know of it?"

"I don't know what it entails, but Kayog mentioned we would marry according to your customs after the village was safe," I said. "And I *will* honor my part of the deal. First, because I'm a woman of my word. Second, because if I didn't, the colony and all its people would still end up getting decimated. And third, because ..."

My face heated when I realized what I had almost said. Graith raised one of his feathery eyebrows and tilted his head in a bird-like fashion.

"Because?" he insisted when I failed to continue.

I considered not answering but then changed my mind. There was nothing wrong with being honest about the feelings my husband stirred in me.

"Because both Kayog and Dakas say we are soulmates, and Temerns are never wrong on that front. And so far, the way Dakas makes me feel seems to confirm that he and I could indeed have a wonderful relationship. Since I'm already contractually bound to this marriage for life, I'm not going to fight it just for the sake of doing so. Dakas asked me to keep an open mind and give it a fair go, that's exactly what I intend to do. But I also need you and your people to keep an open mind and not automatically assume I have shady intentions. You can feel my emotions. You know the words I've just spoken are true."

His beak quivered. I couldn't tell if he was smiling, smirking, or pinching his 'lips' in response to my statement.

"You look so delicate, and sometimes appear quite timid," he said pensively. "And yet, a bold, no-nonsense flame burns just beneath the surface. Your body is fragile, but your mind is not."

Although his words deeply flattered me, I shrugged, trying to act nonchalant. "I'm a medical doctor. I don't have time for bullshit or mind games. I say it like it is, and I expect the same in return."

This time, despite the stiffness of his beak, I recognized the smile. It greatly softened his features.

"I like you, Luana Torres. If you weren't Dakas's soulmate, I might have courted you myself."

This time, my jaw dropped. Graith burst out laughing. He'd been so matter-of-fact when he'd spoken those words that I believed them true. But now, seeing his broad shoulders shaking with hilarity made me understand he had simply said it to provoke this shocked reaction from me.

"Now, stop distracting me, human. I have a village to secure," he deadpanned.

With that, the wretched male turned and marched away, leaving me speechless. The sound of an approaching shuttle— correction, make that *three* shuttles—kept me from speculating further about him. As the villagers helped me unload their contents, the insane quantity of things Kayog had sent blew me away. This went well beyond any reasonable dowry. Granted, Kayog had said, since he didn't have to pay for the usual travel to send the bride to her mate's homeworld, that amount would be added to what he would spend on other "wedding gifts" for me. But traveling fees would not account for him being able to spend this much.

While I left Anita, our head farmer, in charge of overseeing the rest of the unloading, I grabbed Lara, our engineer, as she would assist in setting up the numerous state-of-the-art medical pods we had received and that the villagers were helping carry into our medical clinic.

It took far more time than we would have liked to get everything up and running. But when it came to medical equipment, one couldn't be too careful. The slightest mis-calibration could result in worsening a patient's already precarious condition or even death.

As soon as we finished, Lara left to assist the Zelconians outside. Of an age with me, she was also chafing at the technological restrictions imposed on us by those who had founded this colony.

We immediately proceeded to transfer my unconscious father and the other wounded into the new pods in the hope these far more advanced devices would accelerate their recovery. Right now, I'd give anything to have my father well and by my side. Aside from missing him, this business of leading a colony was definitely not for me.

When I walked back outside, I was blown away by the spectacle that awaited me. In a well-coordinated ballet, the Zelconians were setting up the poles at mind-blowing speed. Working in pairs, they held the massive wooden beams—which required six human males to carry—and flew them over the holes the villagers or other Zelconians were digging in the ground with a machine I was unfamiliar with. As soon as it was settled, a couple of Zelconian females would embed a series of strange crystals in the pole before pouring some sort of silver liquid over it. As if animated by a mind of its own, the silver liquid coated the entire length of the beam until it looked like it had always been a metal pole.

It took me a moment to spot my husband, standing with Graith and Skieth by a table. They were engaged in an intense conversation over what I presumed to be the blueprints Kayog had sent us. Lara's presence—so tiny between them—as she also participated in the discussion seemed to confirm my presumption.

With the sun lowering towards the horizon, I shyly approached them. Dakas sensed my presence long before I reached him. He turned and gave me a delighted smile that took my breath away. Aside from the fact that it softened and lit up his face, he seemed so genuinely happy to see me that it made me feel like the greatest treasure in the world.

"Hey!" I said, as I came to a stop next to him.

"Hey," he replied with the same soft smile.

"Hmm ... It's kind of getting late. You have all been working hard for a few hours now. You must be getting hungry," I said, absentmindedly fiddling with the hem of my shirt. "I'm not sure what Zelconians eat. But if you tell me what you'd like, we're going to prepare dinner for all of you."

"Thank you, Luana," Graith said before Dakas could answer. "That's very kind but unnecessary. Phegea is already handling it."

He gestured with his head towards some of his people—two males and a female—near one of the beams. I stiffened and squinted, wondering if my eyes were playing tricks on me. Seconds later, the female's head jerked towards us, and she nodded then took flight. I realized then that someone—likely Graith—had telepathically called her over. She landed in front of Graith who smiled kindly at her.

Although smaller than the males, the Zelconian females weren't delicate little things either. They didn't have a fan-shaped crest like the males, only five narrow feathers like a bouquet at the top of their heads, reminiscent of the 'crown' of a peahen. Their slender curves with flaring hips matched the hour-glass-shaped body of a human female, but they had flat chests. Or so I had assumed from seeing their females at a distance. But now that I was looking up-close at the one I presumed to be called Phegea, I couldn't help but notice the substantial swelling of her upper torso. It wasn't like our pair of boobs but the entire upper-chest area, almost like a frigatebird swelling his red chest to attract a mate.

Graith gave me the strangest look. I couldn't define it and yet, I knew beyond the shadow of a doubt that he was taunting me about something. And then he slightly bent his knees to be at a level with Phegea and opened his beak. My eyes nearly popped out of my head when the female's swollen chest slightly undulated and she poked her beak into Graith's open mouth. Seconds later, she pulled away, and he swallowed.

Poor Lara slapped her hand over her mouth and ran off with an apologetic look, while Skieth chuckled. They repeated this process a couple more times before the Exarch seemed sated. As Phegea turned towards Skieth, Graith faced me, his shoulders shaking with barely repressed laughter.

Although I felt confident my face hid the shock I currently felt, with their empathic abilities, there would be no fooling them. And the wretch was enjoying my dismay. Of course, I should have anticipated this, although I only imagined them doing this for their young, not with adults. My gaze flicked back to her swollen chest. By the time she had also fed Skieth, it had reduced noticeably in size. I realized then that this was her crop, the bag in which she stored food to be softened—not digested—allowing her to either regurgitate it to feed others or pass it on to her own stomach later to feed.

When she turned to face Dakas, too many strong emotions coursed through me. For some stupid reason, I hadn't expected him to feed that way as well, probably because of his more human appearance, especially the absence of a beak. It was narrow-minded of me, but while I found it disturbing between two pureblood Zelconians, it remained a bird thing. Since I saw Dakas as being more like me, it felt as if he would be swallowing vomit, even though I knew better. But the horror of that thought took on a completely different edge when Phegea cupped my husband's face between her hands and poked her beak into his open mouth.

Instead of the disgust I'd expected, a violent wave of jealousy slammed into me. I barely held back from yanking her hands away from his face. I hated her beak in his mouth, but I hated even more that she was touching him when she hadn't done so with the others. All amusement faded from Graith's face. He frowned, both he and Skieth cocking their heads to the side to observe me.

Dakas swallowed, but as Phegea leaned forward to give him more, he shook his head and turned to face me. He gave me an inquisitive look then took on a troubled expression.

My face burned with embarrassment. I'd never considered myself the jealous type. If this had been something inappropriate, he wouldn't have done it in front of me.

But why did she touch him?

"You haven't fed enough, Dakas," Phegea said.

"It's okay—"

"No," I interrupted, knowing he was refusing because of my stupid reaction. "You need proper sustenance with all the work you are doing. Don't mind me. I insist," I added when he seemed to hesitate.

He nodded with obvious reluctance. But as soon as she cupped his face again, my jealousy reared its ugly head. This time, Phegea looked at me with an amused expression.

"Dakas is my cousin, and I am already mated," Phegea said in a soft, musical voice. "Our Exarch was just being his insufferable self, trying to gross you out or stir some sort of strong reaction out of you. He didn't mean to make you jealous. But I'm glad it did."

"What?" I asked, my cheeks all but bursting into flames. "Why?"

"Because possessiveness proves you already care for Dakas," Phegea said matter-of-factly. "I hold his face because he doesn't have a beak. It helps me assess the distance to avoid stabbing him in the throat."

I scrunched my face, feeling stupid for my jealousy. "Thanks for explaining," I mumbled.

She winked while Dakas gave me a smile that was both smug and approving. Then he opened his mouth for Phegea to feed him some more. As soon as she was done, Graith gestured at me with his head.

"Why don't you give the new member of our tribe a taste?" he said to Phegea.

This time, my face utterly failed to hide my horror. Skieth and Graith burst out laughing while Dakas glared at them, and Phegea shook her head.

"If it's any consolation, Graith only picks on the people he likes," Dakas said. "And for what it's worth, feeding from the crop isn't so bad. It's like eating pureed food, all blended together."

"Just 'not-so-bad'?" I asked with a shudder. "You don't make much of a convincing argument. I'm happy to simply take your word for it."

"Dakas always had a fancy human palate," Phegea said with a chuckle. "He's never been too crazy about it either, so I think you'd enjoy it even less. If it's any consolation, our people usually eat their own meals. We only use crop-feeding in instances like today where we're on a tight schedule. This way, people can keep working without meal breaks. Now, off I go to feed the others. They will be ready to activate the fields in about thirty to forty minutes."

My heart soared. Although I had a semi-clear understanding of what they were doing, I would remain on edge until we had an effective wall protecting us.

"Go eat, my mate. I can feel your growing hunger. By the time you return, we will be ready," Dakas said.

"Okay," I replied. "But don't start without me!"

"We won't," Dakas said with an amused expression.

I glared at Graith, who was still staring at me with a smirk, then hurried back to my house. The Zelconian leader was growing on me. They all seemed like decent people. So why hadn't our tribes mingled more before this? My youth was filled with so many stories of the native species being hostile. I never really questioned it, but now I wanted answers.

As soon as I entered the house, I made a beeline for the kitchen and quickly slapped together a sandwich. But even as I started eating, I gave the room a critical assessment. Tonight, Dakas would come here and share my bedroom. My stomach knotted with sudden anxiety. Although he had promised not to make any demands, the reality of my situation struck me once more.

To my surprise, it wasn't so much the thought of sharing a bed with him that had me feeling frantic. At a visceral level, I trusted Dakas wouldn't try to get frisky with me until I was ready for it. But I was feeling self-conscious about what he would think of the house I shared with my father.

Like everything in Kastan, our abode was simple. No fancy furniture, designs, or decoration lifted the space. In keeping with the colony's purist ideal, my father had embraced a minimalist lifestyle. I'd just gone along for the ride. Although it made it easy to clean and maintain, the house also lacked spirit … personality.

Over the years, my father had shot down the few improvements I'd suggested. Under different circumstances, I would have held my ground, but Dad was the colony leader. If people entering our home found it to contravene all the basic principles of our founders, it would jeopardize his position. It had not been an important enough issue for me to go to war over it.

Nonetheless, we had increasingly clashed over the introduction and use of clean and responsible technological tools. These conflicts normally led nowhere. But I'd obtained a few minor concessions from him, after long and intense negotiation. Every time, it was because I'd managed to give him convincing enough arguments to sway the others.

Still chewing, I took a stroll through my bedroom, reshuffling some of my things so Dakas wouldn't stumble on a discarded bra or pair of undies. I hastily changed the bedsheets and gave the bedroom an extra cleaning. Unimpressed by the final result, I pursed my lips, resigned, and headed back outside. No amount of polish would turn this rough stone into a diamond.

I yelped when I opened the door and almost crashed into Dakas.

"I was coming to fetch you," Dakas said with a grin. "We're ready."

"Wonderful," I replied, my excitement skyrocketing.

Dakas took my hand and drew me after him. I liked that far too much. We weaved our way through the crowd gathered alongside the beams.

"The silver coating we've added to the poles gives them the same type of resistance as if they'd been built out of Titanium," Dakas explained. "It also absorbs most types of energy damage and channels it into the crystals we've embedded in them to enhance their power. Once activated, the crystals will build the energy fields."

I frowned, giving him a confused look. "But I thought your crystals served as the warp cores of high-end vessels?"

Dakas chuckled. "We have more than one type of crystal. Your UPO only knows of the ones we've told them. Stand here," he added, stopping about five meters from one of the beams. "I'll be back right after it's done."

I noticed then that the Zelconians were standing in pairs next to each of the beams. Dakas went to stand by his half-brother, Renok. They suddenly all moved in sync, each member of each pair facing one of the big crystals at the base of the pole. And then the most amazing melody rose as the Zelconians began to sing. It vaguely resembled a Gregorian chant. Goosebumps erupted all over my skin and shivers ran down my spine in successive waves. Their voices were so incredibly deep and reso-nant, I could have sworn the ground was vibrating beneath my feet as they sang, each pair harmonizing together.

A collective gasp erupted from the villagers as the dark-blue crystals embedded in the beams lit up and began pulsating from the bottom all the way to the top. As the song continued, the pulsations of the various crystals adjusted to each other until they achieved perfect synchrony. Seconds before that, without interrupting their chant, the Zelconians all stepped away from the crystals they were facing. Then a beam of light shot out from each crystal towards it closest neighbor in a pole a few meters away.

My hands flew to my chest, and I clutched them over my heart as bright lights flashed all around the village, the energy field going up between each beam almost like fire spreading along an oil track. Tears pricked my eyes as the Zelconian's chanting faded, and my mate turned to look at me.

While a victorious roar rose behind me, I silently mouthed two simple words to my husband: thank you. But my heart was shouting that he was my fucking hero.

CHAPTER 6
DAKAS

There was something wonderful about basking in the positive emotions of others. But nothing compared to those currently emanating from my mate. I felt like a god. At the same time, my heart filled with pride for my Zelconian brothers and sisters who had made this possible in such record time. The energy field was powerful and should stop all ground attacks. More work was left to do, but it could be tackled in the morning.

I gestured for Luana to approach. She didn't hesitate. But my joyous smile quickly faded as the same slimy aura tainted the air around us. I wanted to ignore Martin, but I kept an eye on him as he once more made his way to the front of the crowd.

"This is wonderful," Luana said as she came to a stop next to me.

"It is only the first step, but it will allow you all to sleep soundly tonight," I replied while removing the bracer attached to my wrist. "This will stop any ground attacks, but the village is still vulnerable to air attacks. Over the next couple of days, we will deploy a series of anti-missile drones to fly over the village until we can set up a more permanent solution. It will likely be a dome and a few turrets."

"That's amazing. Thank you. We never would have been able to do this on our own."

"My pleasure, my mate. Give me your wrist," I said, extending a hand towards her.

She complied, eyeing my armband with curiosity as I wrapped it around her wrist. Martin stood within hearing, making me grind my teeth. But I continued to ignore him.

"Tap here on the interface to display a map of the defensive wall," I explained. "The white dot is your current position. The blue dots indicate the locations where you can deactivate a small section to let people in and out of the village."

"According to this, we're standing right in front of this location," Luana said pensively while studying the interface before looking up at the wall.

"Correct. Tap on it to deactivate it."

My mate complied and whooped with delight when only the segment between the two poles in front of us deactivated, leaving the rest of the energy field standing.

"Simply tap on it again to reactivate it," I said. "If you forget to do so and move out of range, it will give you a 10-second warning for you to confirm that you want to keep it down. Failure to respond will reactivate the field. If you try to deactivate a section of the wall that you are far from, it will require a confirmation. It, too, will be on a timer and will automatically close if no one is in range for a certain amount of time."

"That's really good. The last thing we want is someone forgetting to close it and leaving us vulnerable," Luana said with a frown before glancing back at the wall. "But do we need to set another perimeter inside? There are children and pets running around. Will the wall harm them?"

"No," I said firmly. "This side is safe, although remaining in sustained contact with it will make you want to move away. It doesn't hurt, but its vibrations will create an increasingly unpleasant sensation. Touching the other side will zap you very hard though, unless it is set to lethal, in which case it will reduce you to ashes."

Luana's shoulders drooped with relief. "Perfect."

"But what about the rest of us?" Martin intervened. "Are we all getting a little bracer?"

"No," I said in a tone that brooked no argument. "For the time being, Luana will be the only person with a controller. Eventually, we can provide one for two or three people in total."

"Are you saying we are prisoners inside our own village?" Martin exclaimed loud enough to be heard by all before casting an outraged look at the crowd to gain support.

The urge to bash the man's head in returned with a vengeance. I reined myself in and projected my voice to be heard by all.

"I'm saying, until the situation with the Yurus is under control, you all need to shelter inside the village. There is no reason for the majority of you to be traipsing around the forest. If some of you have valid motives to go out frequently, we can provide you with your own bracer. Otherwise, you can request for one of us to let you out and escort you."

"So, now we need permission to go out, and can't do so without a watchdog? How is that not making us prisoners?" Martin argued.

"Why are you trying so hard to cause trouble?" Luana exclaimed, exasperated. "You know perfectly well they are not turning us into prisoners. *We* issued similar directives a week ago to reduce the risks of people getting hurt. Are you already forgetting that half of our fighters are currently lying in the clinic, severely injured? What could you possibly need to do in the forest that's so urgent you have to try and rile everyone up?"

"I'm a carpenter," Martin argued, suddenly sounding defensive. "I need wood to—"

"You have the shitload of wood we gathered for the wall,

two-thirds of which we didn't end up using," Luana snapped, interrupting him. "We have no other big construction projects ongoing. What possible need could you have of more wood?"

"Some furniture or repairs could need—"

"*If* someone needs a new piece of furniture, they'll be able to wait a few days for things to be sorted," Luana said, cutting him off again. "And *if* some urgent repairs are needed, a Zelconian will escort you for your own safety. You're inventing issues where there are none. We went to the Zelconians and asked for their help because we're unable to protect ourselves. Let them do their damn job."

Martin opened and closed his mouth, apparently looking for a comeback. But my mate turned to look at the rest of the crowd, dismissing him.

"Currently, I cannot think of anyone who might need to leave the village frequently," Luana said in a strong voice to be heard by all. "We've been diligent about stockpiling everything we might need. If you think you require a bracer, come discuss it with me, and we will address it on a case-by-case basis. Otherwise, if you only have to go out for the occasional specific errand, then go see one of the Zelconians. But keep it to urgent needs only. Going into the forest to pick wildberries for a dessert does *not* qualify. Questions?"

Everyone shook their heads, a few casting commiserating looks at Martin, while others glared at him.

"Good! I believe we are done for tonight?" Luana said, casting a questioning look my way. I nodded. "Thanks everyone for pulling your weight in helping the Zelconians get these defensive walls up and running. You are free to go about your personal business now, but get plenty of rest. We have more work to do in the morning."

The villagers slowly scattered, some of them taking a moment to thank my people, either with words or with a nod.

Graith approached us. "We're heading back to Synsara. I will leave a dozen guards on patrol. They will deploy the drones."

"Thank you, Exarch," I said gratefully.

"Yes, thank you for everything," Luana echoed.

Graith gave her a mischievous grin, although I didn't know how much of it she could perceive. Non-Zelconians had difficulty reading our facial expressions. Still, it warmed my heart to see our leader teasing my mate so much—undeniable proof he approved of her.

"That Martin male is going to be a problem," Graith mindspoke to me. *"He hates you. And the possessiveness he projected towards your female is turning into resentment. Keep a close eye on him."*

"I am aware, and I will," I telepathically replied.

"Enjoy your bonding night," Graith said to Luana in a taunting tone that almost made me chuckle.

This time, she was on to him. She didn't let him get a rise out of her and merely lifted her chin defiantly.

"Thank you, Exarch. I fully intend to," Luana said in a mysterious tone.

With a smirk and a bow of his head, Graith took flight, followed by three-quarters of our people who had come to Kastan.

When they became specks on the horizon, Luana's mood shifted, and she grew intimidated again.

"Well, I guess it's time for me to take you home," my woman said with a nervous laugh.

I smiled and nodded. I almost took her hand again, but decided not to this time. She was stressed enough, and I didn't want her misinterpreting the gesture. With each step, her tension increased, which baffled me. Thankfully, she wasn't afraid of me, but she was fearing something. I couldn't quite figure out what.

As soon as we entered the dwelling, Luana's worry turned into mortification as I gazed at the barren place. And then understanding dawned on me.

Why is she embarrassed of her home?

By Zelconian standards, it was extremely bland, but fully in keeping with what I'd seen so far of the aesthetic adopted by the humans of this colony—which I knew to be different from other humans' style.

"This is the kitchen and dining area, and this is the living area," Luana said, gesturing at them. "As you can see, we keep things minimalist here."

I nodded with a gentle smile as I followed her towards the back of the house.

"This door on the right is my father's bedroom. He has his own ensuite bathroom. This door leads to his office. It was originally designed to be a guest room, but as we don't actually have guests, there was no point. This door leads to the backyard. There isn't much there but a grassy area and the shed where Father keeps his tools. And this is my bedroom."

Her nervousness, which had begun to abate as she was giving me the tour, quickly rose again. I couldn't deny feeling a great deal of curiosity about her personal room. But when she opened the door, the same type of barren space welcomed me: a double bed, a night stand, a desk, and a dresser constituted the only furniture in the room. A single abstract painting adorned the left wall. A giant flat screen and a holographic calendar were the only other two things visible on the walls. Despite my initial disappointment, I could sense this wasn't her personal taste. She was merely conforming with the ways of her people, which was a relief.

"Although you don't have anything with you, and you don't wear clothing, I have freed the top two drawers of my dresser for you in case you need some storage space," Luana said.

"Thank you. That's very thoughtful."

She opened a door to show me a space where various pieces of clothing—mainly dresses—were hanging on a pole. "This is my wardrobe. I didn't make space for you since I doubt you'll have anything to hang there."

"Are you sure? Maybe I'll grow a liking to wearing human pants," I said teasingly.

Luana snorted, and her gaze traveled down my legs. Strangely enough, and for the first time in my life, I felt naked— which I technically was. To my relief, I didn't perceive any disgust from my mate, merely a fascinated curiosity. My legs were identical to a human's, aside from my blue skin, the smattering of feathers around my crotch, and the small blue scales covering my feet and ankles, which tapered off halfway up my calves.

Like every Zelconian, I walked around barefoot. But where the pureblood had bird-like feet with three frontal digits and one in the back—each ending in a vicious talon—my feet looked deceptively human, with five toes. However, where human tarsal bones were fairly long, mine were shorter to accommodate an extra row of metatarsal bones. As a result, I could fully fold my foot around an object the same way I could wrap my hand around a cup. And extruding the talons at the tips of my toes or at the back of my heel gave me a better grip. This was practical to catch something with my feet during a flyby, perch on a branch, or even hang upside-down like a bat.

Luana pursed her lips as she examined me then shook her head, the lovely curls of her long hair bouncing around her face.

"Nope. I can pretty much guarantee you will never develop a taste for that. Aside from the annoyance of doing laundry and ironing—if you don't have non-wrinkle fabric—they can start to feel uncomfortably confining."

"I'll take your word," I said teasingly.

She smiled and led me to the final door in the room. "This is my personal bathroom. I'm not sure how it works in Synsara, but we have the separate shower for a quick wash, the bathtub for relaxing, the sink to brush our teeth and wash our hands, and the toilet to evacuate waste."

The careful way in which she explained, as if she feared offending me, made me smile. "As a human-Zelconian hybrid, I am fairly familiar with all of this. We do not bathe, but we have showers. I use a toilet similar to this one, but without the water tank because of my tail and wings. The pureblood use a different system while standing up."

"Oh?" Luana asked, her eyes widening with curiosity.

Of course, as a medical doctor, our anatomical differences would intrigue her.

"Like most birds, Zelconians have a cloaca that manages both urine and solid wastes," I explained. "They merely stand in front of a waste funnel aligned with their cloaca to relieve themselves."

"But you don't have a cloaca?" Although she worded it like a question, it was more of a statement seeking confirmation.

"Correct. My anatomy is identical to a human's on that front. Well, aside from the fact that my genitals must be extruded and resorbed into my body."

"Fascinating," Luana said.

But I could also feel a certain level of relief emanating from her. Although my mate was showing herself to be very open-minded and accepting of my physical differences, I could sense she dreaded things would get too weird for her. Watching me crop feeding had not exactly been a turn on for Luana.

"Over time, I will be more than happy to teach you all about my people," I said with a grin.

"I would love that."

Silence settled between us. It wasn't awkward, but also not the most comfortable either.

"Since we are here, I actually wouldn't mind taking a shower," I said. "My feathers got quite dirty during today's work."

"Of course! Let me show you how to operate it," Luana quickly offered. "I'm not sure if you use soap or other products on your feathers, but everything I have is here. Feel free to use whatever you want or need. Also, don't worry, it's all unscented, so no risk of you smelling all girly and flowery when you're done."

I chuckled, wondering how she would react when she discovered Zelconian males actually enjoyed washing with fruity and flowery products to seduce their mates.

Luana opened the door of a cabinet and retrieved two large towels. "You can dry yourself with this when you're done."

She hesitated.

"What is it?" I asked.

"Well, while you're showering, I thought I could quickly drop by the clinic to check on the patients. Tilda, the nurse, will have already done it, but I always like doing a final round just in case, especially now, since my father is one of the wounded."

"Of course. Take the time you need. I'll be busy preening and making myself pretty for you."

Luana laughed, her eyes sparkling in the most enticing fashion. "All right, pretty boy. I will be back soon."

As soon as my mate walked out of the room, I went to the shower, turned on the water, then realized I had a major problem. The shower stall was far too small. I had noticed the tiny size of the bathroom, but it hadn't dawned on me just how puny it truly was. In Synsara, my personal shower was bigger than this entire room. There would be no way for me to shower without making a mess.

But sharing Luana's bed for the first time while stinking of sweat and with dirty feathers is out of the question!

I eyed the bath. While it would give me more wiggle room, it wasn't deep enough, and the faucet was much too low. I would need a bowl or bucket to pour water over me. That would be both inefficient and likely even messier than the shower.

I grunted in annoyance. For a split second, the thought of flying back to Synsara to take a proper scented shower crossed my mind. I wondered which fragrance would entice Luana the most. Imagining her rubbing her face all over the down feathers of my chest and neck as she inhaled the unique way the fragrance reacted with my body chemistry had my abdominal muscles contracting with anticipation.

After one last baleful glare at the bath, I returned my attention to the shower. I studied the problem for a few minutes before settling on a course of action. I lay down the second large towel Luana had given me on the floor—not that it would do much good with the deluge I would cause. Satisfied with the slightly-hotter-than-lukewarm water raining down, I stood sideways outside of the shower and stuck my right wing inside. To my dismay, I could only partially unfold it before it hit the walls. Worse still, the showerhead was too low, and the water failed to hit the top of my wing.

Thankfully, I could unhook the showerhead. For a split second, I considered using it over the bath, but the cord wasn't long enough. Then began the worst, messiest, most infuriating contortionist exercise of my life. Twisting this way and that, I ended up on my knees on the towel, the showerhead firmly held in my left hand, my torso leaning slightly inside the stall, and my wing deployed at a diagonal angle for maximum space. But even then, the ceiling kept it from fully expanding. But this was better than nothing.

Aiming the water on my wing at the right angle proved just as insanely challenging. It wasn't so bad on the inner face of my wing, but when it came to the outer side … I used every single curse word I had ever heard in my life and likely invented a few more in the process. Aside from the fact that I couldn't quite aim the water the right way, the wretched thing kept trickling down my back, between my tail feathers, down my butt and legs to soak up the towel under me. In no time, a small pool was forming on the floor, the supersaturated towel having lost its usefulness.

Infuriated, I got back up and managed—accidentally—to aim the showerhead into the room instead of the shower stall before turning off the water. Although my upper wing was waterproof and quickly shed all moisture, the lower feathers were soaked and happily dripped everywhere as I tried to dry the worst of it. They weren't properly clean, some dirt still clinging in-between them. But I'd already spent way too much time on that first wing alone. Luana would return any time now, and I didn't want her to find her bathroom turned into a disaster zone.

I hung the towel on the holder, then picked up the sodden one at my feet. After squeezing the water from it into the shower, I used it to wipe the pool I'd created on the floor. I then proceeded to repeat the dreadful process with my second wing. I was on my knees, in the same awkward position and cursing up a storm when a wave of worry slammed into me.

Luana!

Panicked, I scrambled to my feet, spraying the fuck out of the room with the rogue showerhead before I managed to shove it back in its holder. I cast a distressed glance at my surroundings. I would never have time to clean up enough before Luana reached me. The thought had no sooner crossed my mind than a knock resonated on the door.

"Dakas? Is everything okay? I heard you cussing. May I come in?"

The concern in her voice echoed the one broadcast by her emotions. I closed my eyes and cringed inwardly.

"I … I'm afraid I made a bit of a mess. Do not panic when you enter," I said, defeated.

Judging by the spike of worry I perceived from my mate, my words had the exact opposite effect I'd hoped for. Luana carefully opened the door and poked her head inside. Her jaw dropped as she took in the soaked towel swimming in the puddle on the floor, water dripping down the walls from one of the numerous times I'd accidentally sprayed the room, and me looking like a wet pup with my left wing partially spread inside the shower stall so it wouldn't drip more water on the floor—not that it would have made much of a difference at this point.

As her gaze returned to my mortified face, her bulging eyes clearly asked what in the world had happened here.

"The shower is too small to accommodate my wings, and the cord of the showerhead is too short to reach the bath," I mumbled. "I tried to get creative but... Well, the results speak for themselves."

Luana gaped at me for a second longer before looking over my shoulder at my still dripping left wing in the shower. Then, as if a switch had been flipped, she scrunched up her face like someone about to sneeze, then she burst out laughing. It was the loveliest sound, draping me in an intense feeling of euphoria. Luana's empathy for my trials and amusement at the situation instantly shattered my embarrassment. Instead, infused with my mate's hilarity, I started chuckling.

"I'm so sorry, Dakas. I didn't think of that at all," Luana said apologetically. "The cord of the showerhead actually extends. I used to have a dog, and I would wash him with the showerhead in the bath—not that I'm comparing you to a dog."

I had not taken offense at her words, but something more important held all my attention. My head jerked towards the showerhead, and I looked over the way to extend the cord, wondering how I could have possibly missed it.

"It's not inside the shower," Luana said with a small giggle. "It's the switch next to the sink. Hang on."

She kicked off her shoes in the bedroom, which was still dry, and walked barefoot into the waterlogged bathroom. She reached for a pair of switches on the wall by the sink and flicked the one on the right. A clicking sound resonated inside the stall, and the cord loosened. I picked up the showerhead and, sure enough, at least three more meters of cord poured out of the wall.

I cursed under my breath, making Luana chuckle some more. "I thought those were light switches," I mumbled.

"You had no reason to think otherwise," Luana said in a gentle voice. "I should have explained it to you, but it never crossed my mind that it could be useful to you. But now, you can get in the tub. It will be much easier. Still a little cramped but certainly not as painful."

"Yes, thank you."

"But wait. Give it to me for a second," Luana said, extending a hand towards me.

I gave her the showerhead, and she turned the surrounding ring. A button immediately popped up by the handle.

"This button now controls the water flow," my mate explained. "So, you can turn on the water in the shower, but it won't rain until you press the button."

Just to demonstrate, Luana turned on the water in the shower then held the showerhead over the bath before pressing the button. Water immediately shot out, stopping as soon as she released the button.

"Well, that too would have been practical to know earlier," I said in a dejected voice, which made her laugh again.

I could already tell I would become utterly addicted to her laughter and the emotions that accompanied it. But she quickly sobered and gave me an assessing look.

"What is it?" I asked.

"I was just thinking, considering your wingspan, even with the longer showerhead hose, things will likely be awkward for you. Do you want me to help? I'd be happy to assist."

My heart leapt in my chest at the unexpected offer, and a

powerful emotion coursed through me. Mates preening each other was a great sign of affection. Although Luana entertained no such feelings for me yet, I could sense the sincerity of her desire to help. And underneath it, her desire to take advantage of this to sate her curiosity about my body.

"I would be grateful for your help, my mate."

CHAPTER 7
LUANA

I stared at Dakas getting into the bath while fighting the urge to giggle again. I still couldn't believe what a mess he had made of the bathroom. I wished I could have witnessed how he had accomplished it. Poor thing. He looked so utterly mortified when I entered, like a lost puppy ... or rather a drenched cat. And yet, I was happy this happened. He looked so perfect, so strong, so above the kinds of fuck ups humans got into, I'd almost felt unworthy. This humanized him in the best way and made him feel more accessible and relatable.

He turned to face me with the strangest expression on his face. Although I couldn't begin to interpret it, I liked how it made me feel.

"So ... hmm, what should I do? Just spray you? And do you need soap?" I asked, feeling ridiculously excited about this.

"No soap, never on the wing feathers," he explained gently. "I will require your help for both wings and my back. I'll be able to finish the rest on my own. I will use soap on my skin."

He looked at himself in relation to the relatively small length of the bath and pursed his lips while pondering. He then moved as far left as he could in the bath.

"Let's start with my right wing," he said, spreading it.

I'd known their span to be wide, but in that instant, I realized just how impressive they were. No wonder he'd made such a mess in here. Even now, he had to tilt the tip of the wing up to unfold it fully.

"Your wings are really stunning," I blurted out without thinking.

His eyes widened, then the blue skin of his face took on a slightly darker shade as he smiled. It was beyond adorable.

"Thank you, my mate." He pointed at the tip and gestured in a downward motion. "Apply the water from the tip but always follow the direction of the feathers. Go from top to bottom, then gradually move in closer to me while repeating this motion."

"Okay. Should I rub the feathers as I do?"

"No! You want to avoid messing with the feathers as much as possible to avoid damaging them. It only takes a couple of broken or missing feathers to wreck our flight pattern. Then we look like we're drunk, until we figure out how to compensate," Dakas said with a horrified expression.

I laughed at his overly dramatic description—which I knew he'd done on purpose. He grinned, looking so pleased with himself I realized he sought to make me laugh, or at least smile.

He did say his goal is to make me happy. I can get used to this.

After a few clumsy attempts, I finally got the hang of it. Once I finished with the inner side of his right wing, Dakas folded it just long enough to turn around, move to the opposite side of the bath, and spread his wing again so I could wash its back. We repeated the process with his left wing, then he remained facing away from me so I could get to work on his back.

He bowed his head to lift out of the way the dozen or so straight long feathers at the back of his head which deceptively resembled long blue hair from a distance. Fluffy midnight-blue down feathers covered his nape and shoulders and tapered off in a V between his shoulder blades. A very soft sort of fluff feathers followed the line of where his wings fused into his back. Following the method I'd now all but mastered, I washed the feathers around his nape.

"For these ones, you can gently scrape your nails through them. Very gently. It shouldn't damage them, but even if it did, I don't need them for flying," Dakas said. "Then you can scratch a bit more vigorously the line along my wings."

"Okay," I said with far too much eagerness. "Tell me if it's too much or not enough."

The smile he gave me over his shoulder gave away the fact that he was on to me. I wasn't even ashamed. This whole time, I'd been dying with the urge to touch his feathers. They looked so damn soft! I started carefully scraping his nape. After a few seconds, a strong shiver coursed through him. Alarmed, I stopped, wondering if I had hurt him.

"Don't stop," Dakas said, his voice barely a grumbling whisper, which struck straight at my core.

He's enjoying this!

Rather than making me feel awkward, it emboldened me. Another shiver shook his body, and he pressed his palms against the wall, his head dipping lower. With great reluctance, having washed this section for as long as I reasonably should, I moved down to the upper part of the large muscle where his right wing connected to his back. I started scratching.

"Harder," Dakas said immediately, his voice getting me all hot and bothered again.

I complied. By the fourth or fifth scratch, I recoiled, and my eyes nearly popped out of my head when I heard the most unexpected sound.

I froze. "Did you just coo?"

Dakas stiffened, his wings shifted a bit, then he shrugged. "Maybe?" he said, sounding a little defensive.

"You totally did! So, I guess you like getting the edge of your wings scratched, huh?" I asked, resuming my attentions to that spot.

"It ... it is relaxing," he said, his voice dropping an octave, and he sounded groggy.

Moments later, he cooed again. It was such an unexpected sound from such an intimidating male that it made me chuckle again. It wasn't high pitched like the cooing of a dove, but it wasn't quite deep enough to be considered a purr or a rumble. It was cute, but also sexy as hell. I continued scratching the fluff feathers lining the edge of the right wing all the way down before moving to the left one. I didn't lift my hand, just raked my nails along across his spine to the other side.

I never reached it.

Dakas cried out, throwing his head back and pulling away from my touch. I yelped, jumping back in surprise, before staring at him wide-eyed. He took in a hissing breath and gave me an almost savagely sensual look that had me instantly wet.

"It is best you avoid touching the area in the middle of my lower back," Dakas said in a throaty voice. "Especially with your nails. It is highly erogenous for us."

He didn't need to explain that to me. My inner walls were still throbbing from the way he had sounded when he'd cried out. I suspected he sounded almost the same when he was about to climax.

"Apologies?" I said, not feeling sorry one bit.

He snorted and shook his head at me, not fooled in the least. He turned back, and I finished scratching the edge of his left wing, enjoying more of his sexy cooing. I was tempted to give his mid lower back another good scratch before finishing, but I didn't want to send him the wrong signal. When he turned back to face me, his expression told me that, once again, he knew exactly what naughty thoughts had needled me.

"Thank you, my mate. I will be able to finish on my own," he said with a mysterious smile.

"Okay. Let me get the soap for you." I handed him the showerhead, then reached for the soap by the sink and gave it to him. "While you finish, I'll go take a quick shower in my father's bathroom."

"Thank you. See you soon."

I closed the door behind me, my fingers still tingling from the feeling of his feathers. If they were this soft while wet, how fluffy would they be when dry? How would it feel to rest my head on his chest which was covered with them?

I quickly chased those wandering thoughts and grabbed my least matronly nightgown and clean undies before hurrying to my father's bathroom. Since our relationship wasn't there yet, I wouldn't have worn some sexy lace or silk negligee—not that I owned any. However, after I changed the bedding, I should have gone and bought something a little more alluring. The fact that I wasn't ready to roll in the hay with my husband didn't mean I should wear some kind of potato sack. At least, the sleeveless, white cotton nightgown fell right above my knees and was just sheer enough to give a slight glimpse of my silhouette beneath. Although properly demure, the square, embroidered collar gave just a tiny hint of the curve of my breasts.

Normally, I enjoyed lingering under a hot, almost scalding shower. This time, I sped up a little, but not too much. I wanted to give Dakas a chance to finish and dry himself without feeling pressured. He certainly had quite a large surface to handle.

And a very nice-looking surface at that.

I was really digging my husband. Sure, it was waaay too early to have a crush or any serious feelings, but I was enjoying his personality so far. He seemed sweet, with an easy humor, but also smart, hard-working, efficient, protective, and didn't put up with bullshit. I still felt so proud of the way he'd taken charge in setting up our defenses. Our people could be difficult sometimes when chores needed to be done. But no one challenged him, automatically submitting to his natural aura of authority and obvious competence.

No one but Martin...

That thought completely squashed the happy buzz I'd been floating in since finding Dakas nearly swimming in the watery mess he'd created in my bathroom. I didn't know what the hell was going on with Martin. Or rather, I didn't understand his excessively obnoxious behavior today. He was always a pain in the ass whenever things didn't go his way, but this was extreme, even for him.

I had known Martin my whole life. He wasn't a bad person, just spoiled. I could only hope he would get his shit together soon before things got out of hand. Dakas didn't like him AT ALL. The way he'd looked at Martin when he'd compared me to a gaping fish out of water had scared me. I was convinced Dakas had wanted to inflict the same kind of damage he'd done to that pole to demonstrate how flimsy it was. The other Zelconians, and especially Graith and my brother-in-law Renok, had cast very dark looks in Martin's direction.

I just hope their empathic abilities do not reveal him to be a true monster.

For all his faults, Martin was a valued member of the village, and his widowed mother was the sweetest lady in the world. Losing her beloved husband early had pushed her to dote on their only son, turning him into the insufferably entitled spoiled brat he was today.

Realizing I had lingered long enough. I got out of the shower, put my nightgown on, and dropped by the kitchen to pick up the mop before sauntering back to my room.

"Come in!" Dakas called out before I could even knock on the bathroom door.

I opened it to find him out of the bath, looking dry except for the tips of his wings, and the bathroom almost back to its pre-disaster state. But it was his feet that held my whole attention, more specifically the right one. I'd noticed something odd about them earlier, but now I really got it. He had folded his foot almost like a hand to grip the towel on the floor, which he had used to mop the mess. The abnormal curve definitely qualified as freaky. But to the medical doctor in me, it was beyond fascinating.

Still gripping the towel with his foot, he bent his leg, lifting it sideways so he could take the towel in his hands without bending down. My eyes flicked to his, and I realized he'd been staring at me the whole time, no doubt assessing my reaction to his unique anatomy... by human standards. Did he fear that would turn me off?

"Your anatomy is fascinating to the physician in me and has my human side burning with curiosity," I said matter-of-factly.

His face softened and a mischievous smile stretched his lips. "I'm yours, Luana. We can play doctor-patient whenever you want."

I gasped, wondering if he knew the actual meaning of that saying. His shit-eating grin seemed to say yes, but his starry eyes made him very hard to read. He wrung the water out of the towel in the sink and looked back at the floor for which spot still needed to be wiped.

"No! Don't do that! I was bringing the mop to take care of it," I exclaimed.

"Why should *you* take care of it when *I* made the mess?" he asked, looking surprised.

"Because you're my..."

He raised a feathery eyebrow and cocked his head to the side while waiting to see what I was going to say. I'd almost said he was my guest. In a way, he was, but he was also my husband now. While the colony sought to live in a more traditional way devoid of a noticeable dependence on technology, we weren't old-fashioned in terms of gender roles or gender equality.

"Because if I had been more attentive to your needs earlier, you wouldn't have been put in a position to create this mess to begin with. So, it's my fault," I said.

"I disagree. I know my spatial needs for showering. I should have brought up the issue before you left," he countered. "It was also my choice to try something completely crazy instead of waiting for your return to discuss alternative solutions. So, it was my failure to communicate properly and my poor choices that caused this mess."

"Fine, we both failed," I said with a shrug. "Which means, we'll both clean up. You can have the mop. Since you've already done most of that job, you might as well finish it. I'll get the walls."

To my surprise, this seemed to please him. Dakas took the mop and got the last few damp spots, while I grabbed a cloth to wipe the ones on the wall. We finished almost at the same time while having a laidback conversation about the various types of feathers on his body, and the fact that some were waterproof and others not. Apparently, the waterproof ones were meant to facilitate swimming. I also learned that, in his dwelling in Synsara, he had a state-of-the-art drying system to take care of the ones that got wet.

After sticking the mop in the shower to dry, I whipped out my hair dryer and went to town on his still damp feathers, keeping the heat level low and the device at a reasonable enough distance to avoid damaging them. Dakas's reaction to me caring for him confirmed he loved being pampered. Lucky for him, I was loving every minute of it ... for now.

Once done, I returned to my bedroom ... with my husband. My throat suddenly got super dry as we'd finally reached the moment of truth.

"So ... hmmm ... do you have a preferred side?" I asked with a nervous giggle. "Actually, how do you normally sleep with those wings?"

"Depends. My bed is three times as wide as yours and one meter longer," Dakas said with an amused look. "Sometimes, I sleep on my back, or on my stomach, with my wings spread wide. Sometimes I curl up on my side with them folded behind me. Sometimes, I just crouch on a tree, my wings wrapped around me."

My eyes widened. "You crouch on a tree?!"

"When we're migrating and decide to pause for the night in the middle of nowhere," he said with a shrug.

"And you don't fear falling?"

He shook his head. "My body knows what to do to keep its balance, even if I'm asleep." He turned his gaze back to my bed. "But to answer your question, considering the limited space we'll share, I will sleep on my side with my wings folded behind me. Since your nightstand is on the right, I'm assuming it's your preferred side. So, I'll take the left. It's all the same to me."

"Okay," I said, gesturing nervously for him to proceed.

Watching him get into my bed did the weirdest thing to me. I wasn't a virgin, but I had never slept with a man under the roof I shared with my father. Seeing his feet hang off the end of the bed made me feel guilty and also emphasized just how tall and imposing my mate was.

"I'm sorry you're so cramped," I said sheepishly.

Dakas merely smiled and extended a hand towards me. That should have freaked me out, but I immediately went to him and accepted his hand as I climbed into bed. I lay on my side, facing him. He kept my hand in his.

We stared at each other for a few seconds. The absence of awkwardness or uneasiness baffled me. For a reason I couldn't explain, I felt safe.

"Tell me about yourself, Luana."

I shrugged, scrunching my face. "I was born in this village twenty-six years ago. It was a difficult pregnancy for my mother. She'd had difficulty conceiving before, and again after me. She actually died from complications from another pregnancy when I was five years old."

Dakas gently squeezed my hand in a comforting gesture but spared me the empty apologies for my loss.

"Is that what prompted you to become a healer?" he asked softly.

I nodded. "I was so angry back then. Mother had been sick from the start of her pregnancy. Gunter—our doctor at the time—kept saying she just needed rest, but I knew more could have been done. I just didn't know what. After her passing, I swore I would never be that helpless again. I wouldn't sit there listening to some other person telling me why nothing more could be done to save someone I loved. I would know what to do."

"So, you became this Gunter's student once you were old enough?"

I shook my head. "No. Gunter was one of the hardcore fans of the 'simpler way of life' espoused by the founders of our village. Jenna—the elder woman who challenged you earlier about the defensive wall being high-tech—is his widow. He died from a stupid infection after getting injured during a trek in the forest. We hadn't encountered the specific bacterial strain that he had contracted. More advanced equipment would have allowed us to devise a more effective and timely treatment for him. When we finally did, he was already beyond help."

Dakas shook his head in a way that said "what a waste."

"Back in those days, we had a number of people who ended up either dying or getting stuck with permanent complications or disabilities from injuries that could have been fully mended. Frankly, I feel it was criminal for our medical doctor to want to stick to old, primitive healing methods out of ideology when efficient, far more advanced techniques, methods, and treatments existed."

Dakas nodded slowly, his face lighting up with curiosity. "How did you learn then?"

"I cheated," I confessed shamelessly. "With my father being the colony leader, he's one of the few people with access to the galactic network. I would sneak into his office when he was out to use the online learning site."

He snorted, a glimmer of admiration in his eyes. "Clever. But I'm guessing he eventually caught you?"

I nodded. "I'm not sure when he figured it out. I know it was long before he actually confronted me about it."

"Oh? Why did he allow you to continue?"

"I think my father realized our current ways could not—and frankly would not—continue much longer," I said pensively. "People in my generation and younger are chafing at this primitive lifestyle our ancestors have imposed on us. We understand what drove them to it, but they've gone to the other extreme. However, there's only so much leeway my father can give us without jeopardizing his leadership. But the plague is what really changed things."

"The plague?" Dakas asked, recoiling.

"Mmhmm. When I was seventeen, a bug infestation ravaged the area. It was like a swarm of locusts had descended on us. We'd never seen those bugs before, but they apparently came far from the northeast," I said with a shudder. "Their bites made a lot of us extremely sick. We called it the plague, but it was similar to malaria. I was horribly sick and nearly died. That's when Dad authorized Tilda—the nurse who had taken over Gunter's practice—to reach out to the traveling human doctors of the UPO."

"And they came to your rescue," Dakas said.

"No, they couldn't," I said dejectedly.

"What?" he exclaimed.

"We were an illegal colony. They couldn't help us unless we agreed to be evacuated, which would make us legal citizens again of the United Planets. However, they could analyze a newly discovered lethal disease and make public their recommendations on ways to treat the disease."

Dakas snorted. "Another workaround."

I nodded. "The UPO is pretty big on that. They never break their own rules, but will find alternative solutions when they deem the cause worthy. It confused me, because how could our struggling colony be of any value to them? But I realized today that they were playing the long game. Having humans here could eventually help a rapprochement between our people."

His thumb gently caressed the back of my hand as he smiled. "And that gamble paid off, which I'm grateful to them for."

I smiled back, feeling stupidly shy.

"Tilda downloaded the treatment protocol and was able to save us all," I continued. "When I fully recovered, my father confronted me about my secret studies. He asked how serious I was about it. I told him if he tried to stop me, I would find a way around him and everyone else. He said good, because he wouldn't stop me. He'd already lost my mother and almost lost me. Instead, he provided me with a holographic tutoring system that allowed me to perform some of the more advanced studies, like surgical simulations."

"That's wonderful. It's just unfortunate it took a tragedy for things to change," Dakas said.

I nodded. "It has been a constant struggle, but it opened the door to more progress. At first, Lara had to come to my house to study engineering in secret. But once people started running out of power and freezing due to our solar panels exceeding their life expectancy, and since the UPO merchants refused to trade new ones with us for fear of getting in trouble, they realized we needed to be able to build our own stuff."

"So, what kind of future do you wish for yourself and for the colony?" Dakas asked, the sudden intensity of his gaze indicating my answer was important to him.

"Wow, that's a heavy question," I said with a nervous laugh.

He simply smiled. "Since this morning, the future I have envisioned obviously got completely upended. So, I guess I'll answer about the colony first."

"Fair enough."

"I respect our ancestors' desire to avoid the obsessive dominance of technology that drove them away from the world they lived in," I said carefully. "The way they described it, human contact became almost non-existent because everything was done digitally through emails and vidcoms. Machines did everything, from cleaning, cooking, building, to education, medicine, sex, and even art. Why work on building a healthy relationship with someone, which requires understanding and concessions, when you can have an android exactly designed to your specifications?"

"I can see how the personal relations and interactions could be affected, but why reject the benefits of automating chores?" Dakas asked with some confusion.

"Because it apparently made us too lazy and entitled," I said, rolling my eyes. "Since machines could get things built or done quickly, people started becoming more and more demanding, expecting instant gratification in all things and losing all appreciation for anything since everything was readily available without any effort or sacrifice. But there needs to be a middle ground, not a complete vilification of everything that could improve our way of life."

"Therefore, you want to be able to embrace technology again," Dakas concluded.

"I want us to make use of the technology that will make our lives better and easier, without losing sight of the things that are important, like family and community. I don't want our younger generations to be forced to hide in order to enrich their minds or be made to feel like traitors for wanting more out of life than stagnating in the past. And I want the colony to do it together, united, not through a revolt from our youth. I've already heard too many talks of splitting off into a different colony. Frankly, without the Yurus attack, I think it might have happened."

"Ancestors! We had no idea such tensions were building within your colony."

"It's bubbling under the surface. Despite many hints, the elders have conveniently buried their heads in the sand. But I think recent events are exactly the catalyst we needed. And, from a selfish point of view, I'm ecstatic."

"Oh? Why is that?"

"Because, as the leader's daughter, I was forced to rein myself in not to undermine his authority. But now, as a married woman, and one who will mainly live outside of the colony, I'll finally be able to spread my *virtual* wings," I said with a grin. "The high-tech medical equipment Kayog has sent us is already a gold mine for me. But with your people being open to techno-logical advancement, there will be no limits to all I'll be able to learn and do now."

"You have no idea all the wonders now open to you, Luana," Dakas said with a fervor that moved me deeply. "Many say marriage is a cage. But in our case, you will find it is the key to your freedom. But for now, sleep, my mate. A busy day awaits us in the morning. I want us to be done here quickly so I can show you your new home. You will love Synsara."

I smiled and gently squeezed his hand, which still held mine. "I can't wait to see it."

His thumb caressed the back of my hand again, and he closed his eyes. With a contented sigh, I closed mine as well and dreamt of all the wonders awaiting me.

CHAPTER 8
DAKAS

My eyes snapped open. I couldn't tell what had awakened me, but the lingering sense of urgency instantly faded. The feel of Luana's body pressed against me—her face buried in my neck, her arm possessively wrapped around my waist, a leg entangled with mine—dominated everything else.

Whatever dream had swept away my mate stirred the most delicious emotions within her. She sighed softly, the sensual sound sending a just as delectable shiver down my spine. Luana tightened her hold and gently nuzzled her face against my down feathers before settling again.

I carefully kissed her forehead, wrapped my arm around her, and spread my right wing over her body like a blanket. As I closed my eyes, the sense of urgency which had awakened me surged again right before Renok's alarmed voice resonated in my mind.

"Dakas! Wake up! A raiding party is incoming!"

I immediately tensed. *"On my way!"*

Luana's arm fell from around my waist, and she startled awake, looking confused. "What …?"

"I'm sorry, my Luana. I have to go," I said, disentangling myself from her and getting out of bed.

"What's going on?"

"My brother just informed me a Yurus raid is incoming."

"What? Oh, my God!"

Luana jumped out of bed, fear radiating from her as she rushed to her wardrobe. I circled the bed, grabbed my woman by the shoulders, and gently turned her to face me.

"Calm, my Luana," I said in an appeasing tone. "It is just a raiding party. They will not get past the energy wall. We set the defenses in time. They will soon see your village is no longer helpless. We've turned the alarm off to avoid creating a panic. But if the villagers notice anything, you must reassure them. Keep them calm and well away from the perimeter. In the mean-time, my people and I will chase the Yurus."

"A-all right," Luana said, struggling to rein in her fear. "Promise me you'll be careful."

"I promise, my mate."

To my surprise, Luana cupped my face and drew me down, pressing her lips to mine. I instinctively grasped her hips, tilted my head, and increased the pressure of my mouth on hers. As much as I wanted to indulge further, I forced myself to pull away. My palm resting on her cheek, I caressed her lips with my thumb.

"Do not fear, my mate. I will return to you safely. Trust me."

Luana inhaled deeply and nodded, her beautiful face taking on a determined look. I smiled as the strong little warrior, which lurked behind the timid persona she occasionally wore, came to the fore.

Reluctantly letting go, I retrieved my other armband and left the room.

"How many are there?" I telepathically asked Renok, while placing the bracer on my arm.

"There are three groups of five or six closing in on the village, each heading to a different location."

"They want to force the humans to split their defenses," I said.

"Yep. But they have a surprise coming." My brother's psychic voice had a bloodthirsty edge. *"Sending their position to the defensive wall map. We have four guards at each of the three locations. Should we call for reinforcement from Synsara?"*

I shook my head, even though he couldn't see me. *"No, not yet. There aren't many Yurus attacking. They are expecting an easy bit of fun. Hang on."*

Expanding the psychic connection, I formed a group, linking the minds of all twelve of the Zelconian guards who had stayed to protect Kastan. Creating a psychic group was strenuous for any of us, exacerbated by the number of people included. As a hybrid, it was even harder on me. I wouldn't hold it for very long, but we needed to get everyone up to speed quickly.

"Do not show yourselves," I said to the group. *"Let the Yurus reach the wall and observe how they react. Do not engage until I give the order."*

I felt the acknowledging nudge from each of the guards before disbanding the psychic group. I folded my crest and fanned my darker hackle and shoulder feathers over my chest to cover the brighter colors of my natural adornments. In the darkness, my midnight-blue feathers allowed me to blend with the shadows.

After casting a glance at the anti-missile drones hovering over the village, I flew over the energy wall to the first trees, ten meters away, lining the start of the forest. I extruded the talons at the tips of my toes and back of my heels seconds before I landed on one of the thick, middle branches of a tree. My feet closed around the branch, and I crouched down, wrapping my wings around my body. Their darker color would hide the paler blue hue of my skin, while also blending with the thick leaves of the tree.

"They're approaching, ETA one minute," Renok mentally spoke to his unit and me.

I watched Renok fly silently to a tree across from my position. According to the interface on my bracer, the other three members of Renok's unit—Calluas, Selsan, and Yeiron—were also perched nearby.

My pulse picked up. Based on reports we'd gathered from the villagers throughout the day, we didn't expect the Yurus to have any weapon or scanner. Knowing the humans to be helpless, they usually came empty-handed, except for a couple of nyloths to carry their stolen goods back to their village.

Even now, I could hear the dull thumps of a nyloth's massive front legs striking the ground as it approached and the clicking sound of its smaller back legs. The enthusiastic voices of the Yurus revealed their anticipation of the terror they would instill in the hearts of the villagers as they plundered their riches.

Not today, you won't.

A malicious glee filled my heart as five imposing Yurus and a mature nyloth entered my line of sight. The creature vaguely resembled a three-meter long, grayish-green lobster, with spindly legs the entire length of its flat tail, and a head like a fly. On its back, the Yurus had harnessed a large wooden container they hoped to fill. Their leader's hooved feet pounded the ground, his bull tail wagging with excitement as he spoke loudly to his team. By the size and length of the tusks framing his mouth and the countless scars on his face and visible through the fur covering his body, he was a seasoned fighter, with the ego to go with it. My perfect night vision would allow me to savor the expression on his face the minute he noticed the wall.

"This should be good," Renok telepathically said to the unit. He could maintain the group link for a couple of hours, if necessary. I would have been exhausted in half the time.

I chuckled inwardly and felt the amusement of the others through our mental connection.

"*Jaafan!* What is that?" the Yurus leader exclaimed, his eyes bulging as he came to a sudden stop.

I pinched my lips to stifle my laughter. More *jaafans*—as well as a few other choice Yurus swear words—erupted from his companions.

"Wonjin, go," the leader ordered one of his teammates—no doubt the grunt of the unit—with a gesture of his head towards the wall.

The Yurus named Wonjin looked less than thrilled but obeyed. He scanned the ground until he found a large rock then approached the wall. Stopping a couple of meters away, he threw the rock with all his strength. The projectile shattered against the energy field and turned into dust. An area of effect blasted outward from that section of the wall, knocking over anything within five meters. Wonjin cried out as he flew back a few meters, crashing at the feet of his companions who had barely managed to get out of the way.

"*Jaafan! Jaafan!*" their leader cursed and spat on the ground. "When did those *hoodah* build this? Since when do they have technology?"

"Tarmek, I think we should return to Mutarak and warn Vyrax," one of the males said to their leader while Wonjin rose painfully to his feet.

"Are you stupid, Zulkis?!" Tarmek hissed. "What do you think Vyrax will do to your *jaafing* ass when he finds out you went out on a final raid two days before the attack? Especially since he forbade any raids, so the *hoodahs* would let their guards down?"

"We could be heroes," Wonjin said tentatively. "If we don't warn him, Vyrax will not come sufficiently armed to deal with this level of defense since the humans always cower. He'll be enraged if—"

Tarmek charged Wonjin and punched him in the face so hard, I wouldn't have been surprised if he crushed his cheekbones or dislocated his jaw. Blood exploded from Wonjin's mouth as he fell to the ground, but he sat up immediately, wiping his mouth with the back of his hand, looking no worse for wear. The three other males had seemed to concur with the grunt, but they quickly slapped neutral expressions on their faces.

"Vyrax will thank you for this information, seconds before he tears you limb from limb and eats your still bleeding flesh right off your bones, you *jaafing* slit."

Minkus's voice in my head startled me as he reported a similar scenario happening at his team's location. Garok reported the same.

"Do not interfere," I ordered.

The Yurus argued a short while longer before starting to throw whatever they could get their hands on at the wall. I savored their rage at being denied a night of fun, bullying humans, and looting. But their emotions confirmed they had no real hope of breaching the wall. They just wanted to test it.

"Tarmek, what of the others?" Zulkis suddenly asked after yet another large rock failed to even remotely damage the energy field. "Did they also encounter a wall? The village is still quiet, so I can only assume they haven't been able to raid from their end."

"What's your point?" Tarmek asked angrily.

"What if *they* decide to run back to Mutarak and warn Vyrax?" he asked.

Tarmek froze, horror descending on his features. "Back to the city at once! We were *never* here! Is that understood?"

"Yes, Tarmek," the four males said obediently.

But even as they turned back, Tarmek unclipped from his belt what I presumed to be a personal com device. Moments later, Minkus confirmed his team of Yurus had been contacted and was pulling out.

"Let them go. Remain unseen," I ordered our units.

"We could try to beat them to their village to draw attention to their return so Vyrax would butcher them. Fewer enemies for us to deal with," Renok suggested.

"A tempting thought, but it would also alert Vyrax to the defenses we've set up," I countered. *"They plan to attack the day after tomorrow, presumably without their technological weapons. I want him to remain blissfully ignorant. We have until then to make as many weapons as we can from the blueprints Kayog gave us. We'll scare the living daylights out of the Yurus when they show up."*

"Understood."

When the Yurus were far enough away, we came out of our hiding places and flew back into the village. Still sound asleep, none of the villagers had even noticed the threat that the wall had averted. Covered in a thick robe and standing at the edge of the village square, Luana pressed both her palms to her chest as if to hold in her frantically beating heart while watching us land safely.

"Go back to bed with your mate, Dakas. We'll warn you if any more trouble arises," Renok said.

"Thank you, brother," I said, letting him feel my gratitude.

The joy and relief emanating from my woman as I approached her filled me with the most wondrous sensation. I smiled and something seemed to break inside of her. Luana ran, crossing the short distance between us, and threw herself into my arms. I closed my arms and wings around her in a comforting gesture before kissing the top of her head.

"All is well, my mate. The wall confounded them. They gave up and turned back."

She tightened her hold for a second then loosened it to peer up at me. "Thank you so much."

"I didn't do anything tonight but watch them fail miserably at weakening our defenses," I said smugly. "But you are welcome.

88

Let's get back to bed. We're going to have a lot of work to do tomorrow."

Luana yelped in surprise then giggled when I lifted her into my arms and carried her home. Along the way, I gave her a quick summary of what had transpired by the wall.

"This is actually good," Luana said as I set her back on her feet. She removed the thick robe she had put on and hung it in her wardrobe while I circled around to the other side of the bed. "We now know when they want to attack. We have all of tomorrow to build weapons. Actually, I suspect it will be a few more days because Vyrax will waste a stupid amount of time trying to breach our defenses without weapons before turning tail. But then, he'll probably come back a couple of days later with his maximum arsenal. Do you think we will be able to thwart him?"

The hope mixed with uncertainty in her voice, gaze, and emotions made me want to pull her into my embrace, but I forced myself to simply lie next to her.

"The blueprints we've been studying with Lara are phenomenal," I said in a reassuring tone. "Kayog made sure we had the type of weapons that would discourage even Vyrax. Lara said she would have all the weapon molds ready for the morning so we can start casting them at first light. I am confident all will go well. Sleep now, my mate. I need you well rested."

To my delightful surprise, Luana snuggled closer, gently pressed her lips to mine, then buried her face in my neck. I swallowed back a coo, wrapped a possessive arm around her back, and closed my eyes, a contented smile on my face.

CHAPTER 9

LUANA

Morning found me wrapped all around Dakas, his right wing serving as our blanket. When I told him I would give our relationship an honest and fair try, I hadn't known how it would go. But this easy chemistry between us exceeded all my hopes. Sure, the shower mess had significantly helped us grow even more comfortable with each other, but his personality played the biggest part.

The lazy way his thumb began caressing my lower back confirmed he was also awake. Knowing it was time to rise, I heaved a half-sigh, half-groan that made him chuckle. But he was so warm, so cuddly ... Despite the hardness of his muscular body, Dakas had been made to snuggle with. I inhaled his fresh, slightly spicy scent then rubbed my face against the soft, feathers on his chest. Dakas immediately started cooing.

I burst out laughing, and he chuckled again. Unlike last night when his pleasure from me scratching his wing fluff feathers had prompted the cooing, this time, I was convinced he had deliberately done it to get this reaction out of me. I lifted my head to look at him and instantly drowned in the sea of stars in his eyes.

"I love the feel of your laughter," Dakas said in a deep voice.

"I love the feel of all of your happy emotions, but your laughter is my new addiction."

"I can think of far worse things to get hooked on. Lucky for you, I like when you make me laugh," I said, my stomach fluttering. "You therefore have my permission to do so as often as you desire."

"Good, because I intend to do so frequently."

His gaze lowered to my mouth, and he leaned forward. He remained hovering just above my lips, his wishes clear. I loved that he sought my consent first. Remembering how I had kissed him last night without asking shamed me. Then again, I knew at a visceral level that Dakas was ready to go all the way but was allowing me to set the pace, which made me like him even more.

I closed the distance between us and pressed my mouth to his. Dakas instantly took control of the kiss. Despite his obvious lack of experience on that front—since all Zelconian females had beaks—my husband wasn't clueless or clumsy. Tentative would be a more accurate description. He paid close attention, both physically and empathically, to my reactions and adjusted accordingly.

Knowing Dakas could feel my emotions made me instantly hot at the thought of sex with him. What would it be like making love with someone who could feel what I felt? He wouldn't have to guess if I liked what he was doing.

And right now, I wanted Dakas to deepen the kiss and for his hands to get a bit more daring. He couldn't read minds, but he did exactly that. My lips parted to welcome his tongue while his hand slid down my back, over the curve of my bum, and down my thigh to settle on my bare skin right above my knee.

Without interrupting the kiss, Dakas further leaned over me, forcing me to lie back. As our tongues gently mingled, quickly adapting to each other, his hand started moving back up my body, this time directly on my skin, under the fabric of my nightgown. My abdominal muscles contracted as the calloused warmth of his palm ventured up my thigh. An odd mixture of relief and disappointment swirled inside me when his hand didn't linger on my panties but kept moving up my waist.

A moan tore out of my throat as his kiss became more passionate. My nipples ached, waiting for the moment his palm would close over my breast, but it stopped right below it, slipping to the edge of my back before caressing a path back down my body to my leg. Dakas broke the kiss and gave me a look so full of desire that I felt moisture pool between my thighs.

"Do you have any idea how beautiful you are?" Dakas whispered with an intensity that turned me upside down. "I cannot wait to take you home and bond with you, for my soul to be one with yours. Then ... then you will truly know my heart and how your mere presence makes me feel."

"I look forward to it," I whispered back, my chest filled with the most wondrous heat.

"But for now, stop trying to tempt me, you seductress. I have distressed villagers to protect and evil to thwart before I can drag you to my lair and have my way with you!" Dakas said teasingly.

I laughed. "Apologies, oh valiant hero. Go forth and thwart to your heart's content."

Dakas chuckled, rubbed his nose against mine, and brushed my lips again before reluctantly untangling himself from my embrace.

"Are you going to have breakfast with me or is Phegea going to do the honors again?" I asked.

Dakas snorted. "I would rather have breakfast with you. Like I said yesterday, adults rarely use that method, although we might today for lunch and dinner considering the amount of work that awaits us."

I perked up. As much as I understood and recognized the value for the Zelconians of leveraging such physiological features, thinking of my husband feeding on regurgitated food was definitely not a turn on. And kissing again the way we just did after he'd done so would be a major turn *off*, maybe even a deal-breaker.

"Awesome—about breakfast! For lunch, I'll try to sneak you a sandwich or something you can eat without stopping what you're doing," I said in a sympathetic voice.

"I would welcome that," Dakas replied with a twinkle in his eyes.

"What would you like? I usually have porridge with nuts and fruits, or pancakes. Today, I was thinking of a hearty traditional human breakfast with eggs, bacon, and hash ..."

My voice trailed off, and for a split second, I wondered if I'd said something offensive. Dakas cocked his head in that bird-like fashion again, confused by my sudden mood-swing. But my own thought struck me as so dumb, I felt embarrassed to explain what had made me hesitate.

"Your emotions are such a mess right now! I am truly intrigued. What thought crossed your mind?" Dakas asked with undisguised curiosity.

Squirming on my feet, I scrunched my face while trying to build the courage to confess.

"Well, I don't really know what Zelconians eat. And, for a second there, I wondered if you'd be offended by me suggesting you eat bird eggs," I said sheepishly.

Dakas's eyes widened, then he threw his head back and burst out laughing. While relief flooded through me, I still took on a defensive tone to justify that thought.

"Hey! It was natural for me to wonder! I mean, you're not exactly birds, and you're definitely not a chicken, but still ... I wouldn't eat the meat of most primates because they feel too close to humans. It would be weird."

"You are a gem, Luana," Dakas said, still chuckling. "Many creatures that hatch from eggs also eat eggs. And Zelconians are not oviparous—our females give birth like humans. So, yes, we eat eggs, both cooked and raw. As for our relationship with birds, it's an interesting one. Most birds recognize us as kindred, but also as predators. Some species will come fly alongside us for a bit while others will flee us like they would a raptor."

"Good to know," I replied, still feeling a little silly. "So, what do you want to eat?"

"Aside from eggs, I'm unfamiliar with any of the things you have listed," Dakas said with a shrug. "But I would love to sample whatever you like the most. Generally speaking, Zelconians are omnivores. Fruits and nuts make up 80% of our diet. But we also eat meat, fish, and vegetables, cooked or raw. As a hybrid, I almost always cook my meat a little. It makes it easier to digest."

"Great! That should make it easier for us. I was a bit worried we might have a completely different diet," I admitted.

"Like what, my mate? Did you fear we got up in the wee hours of the morning to go catch some worms before the morning dew evaporated from the leaves?" he asked teasingly while putting on his bracer.

"No!" I exclaimed, giving him a shocked look before grimacing as I pictured Graith, Skieth, and Phegea poking their beaks at the ground to catch an early worm. "Bad visual. Really bad visual. I didn't need that image," I mumbled to myself.

"Is it?" Dakas asked in a mysterious voice.

I stared at him, studying his features in a vain attempt to read his mind. "You don't actually do that, right?"

Dakas's sensuous lips stretched in an almost evil grin. "Renok and the others are being relieved of sentry duty, and my people are setting things up to cast the weapons. I'm going to check on them while you prepare breakfast. I will be back shortly."

"Oh, okay … But you didn't answer," I added, narrowing my eyes at him.

"I know," he deadpanned while approaching me.

I opened my mouth to argue, but he caught my chin in his hand and crushed my lips with a possessive kiss, silencing me. It was brief, just enough for my toes to begin to curl before he ended it, rubbed his nose against mine, and walked out of the room.

Damn the man ...

I was most definitely developing a crush on my husband, wings, feathery tail, scaly feet, and all. Heaving a sigh, I went to the bathroom to wash the lingering sleep from my face, only to be horrified by the bird's nest in my hair—no pun intended. I normally braided my long, curly hair in a single plait before bed or stuffed it into a night cap so it wouldn't be a complete disaster in the morning. I couldn't believe this was the image Dakas had of me on our first morning waking up together. But he, of course, hadn't had a single feather out of place.

Groaning, I splashed water on my face, brushed my teeth, and used a brush to tame my wild mane. After getting dressed, I got busy on breakfast, with homemade hashbrowns, eggs, bacon, beef sausages, toasts, and a side of freshly cut fruits. I hesitated on the amount of seasoning. As he mentioned the pure-blood sometimes ate their meat raw, I suspected they did so without any spices on them. I decided to err on the side of caution and only put a small amount of salt and pepper on his portion. Adding more would be easy, removing some, not so much.

I was pressing some fresh orange juice while brewing a pot of coffee when Dakas returned. His nostrils flared, and a pleasantly intrigued expression spread across his face.

"This smells very nice," he said.

I beamed and gestured for him to take a seat at the table. After he settled down, he eyed the plate I placed before him with undisguised curiosity. But his face fell when he saw the set of utensils.

"Right," he whispered to himself.

"Are you not familiar with knives and forks?" I asked cautiously as I took a seat across the table from him.

"I am aware of what they are," Dakas conceded. "But we don't use them to eat. We use spoons for broths, pastes, creams, jellies, and grains. Otherwise, we use our talons both to pick up our food and to cut it." He looked at the contents of his plate, especially the eggs sunny side up. "These eggs, and potatoes, we would eat with a spoon. The rest, we would eat with our hands."

"Oh, I see. Let me get you a spoon then," I said, standing up.

"No," Dakas said in a tone that brooked no argument. "Human food shall be eaten the human way. Teach me, my mate. How do I use these?"

But even as he spoke those words, Dakas picked up the fork with his left hand, testing various positions before settling for holding the handle like a dagger to stab into the beef sausage while picking up his knife. Every single muscle in my back seized as this instantly triggered me.

"No! Hell no!" I exclaimed, grabbing my own fork and rushing around the table to stand by his side.

Dakas stared at me with wide eyes, his expression both confused and amused.

"Never, *ever* hold a fork like that. It's a crime against humanity and proper table etiquette. A fork is *not* a dagger. You also don't hold it like it's a straw, and you especially don't stick the knife between the teeth of your fork to cut. There are two ways to handle it: one to prick, the other to scoop. To prick, you hold it mainly with your fingers. You could hold up your pinkie if you want to look fancy," I said, demonstrating with my own fork.

A smile played on his lips as he carefully imitated me. I knew he was laughing at my outrage over how he had manhandled the fork. But it featured very high on my short lists of pet peeves, which included people chewing with their mouths open or being loud eaters. The worst were those who felt the need to create their own soundtrack by moaning, nom-noming, or smacking their lips while they ate. Just thinking about it made me twitch.

This time Dakas chuckled, and I glared at him.

"Whoever tortured you with their poor table manners must have done quite a number on you," he said mockingly. "You will have to give me an extensive list of what not to do for days when I want to rile you up."

"HEY!"

Dakas laughed again. I elbowed him playfully then also grinned.

"Now, stop emitting such annoyed emotions over past grievances and finish teaching me how to use these before this food gets tired of being neglected and walks out on its own," Dakas taunted.

I muttered something under my breath then resumed my demonstration. He took to it with remarkable ease. As scooping with a fork was no different than using a spoon, he needed no practice on that. But the real test came down to taste.

After I resumed my seat, he ate a bit of everything, each one in turn, his expression unreadable. The whole time, I sat watching him, my own food forgotten. I was growing restless when he took a sip of coffee, then one of orange juice, before finally looking back at me.

"So?" I asked, almost holding my breath.

"Is this your usual recipe?"

I squirmed in my chair, wondering how to interpret his reaction. "I prepared everything the same as I always do, aside from the amount of salt in the eggs and spices in the hashbrowns. I normally crank it up a notch. But as I don't know if Zelconians use condiments and spices, I didn't want to risk overwhelming your palate. Why? Is it too much?"

"I'm relieved to hear it. We do use salt and other spices. And for me, this isn't enough."

"Really?! Here, try mine instead," I said, pushing my plate in front of him. "I haven't touched it. And it's spiced the way I normally eat."

Dakas slightly recoiled. "Why would it matter if you had touched it?"

I shrugged. "Some people are germaphobes and are grossed out at the thought of eating from the same plate someone else did."

He gave me a strange look and chuckled. "Luana, I have absolutely no problem with your germs. After all, I had my tongue in your mouth barely half an hour ago."

I gasped then shook my head in disbelief, as he started digging into my food. His eyes widened at the first bite, a smile stretching his lips.

"You like it?" I asked, hope dripping out of my voice.

"That's *much* better. Waaay better," Dakas said with a grin. He pointed to his own plate with his chin. "Those eggs and hashbrowns had me worried, they were so bland. But this is delicious. Now I'm eager to try some of your other recipes."

"Awesome!" I exclaimed with a silly grin on my face. "Finish up my plate, I'll take yours."

"No! There's no reason—"

"Tut-tut! I didn't ask if you *wanted* to," I said, grabbing his plate. "There's a reason I have salt and pepper shakers on the table."

I added some to Dakas's former plate and dug in. We ate in an amiable atmosphere while discussing food. Having him request a second serving of hashbrowns made my day. He wasn't too keen on the coffee, but finding out he loved hot peppers and spicy food in general had the Latina in me doing an internal happy dance.

But as much as I would have loved pursuing our culinary exploration talks, we had to prepare for an attack, and I needed to go check on my father and the other patients. I all but kicked

Dakas out of the house so I could clean up and get over to the clinic.

Despite the early hour, Tilda was already there, caring for the wounded. When I entered, she looked up, her easy smile lighting up her face. Tall and lanky, she had the dark skin of her Kenyan mother and the Asian features of her Japanese father. Looking at her beautiful face, you'd never believe she'd just celebrated her fifty-third birthday. Only a few streaks of gray in her long black hair down to the middle of her back hinted at her age.

"Hey girl, come check this out! These new medical pods are insane," Tilda said, gesturing with her head at one of the pods. "They do absolutely everything and readjust treatments as needed. Remember how bad your dad's leg was yesterday?" At my nod, she tapped the interface of the pod to bring up a holographic display. "Look at the x-ray of his leg!"

"Oh, my God!"

"Oh, my God, indeed! I checked his chart, and the pod has pumped him full of nanites that have essentially stitched the bone back together," Tilda said, ecstatic. "The painful limp we thought he'd be stuck with? History! He's going to be as good as new."

Tears pricked my eyes, and my throat tightened. Tilda gave me a sympathetic look, caressed my hair in a maternal fashion, then squeezed my shoulder. I replied with a quivering smile while eyeing the chart, then my father's vitals and stats.

"Your daddy's going to be fine."

"Yeah, this looks really good," I said, my heart filling with gratitude for the Temern, for Dakas, and whatever powers in the universe or stars alignment had brought about this outcome. "There's still some minor swelling in the brain, and a number of wounds to mend. We'll keep him under for at least another twenty-four hours and reassess his status in the morning."

"Agreed."

"How are the others?" I asked marching towards the next pod.

"Julian's guts are neatly tucked back where they need to be. The swelling around his previously dislocated jaw has gone down. And his ligaments no longer show any signs of damage. We should be able to wake him up and release him in a couple of hours."

"That's amazing," I whispered, still unable to believe the wonder of these machines. I tried not to think how much we could have benefitted from them over the years.

What they could have done for my mother and unborn sibling.

"Think all this will inspire Julian to stop systematically cock-blocking our efforts to bring in more technology?" I asked sarcastically.

Tilda snorted. "Doubt it. He'll probably complain about us using technology on him without his consent, even though he was brought to us with half of his gut spilling out."

"Without this medical pod, he wouldn't have made it."

She shrugged. "We know that, but he won't believe it. He'll claim his survival has nothing to do with the machine, just a result of his great constitution, and that he was always meant to survive. This tech was just a cheat to cut corners."

I rolled my eyes and moved on to the other patients. At least four would be released later today, and the others over the course of the next twenty-four to forty-eight hours. The best part of it all was that everyone would make it.

I was finishing the entry of some final notes in their respective files when I sensed Tilda's heavy stare on me. I looked up and gave her an inquisitive look. She rolled her eyes and raised her eyebrows, like someone expecting an answer.

"What?" I asked, confused.

She made a "Come on!" face. "You know what. How was it? Was he good?"

"Oh, my God, Tilda!"

"Don't Tilda me. You knew I would ask you about it. Come on, spill! What is he packing? Is he well hung? Does it have a weird shape? Ridges? Feelers? Oh, my God! Does he have two peens? I read about some alien species that has two peens. And then there's this other one that opens up like a flower." She suddenly paled and eyed me with horror. "Fuck ... he's like a duck, isn't he? He's got that crazy spiraling peen that shoots out like a spring, doesn't he?"

Speechless, I gaped at her in disbelief. For some reason, the look on my face prompted more crazy words to come out of her mouth as she took on a crestfallen expression.

"Oh shit! He *doesn't* have a peen. Is that it? I read that most birds no longer have a penis, or only a tiny thing that barely pokes out. Sex between them literally lasts half a blink: genitals touch for a split second and done! Tell me he's not a half-a-second man? With that hot body and haunting face, it would be a freaking crime. Come on, woman, speak! I'm dying here."

"Whatever happened to the prim and proper Tilda I consider both as a big sister and mother figure?!" I asked.

She waved a dismissive hand. "Pfft, you're the first human friend I know who's banged a truly alien-looking alien. I need deets. I'll be back to being prim and proper after. You do know that everyone and their brother in the colony is speculating about what went down in your bedroom last night and what kind of kinky, scandalous things he did to you. By the happy look on your face when you entered, birdman did all right."

"Ugh!" My elbows resting on top of my desk, I buried my face in my hands while shaking my head.

I hadn't thought of that. But yeah, every single person in Kastan would be wildly speculating about my wedding night with Dakas. The minute I went out, they'd be studying every single one of my movements, including whether I walked bow-legged. The crazy part was that her wild speculations had now planted the seed of insanity in my own mind. What *did* Dakas pack down there? Was it indeed a duck's corkscrew penis? A less scary one like a swan? Next to nothing, like most other birds? Or a standard human peen?

I lifted my head to glare at her.

"Not that it concerns you in any way, but there was no monkey business happening last night. Seriously!" I insisted when she gave me a dubious look. "Before the ceremony yesterday, when Dakas took me into Allan's office, it was to let me know he wouldn't pressure me into anything. We would take it slow and go at my pace."

"Really?" Tilda exclaimed.

I nodded. A funny mix of surprise, disappointment, relief, and admiration fought for dominance on her face.

"So, what did you do?"

"I helped him shower since our stalls are too tiny to accommodate his wings."

Tilda's face lit up, and she clapped her hands with excitement. "So, you did see the goods!"

I rolled my eyes again. "No, woman! I helped with his wings, then gave him privacy to finish the rest, you perv!"

"Bah, you're no fun. And then?"

"And then nothing. We went to bed, talked, then slept. We woke up, had breakfast together, and here I am!"

"Sheesh, talk about boring. You have a hot alien in your bed, to whom you're legally married, and you didn't jump his bone? We need to talk about your priorities," Tilda said with pretend disgust.

I just laughed.

She grinned, her face softening. "Although I *truly am* disappointed not to get any juicy gossip, I am happy to hear he's being kind to you," Tilda said in an affectionate voice. "I won't say I love you like a daughter—I'm not THAT old after all—but I do consider you like a baby sister. I was worried for you."

I smiled, my heart filling with love for the older woman. "Thanks Tilda, but there's no need to worry. He's really wonderful. I think we're going to have a great marriage. Last night would qualify as my best first date ever. He's funny, sweet, super respectful, and he really seems determined to make me happy."

"I'm thrilled for you, sweetie. I seriously feared you'd end up with Martin," Tilda said, coming over to me.

I grimaced at the name but rose from my chair to receive her gentle hug. She released me with a naughty glimmer in her eyes.

"Don't think that gets you off the hook, missy!" Tilda said, wagging a menacing finger at me. "Once you jump your alien's bone, I will expect a full report. Call it medical research."

I burst out laughing and shook my head at her.

CHAPTER 10
DAKAS

The humans, especially Lara, impressed me. Despite some lingering reluctance about using advanced technology, they all worked diligently. We improvised a factory and assembly chains in the blacksmith's shop and Martin's warehouse, which served as both his workshop and lumber yard.

Surprisingly, Martin behaved himself all day. Although his discontent and resentment surged every time he saw me, he otherwise worked as diligently as the others, providing an unexpected amount of guidance and assistance to those who needed help. He clearly thrived on the acknowledgement and admiration of his peers. But while he reveled in their thanks and praises, he'd offered to assist them from a genuine desire to help.

Could Luana be right about him not being such a bad man?

I would reserve judgement for later and not let my guard down. The sliminess of the emotions he'd broadcast yesterday still stuck to my psychic mind.

While I supervised the building of the protective dome, Skieth oversaw the construction of the turrets, and Graith—with the assistance of Lara—handled the weapons and stealth shields. Although these blueprints would help our own technology advance by leaps and bounds, I noticed that Kayog and the UPO chose what to give us with strategic care. The blasters, personal shields, and stealth shields would make us competitive against the Yurus. We even had a basic rocket launcher blueprint for short-range missiles, all clearly geared for planetary warfare. However, we couldn't turn any of it against the UPO or their allies—not that we had any such intentions.

Still, Skieth and I had already modified the rocket launchers —using one of our offensive crystals—and turned them into lasers.

By the time half the humans had returned from their lunch break, my brother Renok and cousin Minkus had returned from their rest. They set up a shooting gallery in the town square for the human volunteers who wished to learn how to shoot the blasters we'd been building—all of them set to the lowest stun to avoid accidents.

That evening, my fellow Zelconians and I trained in aerial battle using our brand-new blasters and personal shields. Like with the rocket launchers, we had modified the personal shields, which deployed in front of our armbands. Using our crystals, we'd given it similar strength and properties as those of the energy field we'd erected around the village.

It would take both humans and us far more practice than the few hours we'd had today to master these new weapons and tools. But it was a start, and a good one. If our assessment of the situation was accurate, we wouldn't have a real battle with the Yurus for two or three days. With luck, it could even be a full week.

By the time we called it a night, Skieth had five of the twelve planned turrets fully operational, including long-range scanners, which would track the movements of any Yurus party within a three-kilometer radius from the village. After equipping a couple of drones with our freshly built stealth-shields, we sent them out to Mutarak to verify that they hadn't moved up their attack plans —which they thankfully confirmed.

Exhausted and aching to see my mate, I still took a flight to Synsara to shower before returning to Luana. As much as I had loved her showering me last night and the exquisite feel of her delicate hands, it would take too much time at this late hour. Right now, I just wanted to feel the warm softness of her body against mine while we still had the house all to ourselves.

Tomorrow, Luana would pull her father out of his induced coma. How would he react upon finding out that his only daughter was now married to one of us? And how would he feel when I took her away from him to live with me in Synsara— ideally, tomorrow night after we'd turned back the Yurus?

That should go down well...

I entered Luana's house to find her sitting on the couch of her living area, her legs crossed under her while she read something on a datapad. The way her face lit up, her sincere joy upon seeing me turned me upside down. A burst of affection exploded in my chest, and my nape tingled with the urge to soul-bind with her.

Luana tossed her datapad aside and rose to greet me.

My mouth went dry as I took her in. She was barefoot and dressed in a different nightgown than last night. The dark-gray, shiny fabric fell loosely around her body, revealing her curves in the most enticing fashion. The shorter skirt stopped mid-thigh, exposing her long and shapely legs. The slightest gust of wind would expose her pelvic area. Two flimsy strings held the dress up at her shoulders. The low V-shaped collar gave a sinful glimpse of the curves of her perky breasts.

That part of her anatomy fascinated me as much as kissing had. My palm ached with the desire to cup them, but I didn't dare without her explicit consent. Her behind also constituted a major source of distraction. As our tails covered ours, I'd never noticed the appeal of the roundness of a female's behind. And Luana's definitely made my fingers twitch.

"You look beautiful," I whispered.

The familiar timid expression flitted over her face as she smiled shyly and took a step closer to me. I drew her into my embrace, and she came willingly. Luana lifted her face as I lowered mine, and our lips met halfway, hers parting almost immediately. I didn't resist the invitation and slipped my tongue between them. I'd feared my female would be turned off by my lack of kissing experience. But her emotional responses to my tentative efforts guided me. I'd quickly adjusted, and her pleasure confirmed my performance was adequate.

While one arm held her firmly against my body, the other caressed a path up her back to her nape. I'd wanted to sink my fingers into her soft curls, but she had bound her lovely hair in a single, long braid. As much as her new outfit aroused me, this new hairdo disagreed with me.

I broke the kiss and frowned at her hair. "Why did you braid your hair?"

She touched her braid with a sliver of worry. "Because it turns into a mess overnight. It was a complete disaster this morning, like a hurricane had blown through it. Why? You don't like it?"

I scoffed. "Not at all! It was beautiful this morning. This hairdo is lovely. I don't mind if you wear it during the day. But not at night. Please leave it unbound for me. I love it wild, fanning over my chest, and to be able to slip my fingers through it, unimpeded," I said in a pleading tone.

And I can't wait to see how much wilder it will get after I've made love to you.

An adorable tinge of pink crept over her cheeks as she nodded. Luana started undoing the braid, but my hand covered hers.

"Let me," I said.

She let go, and I carefully unraveled the plaiting, running my fingers through the long, curly strands to fan them behind her and over her shoulders.

"Beautiful," I whispered to myself.

The surge of emotion emanating from her made my skin tingle and my body hum with pleasure. Ancestors … I never imagined pleasing my mate—and I hadn't even been trying—could bring me such a blissful sense of well-being. Wrapping my arms around Luana, I picked her up. She wrapped her legs around my waist and clasped her hands behind my neck.

"You smell good," Luana said, inhaling deeply.

"I went to Synsara to shower," I confessed while carrying her to the bedroom.

She recoiled. An air of hurt, disappointment, and confusion crossing her features.

"I would have been happy to help you again. I didn't mind. In fact, I enjoyed it," she said, trying to keep a neutral tone.

"Luana, I assure you, I enjoyed it even more than you did. Have you forgotten my cooing?" I asked teasingly.

She snorted, the hurt fading, while her confusion grew.

"I was too sweaty from all the training to come to you unwashed. But it is late. We've both had a long and exhausting day," I explained. "Showering here would have taken us too long, not to mention created a mess. But you can still scratch my fluff and down feathers to your heart's content."

Luana chuckled and rubbed her nose against mine like I had previously done to her. I recaptured her lips as we entered the bedroom. A blast of desire radiated from my mate, her arousal fanning the burning flame of mine. However, as much as I wanted to make love to her, Luana wasn't quite ready yet. Still, she needed something more from me.

And I will gladly give it to her.

Without interrupting the kiss, I carefully laid her on the mattress. This time, she didn't drop her hands from behind my neck, but held on tighter, making it clear she didn't want me moving away. With my tongue still plundering her mouth, I climbed on top of the bed. Luana parted her legs to let me settle between them, the fingers of one hand gently teasing the down feathers on my nape and nestling in the valley between my shoulder blades.

Sustaining my weight with one hand, I let the other venture down the length of Luana's body. As soft as the lustrous fabric of her nightgown felt under my hand, it was the burning heat of her bare skin I wanted against my palm. Breaking the kiss, my mouth explored on its own, kissing and nipping at the softness of her neck.

At the same time, I shamelessly slipped my hand under her skirt again. Luana didn't rebuff my daring touch. But where the night before her sliver of tension had restrained my boldness, tonight her emotions screamed for me to go further. My mate's need, like a dull ache, clawed at me, making me throb with a burning desire of my own.

A moan escaped her as my hand finally settled on the soft mound of her breast. Ancestors! It was so soft. The hardening nub of her nipple tickled my palm as I gently caressed it. Luana didn't resist when I raised her nightgown, my mouth replacing my hand on her breast. Instead, she lifted her head and torso to get rid of it herself.

This time, my moan joined hers at the exquisite feel of her naked body against mine—aside from the flimsy, nearly non-existent piece of fabric that served as her panties. Luana held my head against her breast, her back slightly arching to increase contact as I sucked and licked her nipple. I loved its strange texture under my tongue. Who would have thought it would be so sensitive and erogenous?

Echoes of her pleasure resonated through me. As an empath, I felt what she did at an emotional level, not in a sensory or physical way. I didn't feel my own mouth on her, only the emotions it stirred within her and the enjoyment she derived from it. And right now, her body was telling me to grow bolder.

I gladly complied. As my mouth worshipped her body, my hand ventured lower over her stomach, her adorable outie navel, and under the tiny triangle of her underwear. The heady scent of her growing arousal made my head spin as my palm settled between her thighs. I had expected some curls there, but only bare, smooth skin, and some slickness around her slit welcomed me.

Luana moaned again, a shiver running through her as my fingers explored her hidden treasure. The little nub there intrigued me. The way she reacted to my touching it emboldened me. Soon, I was rubbing it, increasing the pressure and speed of my fingers, as waves of pleasure rose inside of her, the echo of each driving me mad with lust.

I kissed my way down to her pelvis, simultaneously lowering her panties with my free hand. The scent of her musk made my mouth water and my abdominal muscles contract with the need for my penis to extrude. I slipped two fingers inside Luana's slit, making room for my lips to settle on her little nub. My mate cried out, and the intensity of her pleasure slammed into me, wresting from me an almost painful growl as I fought to rein in the urge to unleash my passion.

I licked and sucked on my female with a frenzy, moving my fingers in and out of her faster. And then I grazed a little bundle of nerves. The bolt of pleasure it triggered within Luana coursed through me, making me moan. Ancestors, how would I ever be able to handle my own pleasure when my female's alone drowned me in a maelstrom of bliss? I zeroed in on the sensitive spot until Luana fell apart, shouting my name. A blinding light exploded before my eyes as the strength of my woman's climax smashed into me.

My head spun from the endless flow of ecstasy pouring out of my female and into me. I gathered Luana into my arms, still shaking with the spasms of her orgasm. I rolled onto my back with her on top and closed my wings around her like a cocoon. At that moment, I knew that I would never allow her nightwear between us ever again. The tingling at the back of my head intensified with the need to bind her. But I silenced it, gently caressing my mate's hair while humming a Zelconian love song in her ear as she fell asleep.

CHAPTER 11
LUANA

Heart pounding, I watched my father stir from his medical pod. We lowered the sides so he could turn and sit at the edge. He touched his previously shattered leg with an air of disbelief before looking up at me.

"Lulu," he said, using my pet name, his eyes wide and incredulous. "My leg ... I don't feel any pain. How did you fix—"

The words died in his throat as he caught a glimpse of the dozen high-tech medical pods filling the space. The seven empty ones stood vertically alongside the walls to make more room. Four others contained the remaining patients still under sedation. He looked down in confusion at the fifth one he was sitting on. The way he glanced around the room, his head jerking this way and that, I figured he was trying to make sure he was still in Kastan in our own medical clinic.

"What is this? Where did all this come from? Where are the others? How long have I been out?"

I placed a calming hand on his chest and smiled reassuringly as he fired questions at me.

"Everything is fine, Dad. All the wounded who made it back

to the village have been saved. The five of you are the only ones that still needed some mending," I explained. "You're as good as new now, and the other four should be up before nightfall."

"Good. Good," my father said distractedly. "But where did all of this come from? Did the Yurus—?"

"No, Dad. The Yurus have not taken over, and they never will. I need you to listen to me carefully, all the way to the end, okay? A *lot* has happened over the past few days, all of it for the best."

From the look on his face, my father was bracing for what he'd accurately guessed would be a major shock. I launched into a detailed recounting of what had transpired since his return from that disastrous scouting expedition, I described my meeting with the Zelconian Council, Kayog's intervention, my rushed marriage, the defenses our people had helped the Zelconians erect around Kastan, the failed raid attempt, and today's impending attack.

I swallowed hard as a heavy silence settled between us when I finally shut up. He hadn't said a single word while I spoke, though a flurry of unreadable emotions swept across his features before he hid them.

"Dad, please say something," I said at last when the silence stretched too long.

An odd glint shimmered in his eyes before his gaze slowly roamed over me. To my utter relief, despite its intensity, it contained no disgust or anger.

"You look unharmed. Is he kind to you?"

My shoulders slumped with relief, and I exhaled loudly. "Yes, Dad. Dakas is wonderful to me. Both he and Kayog say we are soulmates, and I think they're right. I mean, I agreed to this marriage to save the village. But if he had courted me without any of these constraints, I still would have been very much into him. I'm getting to know him, and he's a really good man. He's not pressuring me into anything. You're going to like him."

My father's eyes flicked between mine as if to assess the truth of my words. I held his gaze unwaveringly. He nodded slowly, hopped off the medical pod, and walked towards one of the closest pods. He rested his hand on the lid, looking at Hakeem's unconscious form within.

"You said everyone made it, even Julian?" he asked, glancing over his shoulder.

"Even Julian. His guts are right back where they should be, and he doesn't have a single scar. He was released yesterday around lunch. He not only helped build more weapons, he's also training to use them along with our small militia."

He snorted, shook his head, and looked back at Hakeem through the glass dome. "You did good, kid."

My throat tightened. My father was a man of few words. And while he'd always been a supportive and loving single parent, he'd never been overly generous with compliments.

"Thanks, Dad."

"Give me some clothes so I can see what all of you have done with the village, and so I can meet this husband of yours," he mumbled.

I complied, giving him a bit more detail on the types of weapons we had been building and especially answering his questions about the villagers' response to so much technology. My father had always been a moderate on that front. I believed he would be more progressive in many ways, if allowed. Making sure I never undermined his authority had been more than just out of a daughter's duty or out of love for him. Had the colony replaced him with a different leader, things would have moved further backward.

The minute we stepped out of the clinic, a joyous roar rose through the villagers, spreading like a wave as people came to welcome him back and express their joy that he looked so well.

It didn't offend me in the least. I was extremely relieved to be able to return leadership of the colony to him and to go back to focusing on caring for patients. I'd never fully comprehended the amount of administrative juggling his role required, especially now with resource expenditures, monitoring people's comings and goings, and managing volatile tempers that had gone into hyperdrive with the looming attack.

Although I believed I'd done a decent job of holding down the fort in his absence, my father embodied an experience and stability I couldn't offer. I was no longer the colony leader's daughter or Kastan's young doctor. I was the Zelconian's wife— a woman who would soon leave them to start her new life elsewhere. I suspected that contributed to how few complaints we received about the medical pods. As much as the colony balked at technology, you couldn't bitch about something that would literally save your life, especially when you could no longer be certain how available your resident doctor would be, going forward.

The look on my father's face was priceless as he took in the turret towers, the energy field enclosing the village, and the posts strategically positioned on various buildings to create the protective dome. He walked through the village square and stopped to examine the blasters our militia was training with. My throat tightened as our people followed him, reveling in his sparse words of approval for the work they had done. They reminded me of children seeking their father's blessing.

I tagged along with him, chiming in when needed, but my eyes kept flicking around, looking for my husband. The Zelconians were mostly on the other side of the village, finishing the work on the last turrets. The others were inside the 'factories' where more weapons and back up personal and stealth shields were being built.

Then movement at the edge of my vision caught my attention. I froze at the sight of Graith, Dakas, Skieth, and Renok flying towards us. The crowd moved aside to allow the four Zelconians to land near us.

My father's face closed off in an instinctive attempt to hide his thoughts. But of course, they wouldn't fool the empathic abilities of our protectors.

Graith landed gracefully, followed by the other three, only a few steps behind him. Dakas came to stand by my side, his hand reaching for mine although his gaze never strayed from my father. I didn't pull away. Dad's eyes flicked towards Dakas then zeroed in on our joined hands before focusing on Graith. In this instant, I would have killed for empathic abilities to know what emotions were coursing behind my father's impassive face.

"Salutations, Colony Leader Mateo Torres. It is good to see you fully recovered," Graith said, sounding as formal as the day of our first meeting in his Council chamber.

"Greetings, Exarch Graith Devago," my father replied. "Thank you for your kind words and the assistance you have provided my people while I was incapacitated."

"Do not thank me. All the merit goes to your daughter and her mate. They made this possible, and he has spearheaded the defenses of the colony. I do not believe you have formally met him yet," Graith said, casting a sideways glance at us.

"I have not," my father confirmed, this time facing Dakas straight on.

My pulse picked up as we drew nearer my father. He thoroughly examined Dakas from head to toe, making no effort to hide it. Thankfully, my mate didn't seem to take offense.

"Dad, this is Dakas Wakaro, my husband. Dakas, this is my father, Mateo Torres," I said, hating the subtle tremor in my voice.

"Colony Leader Mateo, it is a pleasure to see you again, and looking so well," Dakas said.

Again?!

My eyes widened as I stared at my father. He didn't keep me apprised of everything he did. Had he flown to Synsara in the past to meet the Zelconian Council?

"Thank you, Councilor Dakas Wakaro. As you are now my son-in-law, you may call me Mateo," my father said.

"Only if you call me Dakas," my husband replied.

My eyes flicked between the two most important men in my life, studying their expressions for any signs of animosity. It was stupid how much I felt like a fourteen-year-old girl bringing her first boyfriend home to meet her parents.

"Dakas it is," my father said with a nod. "Thank you for securing my village. This was not how I had expected my daughter to leave the nest. But she tells me you are very kind and respectful to her. I therefore welcome you into our family and offer you my friendship."

Tears pricked my eyes, and I blinked them away as my father extended a hand towards Dakas. For a split second, I wondered if my husband knew what that gesture meant, but he smiled and didn't hesitate to shake my dad's hand. Relief flooded through me as my father greeted the others and Dakas introduced him to his brother Renok.

For the rest of the morning, the four Zelconians and Lara walked my father through all the defenses they'd set up around the village and explained Dakas's plan for when Vyrax would attack. A couple of hours after lunch, Tilda and I released the last of the injured men from their pods.

I turned off the 3D holographic projector, shutting down the display of one of the blueprints Kayog had included in my "dowry." On top of the medical equipment, weapons blueprints, and materials, the Temern had included the blueprints of various technological tools and machinery that would significantly improve our quality of life without undermining the colony's determination to put meaningful human interactions before technological innovation.

Since their use would likely be more controversial, I had kept them aside so he could present them to our people for a vote. As was his wont, my father remained mostly quiet while I described the purpose of each device. I hated that a vote or discussion was even needed. All of this should simply be made available to anyone who wanted it, and those who didn't could simply ignore it. I realized then that the events of the past few days had truly eroded my patience and tolerance for the backward way of life imposed on us.

My father was opening his mouth to share his thoughts when the town alarm resounded, nearly making me jump out of my skin. Dad stood, a determined look on his face.

Pride filled my heart. My father was badass. Tall, broad-shouldered, with a ruggedly handsome face, he never backed away from a challenge. I'd inherited my curly hair and dark brown eyes from him, but had my mother's more delicate frame. He was muscular, but not in the sharply defined way my husband and the other Zelconians were. Dad also didn't have to raise his voice for people to shut up and pay attention. Usually, a single hard stare from him sufficed to make anyone squirm. But if he did raise his voice, you had better have your last will and testament written out and your house in order, because hell was about to break loose.

We marched out of the house to find a terrified crowd assembled on the square. At least a hundred Zelconians stood on the roofs of buildings close to the protective wall. As expected, Vyrax's "army" was coming directly towards the square. No other units flanked us, testifying to the arrogant certainty the Yurus leader held that this would be a cakewalk.

I glanced overhead. The shimmer of the protective dome reassured me. Although convinced there would be no missile attacks, Dakas had not wanted to take any chances. I believed he also meant to put on a show to make Vyrax think twice about taking us on. And even if he still did attack—which he more than likely would—he would spend time preparing, which would give us more time to get our shit together.

I hated not having Dakas by my side, but he was with Graith, coordinating the Zelconians. While they wanted Vyrax to see them and be aware of the alliance between our people, they weren't planning on interfering. The humans of Kastan were sovereign, and that needed to be properly conveyed.

I stopped in the square, just ahead of the rest of the crowd, while my father advanced alone. I exchanged nervous glances with Tilda. She and I had spent most of the day yesterday setting up emergency medical stations at various rally points in the village in case things turned ugly. We could only pray it had been unnecessary.

Too soon—and yet, it felt like forever—the thumping sound of the front legs of numerous nyloths approaching sent a cold shiver down my spine. It was almost like military drums announcing the incoming army. Moments later, war cries erupted in the distance, accompanied by the clopping of countless hooves. And then the tall, furry silhouettes of hundreds of Yurus broke through the tree line of the forest.

Their conquering cries died in their throats as they set eyes on the wall. The Yurus in front stopped abruptly. Some of their companions behind, not expecting this, ran into them, involuntarily shoving them forward. Carried by the momentum, a handful of Yurus stumbled to the ground barely a meter from the energy field. A malicious part of me wished they had struck it just for the pleasure of seeing dozens of them get blasted by the wall's defensive area of effect.

Outraged cries and shouts rose from the masses, with copious amounts of *jaafans* tossed around along with other choice swear words in Yurusian. Some of the would-be invaders who had been knocked down got up, turned around, and struck whoever stood closest to them in random retaliation. For a far-too-brief moment

I hoped this would turn into an all-out brawl—a common occurrence with this volatile species.

But a thundering roar from the rear silenced them.

Mounted on a krogi—an armored, scale-covered, buffalo-looking beast with red eyes and mouth tusks reminiscent of its master's—Vyrax charged forward, trampling some of his troops in the process. I nearly burst out laughing at the slack-jawed disbelief on his face as he jerked on the reins and came to an abrupt halt. He jumped down from his mount, landing on his thick black hooves with a thud. He drew out a highly ornate double-axe from the strap around his back and brandished it as he marched resolutely towards the wall. It looked like it had seen countless battles and been passed down from his ancestors.

Vyrax was terrible to behold. At least seven feet tall, with mountains of muscles his shaggy reddish-brown fur couldn't hide, he was one scary son of a bitch. A network of scars marred his body, but he displayed them like a badge of honor. The length and thickness of his recurved black bull horns indicated he was at least in his forties. He didn't have the bull snout of a minotaur, but the snarling face of an Orc. The tip of his left mouth tusk was chipped.

Two meters from the wall, he stood directly facing my stoic father, who stood at a similar distance on our side. While the Yurus leader examined the wall, the nearby turrets, and the protective dome with blatant fury, another mounted krogi walked up to the edge of the forest. I easily recognized the white fur of Zatruk, the second male in the pecking order of the Yurus leadership. The albino male had the reputation of being ruthless, merciless, and vicious as fuck. He remained mounted on his beast.

Vyrax returned his focus to the wall and began spinning his battle-axe like a drum major.

"Don't do it," I whispered to myself.

That weapon would disintegrate on the wall, and we didn't need him any more enraged than he already was. To my relief, he gestured to one of his goons. As predicted, they hadn't come armed with high-tech weapons. Most appeared either unarmed or equipped with the standard cold weapons they usually carried on their person.

The goon, standing five meters or so from his leader, took a couple of steps towards the wall, stopping maybe one meter from it. He removed what looked like a standard dagger from his belt and threw it with all his strength at the energy field. I braced for it. As with last night's incident, the blade disintegrated on impact. But the outward energy blast sent the Yurus, and a handful of others caught within the blast radius, flying backwards and crashing into others.

Roars of pain and rage rose all around. Thankfully, Vyrax had been standing outside of the area of effect. But even so, his expression frightened me. His face spelled murder. He raised a hand to silence the deafening shouts of his troops, and they all quieted. The discipline that demonstrated took me aback.

"As you can see, Chieftain Vyrax, you cannot pass," my father said, his voice broadcasting loud and clear through the com system Lara had cleverly set up specifically for this purpose. "Your days of bullying us are over. The wall surrounds the entire village. If we were belligerent, our turrets could have cut down half your troops before you could flee. But we haven't opened fire. We have no quarrel with your people. We just want to be left in peace. Turn around, leave, and don't come back."

"You think you can command *me*, and on my own planet, you *jaafan hoodah?*" Vyrax hissed, taking a menacing step forward.

My father shrugged. "If you want to sit out here and pout, knock yourself out."

"You think we do not have the means to counter this technology?" Vyrax asked. "Bring down this *jaafan* wall and submit to my rule. Resist and, when we destroy it, you will receive none of the mercy I initially planned on granting you."

"You do not know the meaning of mercy," my father said with a dismissive wave. "As you can see by the extreme measures we've taken, we will never submit to you."

Vyrax's gaze flicked again to the wall, turrets, and dome before returning to my father. He narrowed his eyes. "And where did that come from? The UPO? They have no right to interfere with local conflicts! They cannot arm you against your betters to tilt the balance of power!"

"The UPO isn't meddling. As humans, our people have already developed all the technology you see here, and some even more advanced," my father replied calmly, before gesturing at the Zelconians still standing on the roofs. "We have also formed an alliance with one of this planet's indigenous people, which has put our colony in good standing with the UPO. This means, we can now freely trade with any of the members of the Organization. We acquired legally all the technology you see here."

Technically that was true, although we hadn't so much acquired it as it had been given to us as my wedding gift. But that was all semantics.

"Keep pushing us, and we'll acquire more weapons and defenses," my father said, his tone hardening. "The mercenaries you are doing business with cannot provide you with even a tenth of the type of arsenal *we* can tap into as official members of the UPO. *You* drove us to this. Be grateful we have no desire for conquest and merely want to live in peace. But keep attacking us, and you will be responsible for what happens next."

I stared in awe at my father, pride filling my heart to bursting. I had known him to be a tough guy, but I'd never seen this side of him. I thanked God, Kayog, and all the powers that had allowed him to recover in time. I never could have delivered this speech in such an impassive and ballsy fashion.

By the way Vyrax looked at my father, I had no doubt he would have bashed his skull in and torn him limb from limb had

Dad been within his reach. The silence lasted for mere seconds, but it was so filled with hatred, it felt like it stretched on forever. Then Vyrax switched from Universal to bark a command in Yurusian. I didn't speak that language any more than I did Zelconian.

For a brief moment, hope blossomed in my heart as all of the Yurus appeared to turn around and head back into the forest. But that was short-lived as loud noises emanated from the forest, soon followed by the sight and sound of some falling trees. My innards twisted as I tried to speculate what they were up to. Heave-ho types of shouts reached us, accompanied by the growling cries of the nyloths. The malicious grin stretching Vyrax's wide mouth and making his tusks stand out even more, did not bode well.

Unsurprisingly, worried whispers rose behind me from the crowd. But thankfully, no one sounded on the verge of panic … yet.

I cast a glance at the roof of the Great Hall where Dakas stood. By the movement of his lips, he was talking, but the other Zelconian nearest him seemed a little too far away. Plus, why would he be using words when his people could communicate telepathically? My father pressed two fingers to his ear, and I realized Dakas was probably talking to him through an earpiece.

From what Dakas had told me, humans could hear their mind-speak even though they couldn't respond. But doing so without prior practice could cause debilitating migraines, which was why they had given my father an earpiece so they could communicate with him discreetly during the attack, if needed.

My father moved his head in a subtle nod before tapping some instruction on the wall control armband he had also been given. I automatically raised my arm to look at mine. He had set a series of defense mechanisms within the wall to ready. A single vocal command—or an attack against it—would trigger them.

None of them were set to lethal. Killing any Yurus today would only escalate the situation.

The missile launchers in the turrets were also sitting at the ready. Although we had people manning the towers, my father had locked the projectiles uniquely to our version of a flash grenade.

Sudden movement on the other side had the invaders parting to let through a pair of massive nyloths followed by a dozen Yurus carrying huge branches or narrow tree trunks. It took me a moment to realize what they were doing, and then my blood turned to ice. Upon the vocal command of their masters, the nyloths stopped a meter from the wall. A second command had them place the tips of their giant pincers—each one larger and taller than me—directly on the ground before pushing themselves up.

Between the pincer claws and the arm segments they were attached to, each pincer measured a little over three meters, only a couple of feet shy of the top of the wall. Propped in that position, the nyloth effectively created a ramp wide enough for two Yurus to comfortably run up side by side. But a single Yurus climbed on each of the nyloths, carrying a thick trunk with both hands over their heads, like a giant javelin they intended to throw.

Panicked cries rose behind me as the two Yurus were about to reach the fly head of their respective nyloth, looking determined to use their momentum to jump over the wall. The fall on the other side wouldn't kill them, let alone injure them. I had not foreseen this. But then why the trunk? Were they going to throw them first to make sure it was safe? And was it? Wouldn't the protective dome cover block it? Or had we left a gap between the wall and the dome?

Time seemed to slow as I processed all of these thoughts. But a single word from my father put an end to it all.

A blinding light along the two sections of walls in front of the nyloths was followed by a whooshing sound and then screams. Once again, the wall knocked back everything within range. The nyloth fell backwards, landing belly up, one of them all but crushing the Yurus that had been standing on its head. Despite its countless legs and long pincers, its body seemed too wide to allow it to flip back onto its belly.

The Yurus in the front covered their eyes with their forearms, many of them shaking their heads as if to clear their vision—Vyrax included. To my shock, his right hand, Zatruk—or was he his rival?—remained seated at a safe distance on his krogi, an amused expression on his face.

He issued a command, and the unaffected Yurus in the back rushed to the front to help turn the nyloths and get them back onto their legs.

"Leave while you still can," my father ordered to the scrambling Yurus.

Vyrax responded with a savage roar.

As sole response, my father raised a hand. A volley of bright lights shot out of the two turrets to the left and right of the invaders and converged towards them. A series of explosion right above the Yurus, emitting both a blinding light and deafening sound, had their troops shouting in pain as they covered their ears and scrambled to retreat.

Zatruk winced but held his position. He only moved to stop his leader's krogi from fleeing as well. Vyrax stood in front of the wall for a few seconds longer, snarling, apparently immune to the pain of the flash bang grenades. A world of hatred burned in his eyes as he began backing away, taking at least five steps with his gaze still locked on my father before he finally turned around. With a determined gait, still apparently impervious to the explosions overhead, he stuck his battle axe into the strap on his back, mounted his krogi, and rode off with his right hand.

A collective roar of victory shot out all around me as we watched the receding backs of those who had sought to enslave us. My father turned around to look at me. The neutral mask he almost always had plastered on his face suddenly fell, revealing a vulnerability I couldn't recall seeing since my mother's death.

Something broke inside of me, and I ran to him like I had ached to do so many times over the years, especially this morning when he had finally emerged from the medical pod. I threw myself into his arms, and he caught me, taking a step back to absorb the force of the impact. Holding me tightly, he kissed the top of my head before resting his cheek on it.

"My baby girl … Thank you for achieving what I couldn't. You made this possible. You saved us."

CHAPTER 12

LUANA

Wild celebrations raged throughout the village. Our farmers spit-roasted some pork, lamb, and goat while everyone else prepared large quantities of accompanying dishes for the celebratory feast.

My father sat down with Dakas and Graith to discuss strategy, while Tilda and I did a mental health check of our more fragile villagers to make sure they were properly handling the stress of the recent days.

To my delight, the Zelconians shared in our feast. Nobody seemed to mind them eating with their hands. I didn't know if Dakas had warned them about my utensils pet peeve, but they only ate the side dishes using spoons. I almost felt like a bully over it.

But as the sun bowed down to the moon and the stars filled the skies, our protectors left to return to their city. We quickly appeased the villagers' initial worry upon hearing that I, too, would be flying to Synsara with Dakas. A dozen Zelconian guards would once again stand watch overnight, and more advanced defenses would continue to be set up around the colony on top of pursuing combat training drills.

Today had only been the first salvo. Vyrax had been publicly humiliated. If he didn't manage to save face, his rule would be challenged, and he could be deposed. My gut told me Zatruk—the albino Yurus—was merely biding his time before usurping his place. I couldn't tell if it would be a better or worse thing for us. Either way, it meant Vyrax would come back at us with guns blazing and the full power of his military arsenal.

Although I understood my father's reasoning for only forcing them to leave without inflicting actual injuries, a part of me wondered if it had been a mistake. We could have killed Vyrax and eliminated the core of his forces while they had stood essentially unarmed and within range of the deadly weapons we had built, enhanced by the Zelconians' crystals and technological expertise. But it would have been a massacre. There was still hope for us to achieve peace without bloodshed.

Right now, however, Vyrax was the least of my concerns. I had expected pushback and maybe even outrage from my father when Dakas informed him he would be taking me to Synsara tonight to settle there permanently. I would transfer my things gradually over the next few days.

Surprisingly, Dad merely nodded, a hint of resignation and sadness in his eyes. But at the same time, I'd seen a glimmer of relief—a sentiment I shared.

Dakas and I were growing closer. We weren't in love—it was far too early for that—but our mutual attraction was moving in a healthy direction. I would never be comfortable exploring my sensuality with my new husband with my father sleeping across the hall.

And, to be honest, I was beyond eager to discover Dakas's home.

Although we tried to sneak out amidst the festivities, a number of people came to see us off, including Dad. Initially, Dakas had wanted to fly me to Synsara in his arms. While I didn't doubt he possessed the strength to do so, it was a long flight, and the look on my father's face made it clear he didn't approve. Since I wanted to bring a number of basic essentials—which meant far too many things I probably wouldn't need in the foreseeable future—I ended up flying my zeebis Goro, a huge bag tucked in front of me. Another zeebis was supposed to carry a medium-sized crate with my other stuff, but Dakas made a show of bringing it himself to erase any question about his ability to carry me over such a long distance.

It was cute.

I'd never flown so high and so far at night. While Cibbos resembled Earth with its greenery, blue sky, single sun, and fat moon hanging overhead at night; its flora revealed its true visage after dusk. Many plants gained a fluorescent glow as darkness fell over the world. From a bird's eye view, the land took on the appearance of the most stunning abstract painting whose shapes gently heaved and swayed following the whims of the wind.

"This is breathtaking!" I shouted to Dakas who was flying a little too far from me for my liking. However, he didn't have much of a choice with his and Goro's large wing spans.

A wide grin stretched his sexy lips. "Wait until you see the view from Synsara!"

I could only imagine how magnificent it would be. From the colony, the night view of Synsara was always mesmerizing. It looked as if the Northern Lights were shooting out of the three main peaks of the mountain that served as home to the Zelconians. Even now, the shimmering colors—primarily pale-blue, white, and turquoise—mesmerized me.

As we made our approach, it struck me that I didn't really know what was about to happen. It was still early enough for Dakas to want to introduce me to some of his peers before we retired to his home, but I was feeling a little too overwhelmed for that. It made me wonder how he felt on our wedding day, having all of this thrown at him on top of having to deal with our village's woes.

But Dakas seemed adamant that we would perform our binding ceremony tonight. It rather pleased me that it was meant to be private instead of the usual extravagance of a human wedding. To my relief, we didn't fly towards the grand plaza on the plateau, or the Council chamber. Instead, we flew up towards one of the upper levels at the edge of the southern mountain peak and landed on one of many huge balconies. It followed the curve of the mountain on a 50° arc, giving us a breathtaking view of the valley of Kastan and of the wild territory to the south.

Carved directly into the mountain, the Zelconian homes had a medieval feel to them with their stone façades. The clever design made it so the balcony above didn't fully cover this one, its railing ending barely a fifth in on an overhang. But with the great height, at least four meters, the neighbors above would really have to bend over the railing to spy on what was going on below, and even then, they would only get a glimpse of the edge.

A series of tall arched French windows lined the entire exterior wall. A few of them acted as double doors, giving multiple entry points to the dwelling. Small crystals had been carefully embedded along the window frames, giving them a soft glow. I couldn't tell if they were merely decorative or defensive. I suspected they could be both. Some of the crystals looked like they formed runic letters above the windows that served as doors.

My jaw dropped as I entered the house. My brain barely noticed the minimalist décor which left plenty of space to accommodate the Zelconians' wings. But the insane carvings on the walls left me speechless. Exquisite 3D sculptures of fantasy creatures adorned some of the polished stone walls. The most mind-blowing doorways opened onto the other rooms of the house. They weren't arched or square but had an organic shape that gave the impression they came straight out of a fairy tale or an elven village.

Ample seating without backrests—mostly large cushions, benches, and poufs—surrounded a white wooden coffee table, its edges and legs just as beautifully decorated. One wall appeared to be a huge window but was in fact a giant vidscreen in disguise. It took me a little while to realize the amount of technology that had been discreetly incorporated into the house and cleverly woven into the decor.

And everywhere, crystals of varying sizes had been embedded in the walls and furniture.

Dakas put my crate down by the entrance to the living area, relieved me of the baggage I was carrying, then took my hand to give me a tour of the gourmet kitchen and dining area. My eyes popped at the sight of the herb garden nook right next to his cooling unit.

"You cook?" I asked, blown away by the heating plate, indoor grill, and large oven.

"Of course," Dakas said smugly. "And I'm quite good at it, if I may say so myself. I intend to impress you."

"I'm looking forward to being impressed," I said before wrinkling my nose in distaste. "As long as it is not worms. Don't think I've forgotten you still haven't answered that question."

Dakas snorted and gave me an enigmatic look. "Why so much hate for worms? Don't humans eat snails as a delicacy? Don't you also eat mopane worms, which I believe you call edible maggots?"

I scrunched my face, wishing he hadn't reminded me of those. "Is that a confirmation that Zelconians do eat worms?"

"I'm neither confirming nor denying. I'm merely asking a question to understand why out of two similar things you deem one disgusting and the other refined."

"You're dodging," I said, itching to kick him. "Why won't you answer?"

"Because not knowing is driving you insane, and I find it infinitely entertaining," he deadpanned. "Come, let me show you the rest of the house."

As much as I wanted to throw things at him, I let him take my hand and lead me through the rest of the tour. The next room that made my jaw drop was what he casually called his office. It was a large space with a massive holographic 3D map of Cibbos. He apparently used it not only to coordinate hunts, but also migrations, and the crystal culture. Over the next few days, assuming the mess with the Yurus allowed it, Dakas had promised to reveal all the mystery surrounding Zelconian crystals.

He then showed me three guest rooms, which he hoped to turn into kid rooms in the not-too-distant future. The water closet broke my brain. Although Dakas had warned me, it still threw me for a loop to see the equivalent of a tiny urinal with an adjustable height, like a showerhead, instead of a toilet bowl. While the size of the guest hygiene room was comparable to that of a human's, the guest shower room took it to another level. It was large enough to be a child's bedroom, with multiple adjustable showerheads.

"If that impresses you, wait until you see our ensuite hygiene room," Dakas said with a grin.

Another shock awaited me the minute I entered his bedroom. "Oh, my God! That's not a bed! It's a freaking football field!"

Dakas threw his head back and laughed while I proceeded to examine the massive thing up-close. It could easily accommodate five or six adult human men.

"I need room to spread these wings, my mate," Dakas said teasingly. He went to stand at the foot of the bed, put my bag down on the floor, and spread his wings wide. "See?"

Sure enough, they took almost the entire width, with only

about a foot to spare on each side of the mattress. Two ornate wooden nightstands framed the bed. But no lamp sat on top. Instead, crystals shaped like water gushing out of the wall before it suddenly froze appeared to serve that purpose. Moonlight flooded the room through four humongous windows—two of them actually doors which opened onto the balcony. Unsurprisingly, the spacious room contained no closet—walk-in or otherwise—only a small dresser.

Dakas pointed at the very long right wall against which the dresser was propped. "I will build a wardrobe for you here," he said as if he'd read my mind. "There is enough room to make it the entire length and two meters deep. I will only need a couple of shelves for my accessories."

"You sure know how to speak a woman's language," I said with gratitude.

Although I felt guilty about him having to modify his bedroom, even with that addition, the room would remain insanely spacious.

"And this is the hygiene room," Dakas said, waving me into the large adjoining room.

It also had the stunningly carved archway but with an actual set of doors. Like the guest bathroom, the space was ridiculous—but even more so. It was easily as big as my bedroom in Kastan. Here, too, multiple showerheads promised a memorable experience. A separate room with a closed door contained the toilet. To my relief, it resembled a human toilet but without water tank and not propped against the wall. It sat in the middle of the space on a small pedestal, with enough room behind it for a pair of wings. I realized then that the pedestal was so that the wings at the back wouldn't drag on the floor.

"We don't usually bathe, although we enjoy a good swim. There is enough room to add a human tub here," Dakas said, pointing at one side of the room. "But if you want something bigger—something we could share—I can take down the wall here. It goes to a storage space."

"Ooh, I don't want you to go to all this trouble just for me. A normal tub would be fine, or even none at all. I mostly shower, anyway."

A wicked grin settled on his lips, and his gaze smoldered. "I think saying it aloud made me realize I actually *want* to soak in a bath with you naked in my arms."

My skin heated as a sudden arousal and embarrassment flooded me. After last night, I had no reason to feel shy. The atmosphere shifted, and I realized the tour had ended. Dakas was ready to move on to serious business.

"There is one last room for you to see," my husband said, his voice no longer playful. "We must purify ourselves before we enter, and there, we will bind our fates for eternity."

"Okay," I said in a breathy voice.

"Please, discard your clothes. We will shower together," Dakas said in a soft voice.

As much as the thought thrilled me, something in the solemn way Dakas spoke those words tempered the salacious side of me. We walked back into the bedroom where I removed my clothes, folding them neatly atop of the dresser while he got rid of his bracer and the weapons belt he'd worn for combat training earlier.

I was neither an exhibitionist nor a prude. I felt comfortable with my own body, and routinely saw naked patients, sometimes in positions people deemed embarrassing or even humiliating. This had helped free me of the usual reservations one feels when stripping in front of others. As soon as I was done, Dakas took my hand again and led me back into the shower room.

I didn't quite know what I had expected. Initially, before he asked me to strip in that serious voice, I thought he would get frisky. But his tone had made it clear this was serious—maybe even sacred—to him.

From a shelf carved directly into the stone, he retrieved what I thought must be a bar of soap. As the water rained down on us, Dakas spread his wings wide, and the showerheads targeted them, spraying both the front and the back at the downward angle he had taught me. He gestured for me to approach while building a lather of soap. The flow of the overhead water died, but the side ones continued to work on his wings. Dakas began washing me, covering every inch of my body in soap. The way the water continued to hit his wings just right convinced me some sort of motion sensor or tracker directed their aim.

There was nothing sensual in the way Dakas touched me, even when his hands ran over my breasts, my bum, and my sex. Clinical definitely didn't apply either. Dakas was reverent and solemn in the way he washed me, making me feel worshipped. The water on his wings stopped on its own while my husband finished washing my hair. After rinsing me thoroughly, he made me face him, handed me the bar of soap and spread his arms wide.

For a reason I couldn't explain, my throat suddenly felt constricted, and my mouth went dry. Remembering his words about not using soap on his feathers, I built up a lather and applied it to all of his human skin parts.

My eyes widened when the slightly feathery skin between his thighs parted and his penis extruded. It was my first time seeing it. As much as I would have wanted to fuss over it, I was too caught up in the sacred feeling of the moment to do so.

I didn't know if that kept me clinical about it, or if my years of medical practice had an impact. Either way, my brain registered its human shape, aside from the spiraling ridge around the length. For a second, I wondered if it was an evolution of the coiled duck penis or simply a hybridization because of his human parent. But I quickly dismissed that passing thought.

I gently washed his genitals then his legs and feet like he had done for me before rinsing him.

Dakas quickly flapped his wings and shook his crest and tail to get rid of some of the excess water. Holding both my hands in his as we stood face to face, he spoke a vocal command. Delightfully warm air blew all around us in a wonderful whirlwind, drying off all the moisture on our bodies.

I was drowning in the ocean of stars that sparkled in his eyes. We didn't say a single word, and yet a million silent communications passed between us. At the back of my head, I felt a light tingling that I knew to be Dakas's soul brushing against mine, eager for us to bind.

When the drying fans stopped, Dakas drew me to him and kissed me, long and deep. No passion or lust fueled it, only a world of tenderness. I melted against him. He picked me up and carried me like a bride to the back of the house, up a wide set of stairs, and into a circular room that I immediately recognized as some sort of temple or meditation area. It had no windows, only intricate symbols carved into the walls and encrusted with glowing crystals. In the center sat two cushions facing each other. Between them, four large crystals stood erect.

Dakas put me back on my feet right at the entrance then led me inside. We both kneeled on our respective cushions and sat back on our haunches.

"This is the soul room," Dakas said in a soft voice. "As Empaths, we often need a holy place to center ourselves and realign our emotions with our true self, separate from the feelings of others. This room is attuned to me. You and I are here today to become one soul. And this temple will become attuned to *us*."

I nodded and cast another furtive look around the room, feeling the peaceful energy that reigned within.

"Before we begin, I must reiterate that once the ritual is complete, you and I will be one until the day one of us dies," Dakas warned. "It is *both* a physiological *and* spiritual bond. After we have exchanged our vows, we will kiss. This will pass on to you my mating hormone. It will change you—not your appearance, but your mental powers. It will allow your soul to bond with mine and grant you some empathic abilities."

"You mean that I will be able to feel your emotions and those of others as Zelconians feel ours?" I asked, trying to rein in the excitement this had awakened in me.

"You *will* be able to feel mine, as we will be one," Dakas corrected, "but you will just get a sense of the emotions of other people. It probably won't be much from Zelconians or other species with empathic abilities, but you should be able to get a solid idea of emotions from humans and Yurus, for example, who have no psychic powers."

"Okay, I can live with that."

"Also, know that this bond will make it impossible for you or me to cheat on the other," he added. "Even just considering it will cause you physical discomfort. Doing it will inflict pain."

"I approve of that," I said with a smile.

He returned the smile, his soft expression making me melt inside. He looked like a mythical being in the dreamy glow of the crystals lighting the room, his midnight-blue wings draped beside and behind him like a long, regal cape.

"Normally, we would exchange vows and take turns singing to a crystal to realign it," Dakas explained, glancing at the four crystals between us. "But as you aren't Zelconian, you do not have the ability to feel their response and modulate your voice accordingly. I will therefore do it for all of them. You only need to respond to my pledges with as many or as few words as you desire."

"Very well," I said, starting to feel the jitters of a new bride.

"Let us begin," Dakas said, extending both of his hands towards me above the crystals.

I placed mine in his and locked gazes with him.

"Luana Torres, under the eyes of the Ancestors, I pledge my life to you. You are the other half of my soul. As I bind my spirit to yours, and yours to mine, I promise to always strive to bring happiness to your heart, lift your spirits when darkness would engulf them, share the burdens that could weigh down your mind, and feed your soul with all that it needs and desires to grow and fulfill your deepest aspirations."

As soon as he stopped talking, I took in a deep breath and responded with what I suspected was a themed pledge. The first crystal represented the mind and soul.

"Dakas Wakaro, under the eyes of God, I pledge my life to you. I give you my heart and soul and gladly accept yours in return. I promise to cherish and protect them, to share your pains, sustain you in your endeavors, and bring you joy in all the ways I can."

Dakas smiled then began to sing, his deep voice giving me goosebumps. The first crystal came to life, lighting up from the inside and glowing outwards, while countless waves of pleasant shivers coursed through me. The timid tingling at the back of my head went up a notch.

When my husband stopped singing, he stated a new pledge, this time about my health and welfare, promising to always keep me safe from harm, provide for my needs, do all in his power to mend me when wounded, and to remain steadfast even in my waning years. After I reciprocated, he sang again, igniting the second crystal. This time, the tingling spread across the entire back of my skull and nape.

The third pledge was about children, about being a good father, a good role model, an equal and supportive partner in raising them, and helping them achieve their dreams and aspirations. I once more shared my own vows. When he sang to activate the third crystal, the tingling spread to my spine, but another incredible sense of well-being was engulfing me, like a drug-induced buzz, which I knew came from the effects of the crystals.

The fourth and final pledge was friendship. That took me

aback at first. I'd expected the last one to either be the sharing of wealth or a commitment to love me. But as he expanded on it, I realized it made so much more sense. Friendship encompassed it all. As my truest, bestest friend, he would love me simply for who I was, not who he thought I should be. He would be there in my good and bad times, support me in all ways, including financially, treat me as an equal, and wish the best for me. Being my lover was only the icing on the cake.

When the fourth crystal lit, my entire body was tingling, and I almost felt like I was floating. The crystals began pulsating in sync, and my heartbeat aligned with them as they started lowering into the floor until they were flush with it. I couldn't tell if my eyes were playing tricks on me, but the stars in Dakas's eyes seemed to blink at the same pace.

He leaned forward, and I imitated him. Our lips met then parted, allowing our tongues to mingle. The tingling sensation immediately filled my mouth, but as a real, physical manifestation. A cold wave spread over my tongue, down my throat, and throughout my body. Dakas's taste had changed—fresh ginger dipped in honey came to mind. I knew that it was his bonding hormone being passed to me.

My head spun as the tingling intensified, becoming almost painful around my nape. A sliver of panic blossomed inside me. Had something gone wrong? Was I having a negative reaction to this foreign hormone? I moaned in pain as needles began stabbing the back of my eyes, and my skull felt on the verge of fracturing as the gingery taste intensified. I tried to pull away from Dakas, but he rose to his knees from sitting on his haunches, forcing me to kneel as well and drew my naked body against his before wrapping his wings around us.

A glancing pain slashed through the back of my head, and just as I was about to cry out—and probably lose consciousness —something shattered inside me. The agonizing pain vanished, the tingle faded, and a maelstrom of emotions flooded through me: guilt, protectiveness, and possessiveness, all wrapped in a heavy layer of tenderness. Then joy so profound it nearly brought tears to my eyes—Dakas's joy.

And then his voice resonated in my mind.

"We are one."

CHAPTER 13
DAKAS

I hated that our bonding had caused even the slightest pain to my mate. But it had been inevitable. As most humans, her pineal gland was underdeveloped, which stunted her psychic abilities. But my mating hormone would compensate as my DNA attached to hers over the coming weeks and months, strengthening her powers.

It always struck me as odd that humans hadn't developed this ability. More than three millennia ago, one of their ancient tribes called Egyptians had heavily documented how the pineal gland, the thalamus, and pituitary gland formed their third eye, the Eye of Horus. Combined with the medulla and cerebellum, they formed their inner bird: the Falcon of Horus. They thought the pineal gland remained dormant until the soul reached a high enough spiritual level to awaken and bring them to enlightenment. But awakening it would have given them the empathic abilities that would have brought about the peace their people so desperately needed.

However, right this instant, my woman was all that mattered. Her body relaxed against mine as a sense of wonder filled her, chasing away her previous pain. Holding her tightly, I rose to my feet and carried her to our room. Although she wrapped her arms around my neck, Luana was too languid to do the same with her legs around my waist and just let them dangle.

I loved the naked feel of her and wished that, like me, she could handle living without clothes. I lay Luana down on the bed, stretched out next to her, and gathered her in my arms. She pressed herself against me, rubbing her face against the down feathers of my chest in that way I enjoyed so much.

"You like when I do this," Luana whispered before lifting her head to look at me. I smiled and nodded at the amazed expression on her face. "I can feel it. It's very … blurry, for lack of a better word, but I feel it."

"It will become clearer with time."

My mate started running her palm over my chest, her gaze going out of focus as she concentrated on sensing my reaction to her touch. I completely dropped the walls empaths normally kept up as a courtesy to others. Luana's lips parted as our still nascent connection strengthened. I surrendered to her slow exploration of my body. She studied my responses, devoting a bit more time to areas that triggered the strongest reactions. In no time, she had mapped out my sensitive spots. The funniest part was that, while she was trying to understand what I liked, the pleasure she derived from it through me made her linger a little longer.

Although it had started as an innocent journey of discovery, it soon shifted, my blossoming arousal feeding hers. When her hand landed on my pelvic area, she didn't need to speak for me to know what she wanted. I suddenly felt self-conscious—which made no sense considering she had not only seen my penis, but also washed it. And yet, this was different. Sensing my discomfort, Luana lifted her head and gave me a questioning look laced with worry. I felt silly for that irrational moment of insecurity.

I smiled and sent appeasing waves her way, then extruded. I held my breath as her fingers slid over my thin pubic feathers and wrapped around my length. I hissed with pleasure, and

Luana's gaze darkened while her lips parted in the most sensual fashion. Eyes locked with mine, she gently stroked me, my natural lubrication easing her motion. A shiver ran through Luana as the pleasure she was giving me echoed back through her.

As she accelerated the movement of her hand on me, I closed my eyes with a voluptuous moan. My mate's soft lips began kissing and nipping at the bare skin of my abdomen on a meandering path downwards. A tremor shook me, and I fisted the blanket with one hand while the fingers of the other slipped through Luana's curly hair. As her body moved down alongside mine, her hardening nipples rubbed against my burning skin, sending a jolt of lust to my groin.

When she settled between my parted legs, my female slowed down the movement of her hand to get a good look at my penis. The sliver of self-consciousness that wanted to rear its head again died before it could fully form as Luana's delighted wonder and fascination coursed through me. She stroked me a few more times, her eyes glued to the way the ridges along my length undulated beneath her ministrations before she tentatively poked her tongue out.

My breath caught in my throat, worry and anticipation warring within me—her worry that she might dislike the taste of my natural lubricant enhancing mine. I felt her surprise a split second before her brow shot up. A wave of delight radiated from Luana as she began licking me in earnest. My fingers tightened in her curls, but a strangled cry tore out of me when the wet heat of her mouth wrapped around my length. A pool of lava swirled in the pit of my stomach as my female bobbed over me. Her delicate hand squeezed the base of my shaft before stroking it in counterpoint to the movement of her mouth.

I was cresting too fast. The intensity of my pleasure was messing with Luana in a sensory loop. Her own climax loomed near from those echoes. The growing scent of her arousal was driving me insane. But when she slipped her free hand between her thighs to rub her own ache, the enhanced pleasure she blasted my way nearly made me come undone.

I shouted and yanked on her hair with far more strength than I'd intended to pull her away from me. Luana yelped, and lifted her head to give me a stunned and outraged look, but I was already flipping her onto her back. My mate's attempt at protest died in a blissful shout, quickly followed by a string of moans interspersed with my whispered name as I reciprocated, licking her engorged little nub in a frenzy.

Luana fell apart moments later, her body seizing before her legs began to tremble. I growled as painful cramps twisted my insides with the need to embrace my release. But I resisted, squeezing the base of my penis almost savagely. A few drops of precum still managed to escape, but I reined myself in, reveling in the waves of ecstasy rolling over me from my soulmate.

Still flying high, Luana spread her legs and embraced me when I settled on top of her. She stared at me with hooded eyes, lips parted, and her body still shaken by the occasional spasm of pleasure. Despite her gaze, emotions, and physical stance screaming for me to proceed, I paused.

"Do you accept me, Luana?" I asked, trying to strip my voice of the urgency I felt.

"Yes," she said, hiding none of her impatience and lifting her pelvis towards mine.

It was all the formal consent I needed. I began pushing myself inside. Luana's body resisted me, forcing me to proceed with shallow thrusts. I claimed her lips in a possessive kiss, my tongue tingling as more of my bonding hormone flooded my mouth. I moaned loudly as Luana's nails scraped the highly erogenous area of my lower back. I didn't know if she had done it on purpose, but she repeated the gesture a few more times, drowning the burning feel of my penetration with my pleasure resonating inside of her.

And then her body relaxed, welcoming me in.

I hissed at the exquisite way her inner walls squeezed me from all sides, their burning heat cocooning and massaging my length as they contracted with her arousal. Luana echoed me with a guttural moan, which grew louder as I began to rock in and out of her. Ancestors, this was too intense ... too much. I never imagined that I could die from an excess of pleasure, or that it could threaten to fracture my mind. And yet, there it was.

I felt on the verge of combusting from within, each stroke, each kiss, each caress, conflating the sensory overload already swallowing me. The flow of pleasure emanating from her enhanced mine, before returning to further exacerbate what she felt in an endless loop, threatening to tear us asunder. But I couldn't stop—WE couldn't stop.

Luana's climax slammed into her with dizzying violence, sweeping me away in the process. I threw my head back as I roared my release, my wings spreading wide as my seed shot out into my woman. I thought I would collapse as liquid bliss poured out of me, but it only lessened the pressure that had brought me to the brink of insanity.

Instead of waning, the speed and strength of my thrusts increased as the flow of my seed fell down to a trickle. Before long, I was pounding into my mate, the sound of our flesh meeting buried by our voluptuous moans and shouts of ecstasy. Twice more I spent my seed inside Luana before collapsing next to her, destroyed. I pulled my woman's slick and trembling body on top of me and closed my wings around her. As we gave in to sleep, I basked in the blissful emotions of my mate.

~

I couldn't be more grateful for being an empath. Considering the number of times I'd woken Luana to claim her, had I not been able to feel that she was totally onboard with it, I would be worrying that she was getting fed up with my lustful greed. After showering together—in a less-than-innocent fashion—I'd prepared a Zelconian breakfast for us.

As Renok had confirmed that the coast was still clear down in Kastan, I'd decided to spend the day with Luana in Synsara to give her a tour of her new home. Tilda would hold down the fort at the clinic, while my brother and cousin Minkus spearheaded the improvements we wanted to make to the perimeter of the wall to counter the storming strategy the Yurus had attempted yesterday.

A tender smile stretched my lips as I glanced at my mate, sitting in the living area while talking with her father on the vidcom to let him know she wouldn't come down today. Mateo's conflicting emotions fascinated me. As much as losing his daughter broke his heart, he had rejoiced at her leaving the colony. Although I couldn't read minds, I believed he knew how much their colony's backward ways had been suffocating his Luana.

She came to join me as I was finishing laying out the food on the table. I'd prepared a sampling of various dishes Zelconians traditionally ate. She sat across the table from me, eyeing our meal with greed.

"As you can see, we eat a variety of grains and nuts, usually slightly roasted, some spiced, and normally still warm," I said, pointing at the bowls containing them. "For breakfast, we'll generally have them with a variety of fruits, and a thick juice of either fruits or vegetables. Meat and savory sides are rarely served at breakfast, except if we expect to have a very long day with little opportunities to pause for lunch. But I made an exception for you."

It took every bit of my willpower to control my emotions so that she wouldn't perceive my mischief. I couldn't fully block her out without raising her suspicion. I uncovered one of two plates and nearly burst out laughing when all the excited curiosity fell from Luana's face to be replaced by barely repressed horror.

"These are called doumias," I said, unable to believe I was managing to sound casual when the urge to laugh was almost making my eyes water. "They are a favorite of our people, especially the fledglings as they are soft, easy to digest, and with a unique taste that just makes you beg for more."

Luana swallowed hard, her slightly tan skin turning a shade paler as she eyed the oval-shaped doumias, perfectly golden on the outside and stuffed with mushrooms with only a tiny bit protruding at one end.

"Try one. They're lovely," I insisted before picking one between two fingers and tossing it into my mouth.

To my mate's credit, she swallowed hard again, squared her shoulders, lifted her chin defiantly, and reached for one of the doumias. I'd expected her to decline, at which point I would have confessed my deception, but she pushed through and took a bite. Startled by the taste, Luana's eyes widened with both shock and pleasure before she glared at me in outrage.

"These are not edible maggots! You *knew* what I was thinking!"

This time, I gave in and burst out laughing. The way Luana looked around, she was clearly looking for something—hopefully non-lethal—to throw at me.

"I do not read minds, Luana," I said, still chuckling and without the slightest remorse. "I do not control what thoughts cross your mind. You *chose* to assume this was the 'meat' I was referring to. But I did say meat *and* savory dishes were rarely served at breakfast. *This* is the meat."

I lifted the cover on the second heated plate, this one containing seared slices of hutan, a small mammal commonly found in the wild but which could also be domesticated.

Luana cast a glance at the meat. Her nostrils flared, and I

could almost feel her mouth water. But she turned her beautiful eyes filled with outrage my way, making me chuckle again.

"You're going to tell me that these doumias happened to have the exact shape, size, and dark head of a giant maggot?" Luana challenged.

I shrugged. "I may have carved out pieces of the doumia roots in that shape and stuffed them with grilled mushrooms just the right way to mess with your head," I confessed shamelessly.

She narrowed her eyes at me, her display of anger belied by the relief and amusement that emanated from her. "You know that I will get even, right?"

"I'm counting on it, my mate," I replied with a smug grin.

She shook her head at me, tossed the rest of the half-eaten doumia into her mouth and chewed happily.

"I have provided utensils for you," I said, pointing at them next to her plate.

Luana shook her head, her lovely curls bouncing around her face. "You ate human food the human way. We'll eat Zelconian food the Zelconian way."

"You don't have claws to slice the meat," I argued, although pleased by her comment.

"Nope, but I have teeth," Luana deadpanned, picking up a slice of hutan with two fingers and biting off a big chunk.

Her discreet moan of approval as the spicy taste of the meat exploded on her taste buds pleased me even more.

"So, tell me about yourself. I know that Renok is your brother and that both Phegea and Minkus are your cousins," Luana asked before taking a spoonful of warm, roasted nuts.

I nodded while pouring some thick fruit juice into her glass. "Renok is three years older than me. He is the only child my mother and her husband had. Phegea and Minkus are her brother's offspring. As you can guess, my father is human."

A frown marred Luana's beautiful face while confusion settled in.

"You're wondering how my parents conceived me if my mother was already married, if cheating is impossible for us," I said, matter-of-factly.

Luana's cheeks heated, and she gave me a sheepish smile as she nodded.

"She was widowed when they got together."

"Oh! I'm sorry," she exclaimed.

"It's okay," I replied with a gentle smile. "It all happened decades ago. You see, my father deals in shady business. He's what humans call a mercenary. Thirty-one years ago, he came to Cibbos to try and bribe Karnak—our Exarch at the time—to trade crystals in exchange for technology. But on his way to Synsara, he saw a group of Zelconians in distress. So, he went to assist."

"Your mother …?" Luana asked.

"My mother, Renok and his dad, my cousins and their parents, and a few other people," I replied. "They were down by the river, teaching the young how to swim and diving for fishing. Unfortunately, they had not realized that the Yurus were conducting one of their Wild Hunts in the area. They shouldn't have been as it was Zelconian territory. During lunch break, some of the children went flying into the nearby wood to gather some berries for dessert. Renok's father Tzane was with them. But a shengis had roamed into the area and gave chase."

"Oh no!" Luana said, pressing a hand to her chest.

"Tzane rushed the beast to try and lure it away while the children fled, but as you know, they have very toxic poisons that they can shoot with deadly precision," I continued. "Without weapons, Tzane didn't have much hope. But some of the children couldn't come out of hiding as even taking flight would have exposed them long enough to be killed."

"That's horrible! But where the fuck were the Yurus?"

"Much too far away. Two adults died that day, and many more might have perished if my father hadn't intervened when he did. He was in full stealth gear with advanced weapons—he is an arms dealer after all," I said.

"And thus became a hero," Luana said with a wry smile.

I snorted. "In many ways, yes. But it was too late for Tzane. He had been stung too many times. The tragedy though was that my mother rushed to his side and touched him and his wounds. She must have been wounded herself for the poison to have passed on to her. But it was in a small enough quantity that they didn't realize it at first. My mother's distress at losing her mate moved my father."

"He consoled her from her loss, and they fell in love?" Luana asked.

"In a way, but not exactly," I said carefully. "I didn't get to know my mother. She was barely alive by the time I was born. It took months after the death of her husband for my mother to realize the poison had taken root and was slowly killing her. Meanwhile, even though my father accepted that Karnak would not trade our crystals with him, he continued to come visit my mother and Renok."

"Was it a one-way thing then? Understandable, under the circumstances. She had just lost her soulmate," Luana said sympathetically.

I nodded. "While she only had affection for him, he was falling madly in love with her. In the end, I believe he was trying to come up with a scheme that would get the UPO to recognize her as his mate so they would look into a cure for her. But, as a mercenary, he couldn't even meet with anyone without risking incarceration."

"That's so unfair! Couldn't he take some of her blood samples to an underground doctor to devise an antidote?" Luana asked.

"He tried that, but they knew nothing of the Zelconian anatomy and would have required a pure sample of the shengis' venom," I said with a sigh. "I'm not sure why my mother agreed to bond with him more than a year later. They both knew she was dying. But I'm grateful that I was conceived as a result. After my mother's death, my father left Cibbos."

"Without you?" Luana flinched as soon as the words left her mouth.

I smiled reassuringly. "It's okay," I said before taking a sip of fruit juice. "It's a fair question. And yes, he left without me. His life wasn't appropriate for an infant, and even less for a hybrid like me that required a lot of attention. While my Zelconian features were dominant, some were replaced by human traits that complicated things. Me not having a cloaca was particularly distressing to them."

Luana snorted and slapped her hand over her mouth, amusement sparkling in her eyes. "Oh, God! I can only imagine. They must have thought you were seriously defective!"

"They did at first, but Uncle Alzim quickly found out about human anatomy," I said with a fond smile. "He took me in after my mother's death. But trying to fit an improvised diaper on a fledgling with a tail, making it tight enough to avoid unpleasant leaks, but loose enough to allow me to extrude so that I could urinate was apparently quite the challenge."

This time, Luana burst out laughing. By the way her gaze slightly went out of focus, she was likely visualizing the spectacle.

"I would have paid to witness that."

"You don't need to. You'll get hands-on experience once our little fledglings make their appearance," I deadpanned.

Luana sobered, which only made my own grin broaden. "Right," she said. "We're just going to put you on diaper duty."

I chuckled. "It required a lot of adaptation for them to raise me," I continued, my heart filling with affection for my uncle, his family, and the Zelconians as a whole. "I was never made to feel less although I was different. But I still faced many challenges. I got seriously injured a few times while being crop fed when a beak stabbed the back of my throat. I had major issues regulating my body temperature because so much of it is human. But clothes didn't work for me, and I didn't have a beak to help rid myself of excess heat like the others. Catching a cold, having a runny nose, and dealing with wisdom teeth were all issues that confounded the pureblood."

"Oh wow. I can only imagine. But ..."

Her voice trailed off, and once again I knew what thought had crossed her mind. "My father came to see me a few times in my fledgling years. But I hated it to the point that I asked him not to come anymore."

Luana recoiled. She stared at me, her eyes flicking between mine while trying to guess what could have prompted such a reaction from me.

"I am an empath. He's not," I explained gently. "Being here reminded him too much of my mother. His pain was all I felt around him. Outwardly, he was doing a great job of hiding it. But emotions don't lie. It was like having someone slowly cutting me. We have remained in touch. And over the years, he provided guidance I needed to handle my human side."

"I'm happy to hear you still have a relationship with him," Luana said, reaching across the table to squeeze my hand.

I smiled. "Estranged though he is, I love my father, and he loves me. But now, you need to eat up. I want to show you the city."

We finished our breakfast in an amiable chatter with me telling her about some of my childhood and her sharing some of hers. Then, hand in hand, I led my mate to the back of the house —which humans would have construed as the front—and which connected with the inner city of Synsara.

CHAPTER 14

LUANA

My jaw dropped as Dakas opened the wide set of doors at the back of the house. It was located just past the stairs to the private temple where we'd exchanged our vows and bound our souls. I'd expected some winding dark passage that would lead us to the inner city. Instead, I could have sworn I'd just walked into the most insane shopping mall.

Instead of shops, the front porches of the Zelconians' homes lined the wide walkways over multiple levels. A couple of stories overhead, an energy field served as a protective dome, keeping the rain, wind and other elements from falling into what I believed to be the caldera of a dormant volcano. Although you could walk around the circumference, a massive chasm separated us from the dwellings on the other side. Of course, that didn't faze the locals who simply flew over, many of whom could be seen flying around, and up and down the chasm.

My stomach dropped upon realizing that not a single guardrail protected the pedestrians on the walkways from a deadly fall. I didn't have any particular fear of heights, but this definitely qualified as unsettling. Thankfully, the significant width of the path—which allowed two adult Zelconians to walk side by side with their wings spread, made me feel safe walking in the middle.

Despite being carved directly into the mountain, Synsara was bright and luminous. Between the pale stones, the glowing white crystals embedded into the beautiful carvings on the walls, and the daylight flooding down through the dome of the city, the Zelconians had achieved something I wouldn't have thought possible.

To my pleasant surprise, a number of plants and trees graced the pathways, some looking as if they had grown right through the rock to spread their arms towards the light from above. The façades changed from clearly residential to looking more commercial or official as we approached the center of our current level of Synsara.

"Every level of the city has storage areas, granaries, and what would qualify as businesses," Dakas explained, pointing out each in turn. "We have a form of currency, but it's not much used. Trading remains the dominant form of commerce here. A third of our population works in the more traditional craft trade, but the majority work in crystal shaping and technological research. A series of hover platforms connects them, which is why they are all perfectly aligned on every level."

"Hover platforms?" I asked, perking up.

Dakas chuckled at my reaction. "There are hover platforms everywhere. They're just hiding in plain view. There are many reasons why someone might not want to fly or be unable to do so, and they would be stranded without any transport. You'll be happy to hear that, as soon as a platform starts moving, an energy field is erected around it to keep the object or person from falling."

"Thank you for that!" I said, feeling almost faint with relief.

"Come, let's go try one now."

Intrigued, I let him lead me by the hand to an entrance so ornate you'd think it was a jewelry store.

"Stand on the platform," Dakas said, pointing at a non-remarkable spot on the floor.

As soon as I did, the edges of a large square illuminated around me.

"Oh wow!"

Dakas smiled. "You can use your hand or your foot to control it. The hand is more intuitive. Hold your hand in front of you. To make it go up, gesture upwards as if telling someone to stand up. Gesture downwards to make it go down. And sideways to tell it to stop. The speed of your movement will also affect the speed of the platform. Try it."

I complied, impatient to see what would happen. In my eagerness, I moved my hand down quickly, and I all but felt the floor drop from under me. I yelped, feeling like my stomach was trying to jump right out of my throat, and almost lost my footing. But my bum connected with the energy field that had indeed appeared around the edge of the platform, gently pushing me back to the middle. I waved my hand sideways, again with a bit too much vigor. My stomach lurched once more as the platform came to a sudden stop.

Worst elevator ride ever!

Showing more caution, I slowly moved my hand up, and the platform rose at a pleasant pace this time while Dakas flew around me with an amused expression. But I could feel his pride for me and excitement to show me his world.

Dakas opened his mouth to speak, but a sudden ruckus in the distance caught our attention. It took me a moment to realize it was coming from a lower level. Seconds later a flurry of movements, shouts in Zelconian, and people flying around made me stare at my husband in confusion and worry.

"Oh, this is going to be good," he whispered as if to himself. "I think we have a fledgling gone rogue."

"A what?!"

But he didn't have to answer. His meaning became crystal clear when a little Zelconian—looking no more than five or six years old—flew past us at dizzying speed. Two adult females and one male appeared to be giving chase. The child was insanely fast, making the grown-ups seem like they were lumbering behind. He reminded me of a fly being hunted by three hungry birds.

No, not a fly. He moves like a hummingbird.

"What's going on?" I asked Dakas, as a couple of other passersby joined the fray.

"Juma is misbehaving again," he replied with a chuckle while slowly flapping his wings to hover next to me. "Judging by the current time, he likely tried to dodge school, and the teacher called his mother. And now, the brat is fleeing to avoid being dragged back to class."

Dakas laughed at my flabbergasted expression. But I wasn't paying attention to him anymore. Juma and his pursuers were covering an insane distance, flying up, down, left, right. A few times, I feared they would crash into a tree, a wall, or one of the walkways. After a couple of minutes, at least ten adults were now hunting the slippery little rogue. When the child appeared to be shooting straight for us, Dakas jumped into action. He actually caught him for half a second, but Juma wiggled free.

Soon, complete chaos reigned with too many adults jumping in, getting in each other's way while the little fiend zig-zagged between them with mind-blowing speed and skill. I never saw how he got caught as it happened a little too far from me with his chasers blocking my line of sight. A male held the child firmly while a female I assumed to be his mother berated him. As soon as they landed on the walkway opposite from where I hovered on my platform, the female removed something from the belt hanging on her hip.

Juma became hysterical, trying to break free. I couldn't feel his emotions, but his body language and the high pitch of his voice expressed clear distress. I cast a worried look at Dakas, who gave me a side smile.

"She is clipping his wings," he explained calmly.

"What?! But that's …!" I barely held back the harsh word that had come to mind. "It seems excessively cruel. Won't that hurt him?"

"No, my mate. We do not harm or mutilate our offspring. Juma is merely being overly dramatic," Dakas said in a gentle voice, thankfully not offended by my implied comment. "As long as you do not cut beyond a certain threshold, we feel no more pain when our feathers are clipped than when a human gets· a haircut. But plucking out a feather would hurt the same way as pulling your hair out. Although it may seem like a harsh punishment, it isn't one at all. She's clipping his wings to protect him from himself."

"How so?" I asked genuinely intrigued, although my eyes remained glued on the mother as she removed the tips of a few of her child's flight feathers on each wing.

"This is the phase where fledglings are the fastest, as you've probably noticed by how hard it was to catch him. Such speed is intoxicating and can give you quite an adrenaline rush," Dakas explained. "Most fledglings can handle it, but hyper ones like Juma get hurt. He's already suffered four fractures over the past six months, and nearly killed himself last month when he crashed head first into a wall. He cannot afford another concussion so soon."

I nodded slowly. As a medical doctor, I understood that. I also knew that many pet bird owners clipped their flight feathers to prevent them from flying and getting hurt indoors. And yet …

"His mother isn't taking away his ability to fly, merely limiting his rapid flight. Cheer up, Luana. Look, he has stopped carrying on. He's not even crying, just pouting. It was all a show," Dakas said, pointing at Juma with his chin.

Sure enough, having limited his flight capability, they put the boy back on his feet on the walkway. Even with his beak making it harder to see an actual pout, his entire demeanor, facial expression, and body language screamed exactly that. He wasn't in distress, just unhappy he hadn't gotten his way.

"We're going to have to get you a jetpack," Dakas said pensively.

My eyes widened. "Whatever for?"

"To give you even a chance to catch our brats when they try to flee their chores or homework," he deadpanned.

He barked a laugh at my horrified expression.

Flying kids! That's going to be ... fun.

"Come, my mate. Let's go park that platform. It's time for you to see how we make crystals. Go all the way to the lowest level."

I complied, making my platform travel at a comfortable pace, while feasting my eyes on the inner city. Each level appeared to be decorated based on a different theme related to nature. From the elements, to the flora and fauna, the organic carvings on the walls made the city breathtaking. But the low population surprised me.

"Most of our people are working right now," Dakas replied when I asked. "Anyone who isn't an essential worker or crafter has been temporarily reassigned to upgrading the city's defenses or filling our granaries in preparation for a potential war."

That reminder of the threat that loomed over us dampened my mood, but it reassured me to know they were preparing in case things seriously escalated. I didn't want to think what that might mean for Kastan. Then again, I wouldn't put it past Vyrax to switch his attention to the Zelconians first to take out the head before refocusing on us.

How long would we last without the Zelconians?

We would effectively be trapped inside the village. They could find and cut off our access to our water supply and to the larger orchards, farms, and grazing land for our zeebises that we had not enclosed within the protective wall as it would have been too large an area to cover. But worse still, without the Zelconians as our protectors, would we lose our status as a legitimate colony with all the perks it entailed?

"Whatever dark thoughts are crossing your mind, cast them out, Luana," Dakas ordered in a semi-stern voice. "The Yurus *will not* win. Of this, I am certain."

The conviction in his voice and in the emotions he projected had a surprisingly soothing effect on me.

As we reached the lowest floor, Dakas led me from the platform down a wide hallway. Unlike the upper levels, which were clearly residential and commercial with pretty adornments and luminous crystals, this one was almost clinical—except for a short section of the hallway on the left.

Dakas pointed at it. "Over there, you will find the equivalent of a spa with thermal baths. But we're going in the opposite direction, at the other end of this pathway. Be very careful to always stay on the sides if you are walking here. The center lanes are for high-speed transports in both directions."

I recoiled, casting an incredulous look at the inconspicuous floor. Granted, a clear line of darker colored stones marked the separation between the pathways on each side, and the two 'transport lanes' in the middle. But all of it just looked like larger stone tiles.

"Always make sure there is nothing incoming before getting on the transport."

We stepped into the 'transport lane' on the right, and like with the hover platform, the wide tile beneath us lit up and immediately began to hover by a few centimeters above the floor. Dakas slipped his foot over the surface, and the platform started moving forward, faster than a good walking speed, but slower than a fast jog, and nowhere near enough to be hazardous.

"Sheesh, you guys hardly qualify as primitives," I mumbled, blown away by how much more advanced they were than our colony.

Dakas snorted and shrugged. "Primitive is a relative term. We consider ourselves advanced, but we haven't achieved inter-stellar travel, and that makes us primitive by galactic standards. Then again, before your very convenient dowry, we hadn't figured out how to build a stealth shield. We'd gotten close but the—very simple—solution kept eluding us. We have a ways to go, but we're fine with that. It's part of the fun."

I nodded. "I understand the founding principles of our colony, but denying ourselves such convenience as these trans-port platforms makes no sense to me."

Dakas smiled and caressed my cheek, and I felt his sympathy seeping through our bond.

"Behind these doors, there are either storage facilities, research labs, development centers, or workshops, all mostly or exclusively related to our crystals. And up ahead are the growing chambers."

Our transport platform eventually came to a stop in front of a massive set of doors. We got off, and Dakas waved his hand above the platform, as one would to shoo a fly. The platform took off, settling down on the floor a short distance away where a previous platform had moved away.

The doors parted as soon as we approached. A pleasant heat greeted us when we entered. My steps faltered as I took in the wonders within. A natural hot spring occupied the center of the circular room. A series of small, evenly spaced altars surrounded it. On top of each sat a large glass bowl filled with a clear liquid. A small crystal lay submerged at the bottom. Around the perimeter of the room, at least fifty alcoves had been carved out, and each contained a single crystal of a different size and color.

They dangled on a rope inside a tank filled with a liquid of matching hue. A glass door hermetically sealed each alcove. Within a few of these isolated booths, a Zelconian sang, although we couldn't hear them through the glass door.

A light suddenly lit the surface of the altars surrounding the hot spring.

"We're just in time," Dakas said excitedly but in a hushed tone. "This is when a crystal's vocation is determined. To create our crystals, we pour a large amount of minerals harvested from the bowels of the mountain into these bowls. Then we add water from the spring to create a highly saturated solution. Normally, you need very hot water for crystals, but not for ours. As it cools, the crystals start forming. The natural heat from the spring maintains the ideal room temperature for them to grow."

As Dakas spoke, two dozen Zelconians entered the room from side entrances I hadn't noticed. Each one held a tray with eight small containers filled with what resembled mineral salts of different colors.

"This is the critical phase," Dakas continued. "Each crystal has its own purpose, its own ... aspiration. And they're about to tell the Nurturers." He chuckled at my baffled expression. "Yes, crystals 'speak' to those who have the power to listen. When we sing to them, they respond. The Nurturers simply focus their empathic abilities to figure out what the crystal needs in order to grow into what it desires to be, then feed it accordingly."

Stunned, I stared at the Nurturers who smiled at us before going to stand in front of their respective altar.

"These minerals will grant the crystal different properties. Right now, we're hoping for a lot of black, red, green, and blue."

As soon as he finished speaking those words, Dakas pressed a finger to his lips to indicate that we should now remain quiet. I nodded. Then, in perfect sync, the voices of all twenty-five Zelconians facing the altars rose in the most enchanting melody. Like that first time Dakas and the others had sung to activate the crystals of our protective wall, one shiver after another coursed through me, my skin erupting in goosebumps.

As they sang, all of them scooped mineral salts into their bowls, each at different timings and in different quantities. While some only added from one type of minerals, others mixed two or more different types, coloring the water. The glowing surface of the altars pulsated and the liquid inside the bowl began to swirl, no doubt to help dissolve these new salts. A few Nurturers finished 'feeding' their crystals but continued to sing until everyone had put down their scoop.

Their chant faded, and they each reached for a ladle hooked to their respective altars, took some water from the hot spring, and poured it into their bowl. They didn't dump the whole thing in one shot, but let it trickle down while the liquid continued to swirl. I realized then that the water being already saturated couldn't fully dissolve the new salts, and they were merely adding enough new water to make it possible. They emptied the excess water back into the hot spring, returned their ladle to its spot, then collected their trays before exiting the room.

"These crystals will grow for a couple of days, and then the same process will be repeated as many times as necessary," Dakas explained. He pointed at the isolated booths lining the walls. "Once they reach their first level of maturity, they will be moved to an alcove to continue growing and for their imbued powers to multiply until they reach their full maturity."

"Is that why people are singing to them inside those booths?" I asked.

Dakas smiled with approval at my accurate guess. "Yes. Our Nurturers specialize in different types of crystals. Caya is especially gifted for healing and focus crystals. This is why she sings to this healing crystal. You have to listen to its needs and modulate your voice accordingly to optimize the alignment of the facets of the crystal as it grows. The yellow crystals embedded in each booth act as enhancers for both the maturing crystal's power and the effectiveness of the Nurturer's chant."

"Does the UPO know how you create these crystals?" I asked, blown away.

Dakas smirked. "On some level, yes. They offered to buy the minerals from us and to pay us royalties on every crystal created and sold. When we explained why that wasn't possible, they were quite deflated."

I chuckled. "No wonder they are so keen to forge an alliance with the Zelconians." Then I frowned. "What about the Yurus?"

"They know as well. You're wondering why they would bother trying to take over our crystals then," he said, accurately guessing the thoughts crossing my mind. "You can create the crystals without a Nurturer's chant. They will be half as effective, and the majority will be nothing but junk—so, a lot of waste. However, I suspect the Yurus intend the same thing they have in store for the humans: kill most of the males, enslave the females and skilled crafters to continue to produce the goods they covet. After all, two-thirds of our Nurturers are females."

He gestured to the doors while starting to move towards them., and we left the "nursery."

"Yeah, that makes sense," I said pensively. "But why haven't the Zelconians made a deal with the UPO?"

We crossed over to the left transport lane to go back to the central area.

"Because they didn't have anything good enough to give us in exchange," Dakas said while the platform moved at a pleasant pace. "When they first contacted us, seventy years ago after your colony settled here, our technology was nowhere near where it is today. They were offering us some basic theorems in mathematics and physics so we could try and figure out how to apply them in ways that could be beneficial to us. My people agreed to that first trade to get those theorems."

"Let me guess, they didn't do much for you?" I said in a commiserating voice.

"They were useful, but not revolutionary. After that, since half of our population migrates for winter as food becomes more scarce, they wanted to teach us things such as sustainable farming."

I burst out laughing when he made a disgusted face as he spoke those words.

"We declined. We do some farming, but it is not in our nature, nor is it something we've ever needed. We weren't in a good negotiation position because we weren't advanced enough for them to give us anything worthwhile. So, we waited until we were. Our discoveries and new developments have been growing exponentially over the past couple of decades. We were considering resuming talks with the UPO in the next two to five years."

"But this whole mess with the Yurus has accelerated the process," I said as our transport came to a stop in the central area of the inner city.

"The best thing that could have happened in more ways than one," Dakas said softly, his voice going deeper.

He took my face between his hands and gently kissed me while waves of tenderness and possessiveness flowed out of him. I was totally digging this empathic business.

Dakas released me and led me to an available hover platform so we could go back up. I could feel his desire to carry me instead and to fly up the open space between the levels. But he wanted me to practice using the hover lifts, making me use my feet this time to control it instead of my hand.

We stopped on a few levels along the way for him to show me different shops and services offered. The one that fascinated me the most—although completely useless to me—was the groomer's shop, essentially the Zelconian version of a barber-shop and beauty salon. Seeing people get their overgrown beaks sanded, their cracked beaks patched, their talons filed, and their wings groomed mainly to readjust balance with some trimming for a few broken or missing flight feathers, blew my mind.

Dakas spent the rest of the day showing me more wonders of his world. But it would take me a long time to absorb it all. And that, thankfully, we had plenty of ...

CHAPTER 15
DAKAS

Ten days had gone by since Vyrax's humiliating failure to take over Kastan. While I enjoyed this reprieve, which allowed me to deepen my bond with my mate, it also greatly worried me. Our spy drones had noted a significant increase in interplanetary trade with Mutarak. It spelled bad news. The UPO's Peacekeepers had stepped up their efforts to intercept any mercenary vessel approaching Cibbos, but they didn't have the authority to forbid the Yurus from trading with whomever they wanted.

They were up to something. But whatever it was, the Yurus were doing a fantastic job of hiding it from us. It didn't make sense for Vyrax to allow a slight to go unanswered this long. At least, it gave us more time to reinforce our defenses around both Synsara and the colony, and it gave the humans more time to train.

Luana had been spending all of her time in Synsara, dividing her attention between learning more about Zelconian anatomy with our healer Feylin, and soaking up the latest medical advances and technologies available through the UPO network, which she could now access freely. It had caused some muttering from the colony, some going so far as to imply that I was holding her for nefarious reasons, despite her father's reassurances to the contrary.

Today, as one of the elder humans required a minor surgery, Luana decided to fly down to supervise the procedure. Tilda could have handled it on her own—not to mention the fact that the advanced medical pods Kayog had sent them would perform the whole thing. But having my mate present calmed the female and silenced the growing rumors of foul play against their leader's daughter.

Not wanting to part from Luana, I replaced Minkus, who had been on guard and scout duty for the colony since the day we struck that alliance. To my shock, Martin approached me while I was checking the integrity of the wall.

"We're running low on jiniam wood," Martin said. "Since things have been quiet a while, I'd like to go harvest some, if you or another one of your people wouldn't mind accompanying me."

He spoke the words with a stiff politeness. Although he looked at my face, the way he avoided making direct eye contact felt suspicious. And yet, I couldn't feel the slightest deception from him. Since the first failed attack by the 'rogue' raiding party, and even more so after Vyrax showed up, Martin had dropped his belligerent attitude towards me. In this instant, I would have given anything to be able to read his mind.

"I will escort you," I replied.

"Thanks. I'll go get my harvester," he mumbled.

I mind-spoke with Renok to warn him that I would be heading out.

"Is it wise, brother? None of the humans have gone out since the raid. And this particular one hates you."

I smiled, although he couldn't see it. *"I sense no deception or malice from him. I think it stung his ego to have to ask me of all people. But the humans need that wood for the enhanced arrows they've been stockpiling. Let's gather more wood while things are still quiet."*

My big brother's reluctance flooded our psychic connection. *"Fine. But if you get hurt, I'm pecking his wretched eyes out."*

I laughed out loud. *"Deal,"* I telepathically replied to Renok before disconnecting from his mind.

He'd always been extremely protective of me. He was the muscles, and I the brain. Little Jamu's antics on the day I gave Luana a tour of the city flashed before my mind's eye. Renok and I had not been as dramatic in our misbehaving, but we'd instigated our fair share of chases—not for skipping school, but for Renok to avoid getting his beak sanded and for me to avoid getting my wings trimmed. Like Jamu, I'd been a speed junky. My heart warmed at the thought of the little delinquents Luana and I would have together. I couldn't wait for them to go rogue.

Martin's return, riding a harvester, put an end to my pleasant musing. The name of that vehicle didn't make much sense to me. It didn't harvest anything. It was merely some sort of wide hoverbike attached to a large, rectangular hovering platform to carry stuff in. Trailer or transport vehicle would have been far more appropriate.

As he approached, I tapped a few instructions on my armband, double-checking the wide-range scanners for any sign of trouble. With the coast still being clear, I flew to the closest doorway location and deactivated that part of the defensive wall to let Martin's harvester through, closing it immediately behind us.

I hated how deep into the woods we needed to go to find jiniam trees. A part of me wished I could have simply gone with a couple of my brothers to harvest some for him. However, as much as I disliked Martin, he was skilled in his craft. You couldn't pick just any jiniam tree. You had to find the right ones, at the right maturity level. You also didn't take the entire tree, just specific limbs from it.

We finally reached our destination. Martin descended his vehicle and walked around a few trees before settling on one. After studying its branches, he used some sort of strange, wire-thin rope that he threw like a grappling hook around the limb of his choice. The wire immediately started cutting through the wood. The process was a little slow, but clean and effortless for the human.

Wanting a good vantage point to see any potential incoming threats, I settled in a crouching position on a low branch of a tree across from where Martin was working. My feet wrapped around it, and my toe and heel talons extruded and dug into the bark to stabilize me. Martin turned to look at me, his gaze lingering on my feet. Although he kept a neutral expression, I could feel how much they creeped him out. I could understand why. Their deceptively human appearance made it freaky once they curled well beyond what a normal foot should be able to.

I smirked. He noticed and averted his eyes, his cheeks heating. He shifted on his feet, casting a glance at the branch that was halfway cut, before half turning my way again.

"She seems happy," he suddenly said in a grumbling tone.

I recoiled, taken aback by that comment, but above all by the genuine sadness, maybe even hurt that emanated from him.

"Luana is my soulmate," I said matter-of-factly. "It is impossible for us not to be happy together."

Martin snorted. "Right … I guess that explains why no one else was ever good enough for her."

I frowned at the bitterness in his voice. "Why are you still so upset?" I asked, genuinely confused. "You're not in love with her. I'm not sure that you even like her. And do you really want to become colony leader? To have to handle the kind of mess we're currently facing?"

A slew of emotions flashed through him, many reflected flittingly on his face. The branch falling spared him from answering. I waited patiently as he retrieved his wire and set it to work on a different branch while he pondered his answer. Martin then kneeled in front of the fallen branch to start slicing it in half using a laser knife.

"You're right. I'm not in love with her, but I love her in my own way," Martin said at last. "I don't want to deal with all this political bullshit, but I also don't want to continue to stagnate like this."

I cocked my head to the side, intrigued.

"We were born in this bullshit, retro colony, living like we're still in the fucking medieval era because our grandparents got butthurt by the way people used technology back home," Martin said, anger bubbling within him. "They could have settled on any of the human colonies of the UPO. Plenty of them would have granted them remote lands to live the way they wanted."

"How would that have changed your fate?"

Martin stopped splitting his branch to look up at me. "Those of us who didn't want this shitty lifestyle could have left and moved to one of the other colonies. But they didn't want to risk that. They came here specifically so that we would be trapped. And then they dismantled all our means of transportation out of here, under the pretense of needing the parts to build the colony's infrastructure. But in truth, they just wanted us to be prisoners here."

"The UPO could have relocated those of you who wanted to leave," I offered softly.

Martin snorted then resumed his work. "Our parents refuse to leave. Like us, most of them were born here and got super indoctrinated by their own parents. They're afraid of starting over elsewhere. They think they're too old. I could never leave my mother here. But the reality is that we, the younger generation, are the ones carrying this colony. If one of us leaves, the others will follow, and our parents will die. We're trapped. But with Luana and I as leaders, we could have changed things."

"You don't need to be married to achieve this," I argued.

"We did," he countered stubbornly. "Luana may not have wanted to take charge when her father was down, but she had no choice. Not because she's the leader's daughter, but because there is no one else who could have done the job. We're a small colony. Everyone knows everyone. She's the only person who instills enough confidence for the entire village to follow her. Luana may look timid sometimes, but she's a quiet force. When shit needs to get done, she steps up."

The second branch dropped. Martin stood to go set his wire on a third branch. He returned to the first one he was done splitting and carried the pieces in the back of the harvester.

"We normally choose our leader through an election process. But the day Mateo dies or steps down, there won't be one. It is a well-known fact in Kastan that when it happens, whoever has married Luana will co-inherit that role with her so that she can continue to be our doctor. Your wife is the only person in the colony oblivious to that fact. So, congratulations. You are our future leader."

I gaped at him in disbelief. He snorted again and started working on splitting the second fallen branch.

"But I'm Zelconian!"

"You're half-human," Martin said factually, before lifting his head to look at me. "I wasn't sure what someone like you would do to us. How could we know if you'd be any different than the Yurus? How could we be sure you wouldn't try to enslave us, too?"

"We have no such designs," I said forcefully.

"I believe you now," he replied. A strange look drifted across his features. He shrugged then lowered his head to get back to work. "The way you led your people in building our defenses and all that work you did saved my people. I and most of the men in Kastan would probably be dead right now, and God only knows what would have happened to our women... to my mother... to Luana. You've even gotten that old hag Jenna helping our head-farmer Anita to pluck turkeys and prepare their feathers for our heat-seeking arrows. So, yeah... You marrying Luana is probably the best thing that's ever happened to Kastan."

Although he spoke those words in a grumbling tone, the sincerity emanating from him left me speechless. I searched for an appropriate response, but words failed me. Becoming a colony leader had never featured in my plans.

Would I even enjoy that?

Yes. I loved planning and strategizing. I could do the work and would probably enjoy it, but I didn't think myself appropriate for the role. Sure, I was half-human, but I'd been fully raised Zelconian. I believed in and aspired to the responsible development of technology. I would want to be surrounded by beauty like in Synsara, not this bland, basic village. Then again, many among Luana's and Martin's generation wanted the same thing. Could I be the instrument of their 'liberation'?

But I cast away such musings. Mateo was still young and— thanks to the miraculous work of the high-tech medical pods Kayog had sent—in perfect health. The day he stepped down from his role would likely be long after Luana and I had raised our offspring in Synsara.

"Thank you," I answered at last, failing to find anything better. "I—"

My head jerked left, and I expanded my senses, searching. A sliver of malevolence brushed against my psychic mind, like the spindly legs of a spider. I looked at my bracer, but it failed to detect whoever was closing in on us. A wave of fear emanating from Martin slammed into me.

"What is it?" he asked with a quiver in his voice.

"We're leaving, now," I said, my eyes flicking in every direction as I failed to pinpoint the location of the intruder—something that had never happened before. He was close, and getting closer. But something was interfering with my ability to locate its source.

"Brother, we've got incoming. Stealth. I only sense one for now but can't see him," I mind-spoke to Renok.

Before I could continue, a powerful murderous intent struck me—the type of thought that preceded a predator's killing strike. It wasn't aimed at me, but at Martin who had abandoned his second branch to jump onto the hoverbike of his harvester. On instinct, I dove from the branch I was crouching on and swept Martin off his vehicle in a fly by.

His face took on a terrified expression at seeing me lunging at him. But his frightened cry soon drowned under my shout of pain as something sharp embedded itself between two of my ribs, right where Martin's throat would have been half a second earlier. I almost crashed to the ground from agony and the wiggling weight of the human in my arms. Teeth clenched, I flapped my wings with all my strength, each motion feeling like it was pushing the blade deeper into my flesh. Blood filled my mouth while I struggled to breathe with a perforated lung.

Another searing pain lanced through the back of my right thigh as a second sharp projectile found its mark. Renok's increasingly panicked voice resonated in my psychic mind in reaction to my failure to answer. I didn't mean to ignore him, but I had to focus on not dropping Martin, and fighting through the pain to fly us to safety. Anyway, my big brother would feel echoes of my suffering through our psychic connection.

And so would Luana.

Thoughts of my mate spurred me on. Our bond had been steadily strengthening over the past ten days. Each time we made love—and we did often—I'd share my bonding hormones with her. Her burgeoning empathic connection to me had greatly increased. She would likely panic, maybe not even understand the source of her sudden pain and distress.

Martin started cursing. I almost yelled at him to stop wiggling so much and to hang on properly to me when I felt him pull the blaster from my weapons belt. Aiming over my shoulder, he began shooting at our attackers while cursing them out. I had not expected this from him.

But when a third projectile struck my lower back, I nearly dropped him. I cried out in agony. My legs tingled before going numb. My head swam and savage cramps started twisting my insides while my blood felt as if it had turned to liquid fire.

Poison ...

I looked ahead, still seeing nothing but trees. The village was too far. We'd never make it. I'd known we'd gone too deep into the forest for that damn wood. Even if I dropped Martin, I wouldn't have the strength to make it back to Kastan. Beyond the fact that I was drowning in my own blood, each flap of my wing was making my heart pump faster, spreading the poison even more rapidly through my body.

My vision blurred, my wings grew heavy, and my arms felt like wood. Luana's consciousness brushed against mine. For a split second, I could have sworn I'd heard her voice calling my name in my psychic mind. Could it be? Wasn't it too early for her to develop a telepathic connection with me?

"Hang on, son. We're here."

Graith's voice resonated in my head seconds before five Zelconians dropped their camouflage, their energy shields raised before them to form a wall behind me. I hadn't felt or heard them approach. I was too far gone. I couldn't even tell if Martin had slipped from my arms or if Minkus had taken him from me. I felt myself begin to fall, but Graith caught me. As a veil of darkness descended before my eyes, I tried for one last contact with my mate. I couldn't die without saying goodbye.

But Graith's psychic voice telling me to hang on was all I heard.

CHAPTER 16

LUANA

The oddest feeling of unease slammed into me. Tilda gave me a questioning look as I broke off mid-sentence. I blinked, trying to understand what was wrong, what had triggered such a reaction. But instead of fading away, the sense of doom increased, my back stiffening with tension.

"Something's wrong. No ... something bad is about to happen ... I think," I said.

"What do you mean?" Tilda asked.

"I don't know. This empathic business has been messing with me lately. Maybe it's nothing but ... Stay with Jenna, okay? I need to talk to Dakas about this. The procedure went well. I should be back before she wakes."

"All right," Tilda said, worry filling her eyes.

I took one last glance at Jenna's stats on the medical pod's monitor, then headed towards the door. Just as I was reaching for the handle, a shout rose from my throat as a sharp pain stabbed me in the side.

"Luana!" Tilda exclaimed, rushing to me where I stood hunched over, holding my ribs. "What's wrong?"

The pain vanished as quickly as it appeared, but now I was starting to freak out.

"Dakas," I whispered. "I think something has happened to Dakas."

No sooner did the words cross my lips than I hissed in pain. This time, in the back of my leg. Once again, it disappeared almost instantly.

"He's hurt!"

I rushed outside, calling his name, only for the city alarm to drown out my voice. I felt my blood drain from my face at the sight of Graith, Renok, and four other Zelconians flying out over the wall while attaching their weapons belts around their waists. Seconds later, they activated their stealth shield and vanished from view.

Chaos erupted, and people ran around in panic. My father stormed out of the Great Hall onto the plaza and barked orders through the village's com system, telling all the combatants to arm themselves and man the towers, and for the others to go to their assigned shelters.

I should be readying the emergency medical posts, but a single thought obsessed me: finding my husband. Dakas was in distress. I was running towards one of the towers when the sound of flapping wings made me look up. I nearly wept with relief to see Skieth's dark silhouette descending towards me. But the expression on his face twisted my innards into tight knots.

"Dakas is in trouble," I said before he was done landing.

"Yes, he's under attack," Skieth confirmed. "He accompanied Martin over the wall to gather more wood for arrows. He's bringing him back."

"Over the wall?!" I felt faint as a million questions rushed my mind.

But I needed to focus. Demanding to know why the fuck he had gone there wasn't going to bring him home.

"Yes. Graith and a small unit have gone to assist him. You need to prepare to mend him," Skieth said in a commanding tone.

I nodded stiffly and looked at my wrist before cursing under my breath. As I no longer lived in Kastan, I had surrendered my armband to my father.

"How far are they?" I asked.

Skieth tapped a couple of instructions on his armband. I stretched my neck, tilting my head to try and read its interface.

"At fast flight, they're four minutes away," he replied.

"Okay. I'm going to get a hover stretcher and have Tilda prepare a pod for—"

My mouth opened wide in a silent cry, and my eyes bulged at the searing pain in my lower back. My legs went dead, and I collapsed. Without Skieth's lightning reflexes, I would have crumpled to the ground and probably hurt myself.

Although the numbness in my legs fizzled, a nauseous feeling settled deep within me. Whatever had happened, Dakas was in a critical state.

"He's dying," I whispered, horror taking hold of me.

Skieth straightened me on my feet, grabbed me by the shoulders, and shook me once as if to snap me out of my crushing despair.

"Dakas will *not* die. Not today. Not anytime soon. Reach out to your mate," he ordered in a tone that brooked no argument. "Call out to his soul and hold him. He will seek you."

I didn't know how to do any of it. This whole psychic power stuff was still new to me. And yet, I reached out. I closed my eyes and focused on the way it felt to bask in the tender emotions he always lavished on me, the passion he unleashed when we made love, and the possessive, protective waves that emanated from him when he held me close at night. Through it all, I felt the tiny thread that had been strengthening since our bonding. I latched on and poured into it all the emotions I felt for my husband.

At first, there was nothing. Then a spark turned into a flame and then a blinding light before I connected to Dakas's consciousness. Guilt, pain, and determination flooded our mental link. I called out his name but doubted my telepathic abilities had developed enough for him to hear it. But that didn't stop me. I wanted my husband home, and I'd use every possible method at my disposal to make it happen.

"Dakas," I whispered aloud when his consciousness brushed against mine. He was reaching out to me.

No... He's saying goodbye.

This time, I shouted his name mentally, before his mind disconnected from mine.

"No!"

"He lives," Skieth said firmly, although he almost sounded like he was trying to convince both me and himself. "You must still feel him."

"I don't …" The nauseous feeling surged again. It had to be Dakas's body failing. "Yes. Yes, I do. We need to prepare for him. Tell Graith to get him here *now!*" I ordered, snapping out of my distress and falling back into my medical role.

I didn't wait for his answer, and just ran back to the clinic to find Tilda standing outside the door, eyes wide as she watched the villagers rushing to their respective battle stations.

"What's happening? Where's Dakas?" Tilda asked.

"We need to prepare two medical pods," I ordered, ignoring her questions. "Dakas is injured. Martin could be as well. Set one up and then contact all of our auxiliaries. Tell them to man the emergency medical stations in case we need them."

Despite her burning curiosity, Tilda jumped into action. Working on autopilot, I quickly set up the medical pod, lowering the sides so it would be ready to receive my husband as soon as he arrived. I then snagged a hypospray and rushed back outside. I exited the clinic just in time to see a large Zelconian fly over the wall, carrying Dakas's limp body. By the blue color of his crest, I recognized Graith. Behind him, another Zelconian was carrying Martin.

Heart pounding, I silently urged Graith to hurry. As soon as they cleared the wall, the pillar generating the protective shield of our dome in that area reactivated. At the same time, volleys of missiles fired from our turrets. Under the command of my father, rows of archers started firing our enhanced heat-seeking arrows, and our combatants manned the wall poles to which laser beams and blast cannons had been added.

I couldn't see the army of Yurus rushing forward yet, but I could hear them in the distance. Still, they were currently the least of my concerns. Saving my mate was all that mattered. Dakas's unconscious mind didn't broadcast any emotion, but I could feel our connection, muted though it was. The nauseous feeling didn't abate, nor did it significantly increase. I realized then that my perception of his physical state wasn't proximity-related but severity-based.

Graith landed barely a meter in front of me. I tried to silence the panic trying to surge within me at the sight of all the blood that had trickled down Dakas's mouth, side, back, and leg. His tail feathers were matted with it. The wet sound of his labored breathing confirmed his lung had been punctured. My heart sank at the sight of the odd color of his veins swelling under his skin —poison. And the visual symptoms hinted that it was with the same toxin that had killed his mother and Renok's father.

Even as Graith was carrying my husband into the clinic, I pressed the hypospray to Dakas's neck, injecting him with critical care nanobots. They wouldn't handle the poison but would seek to close any open wounds and to stem severe bleeding.

To my relief, and although I barely spared him a glance,

Martin followed us inside the clinic on his own power. Tilda made a beeline for him, but he waved her away while Graith was laying Dakas down in the medical pod. I tried not to look at my husband's blood covering the Exarch's down feathers.

Once again, I silently thanked Kayog for the precious wedding gifts he sent us. Our previous medical pods couldn't have accommodated a Zelconian with those massive wings. Although they had to remain partially folded behind Dakas, they weren't cramped. Better yet, the advanced medical device could lift the patient on its own to perform procedures on his back without having to flip him over.

"He's infected with shengis venom," Graith said in a tense voice. "We don't have an antidote—only something to slow it down. But—"

"I know," I said while configuring the pod. "I've been studying it since Dakas told me what happened to his mother. For now, I'm going to put him in stasis to prevent the poison from progressing and to stabilize him while we mend his other injuries. A few days ago, I sent some of your pure shengis venom samples to the UPO's labs in the hope of finding an antidote. So, we have a head start."

Although he kept a stoic face, fear and sorrow oozed strongly enough out of Graith for me to perceive them, despite my feeble empathic abilities. I realized then the depth of the Exarch's love for my husband.

"I'm not letting him die, Graith," I said in a forceful tone. "I'll be damned if I'm widowed just when we started making a life together. I'm going to fix him, no matter what it takes."

The strangest expression crossed Graith's features. He lifted a hand and gently caressed my cheek. "Finding you was the happiest day of his life. Bring him back to us, Luana."

My throat tightened at the gentle, paternal way in which he spoke those words. "I will. Now go kick those motherfuckers' asses. Make them rue the day they ever fucked with us."

"Gladly," Graith said, a feral expression settling on his face. He looked at Dakas, caressed the feathers of his crest, then turned and left.

"He saved my life," Martin said with a haunted voice, his eyes glued to Dakas's face, while Tilda joined me in working on my husband. "That blade in his lung was meant for my throat. He could have left me and made it back safe and sound. But he shielded me with his body and carried me while they shot at him. If there's anything, anything at all, I can do to help save him, you only have to ask."

My empathic abilities were too weak to perceive the depth of his emotions, but everything about his body language, voice, and expression screamed the sincerity of his words. That moved me more than I could express.

"You can't help in here, but you can help out there," I said as I painstakingly removed the dagger from Dakas's side while Tilda injected more local nanobots to stitch the wound. "The non-combatants and the children are scared. Word of Dakas's injuries will be spreading fast, frightening people even more. My father is busy leading the battle. You are charismatic. Go reassure our people. You were out there with him. Seeing you safe and sound will appease them."

"You got it," Martin said, turning on his heel and leaving the clinic.

Tilda and I spent the next eternity removing the blades from my husband's body while preventing him from bleeding out. We then closed the medical pod to let it perform its magic with far more accuracy than either my assistant or I could. I addressed another silent thank you to Kayog and the UPO as the machine ran a thorough scan, listing all the procedures it would perform with a suggested priority list for me to approve.

As I had feared, aside from poisoning him, the blade in Dakas's lower back had severed his spine, effectively paralyzing him from the waist down. Prior to my 'dowry' equipment, we wouldn't have been able to fix this type of damage without replacing his lower limbs with cybernetics. But the medical pod's suggested procedure promised a full repair of his spinal cord, with a 97.8% probability of success.

Countless needles poked and prodded him, some injecting, others draining, lasers stitching or cutting ... The whole process felt surreal. I'd had 'illegally' watched plenty of videos on advanced machinery and devices. But this exceeded anything I'd even imagined. I was just grateful that, with the looming war, I'd prepared for the possibility of Zelconians getting injured.

First, I'd uploaded into the medical pods the entire Zelconian medical database provided by their head healer, Feylin. Then I'd spent a lot of time studying the more advanced features of the medical pods as well as the Zelconian anatomy, especially my husband's. There were notable differences between Dakas and a pureblood. Lucky for us, his wounds were all in the human parts of his body, making it easier for the pod to handle.

But the real concern remained the poison. Since Dakas had told me about the death of his mother, I'd devoted a lot of time studying shengis venom. I'd sent the UPO the data from pure samples the Zelconians had acquired over the years after her passing. Their more primitive equipment could not provide as in-depth a breakdown of the toxin's components as the sample I had analyzed six days ago with my new toys.

I reached out to Lillian—my UPO medical contact—once more grateful for all the ways in which becoming a legitimate colony had turned our fate around. She'd been working on the sample I had sent in search of a general antidote. But thanks to the new medical pods that directly connected to their network, I was able to forward her the detailed analysis of Dakas's blood the pod had performed.

Without her help, I would have been forced to try and create an antibody using horses or zeebises for immunization. It was a long process which would require me to mix some of the shengis venom samples in the Zelconian lab to some adjuvant—a chemical that would cause the horse's immune system to produce antibodies capable of binding and neutralizing the venom. Then this would be injected in small amounts to the horse over days and even weeks while closely monitoring its health in order for it to develop the antibodies. Only then could I drain some blood from the horse—who would go on to live a healthy life—to derive a purified serum from it.

That would take too damn long—at least a month, maybe more. Dakas would have to remain in stasis the whole time, which would prevent him from fully healing from his other wounds as they required all his bodily functions to be operational, not frozen in time.

Thankfully, Lillian had at her disposal far more advanced technology and the insanely vast database of toxins, venoms, and poisons—and their antidotes—catalogued from the various planet members of the United Planets Organization. She cross-referenced the shengis venom with them to find the ones that had a similar combination of proteins in their toxins. She then forwarded me the breakdown of the serum used to cure them.

Tilda and I spent a couple more hours encoding nanobots to replicate the potential serums from that list and using them on blood samples drawn from Dakas. It was all the harder to concentrate because we had no idea how things were going outside. The muffled sounds that reached us gave no indication of who had the upper hand. I wanted to believe that if the tide were turning against us, someone would have come to warn us.

After multiple trials and errors, and just when I was starting to lose faith, the antibodies of sample S118 finally started binding to the toxin. I shouted in victory. A few additional tests later to confirm its efficacy, we transferred the protocol to the medical pod. As much as I wanted to flood his system with the antidote, I only gave Dakas a small amount in the area with the biggest concentration of the toxin.

Then the waiting game began. If Dakas responded well, the medical pod would gradually pull him out of stasis and increase the number of antivenin nanobots in his system. Having done all that I could for my husband, I turned my attention to the war raging outside.

CHAPTER 17
LUANA

I stepped out of the clinic to enter a surreal, post-apocalyptic war zone. Missiles flew back and forth between both camps, making the early evening sky look like fireworks battled an endless shower of shooting stars. The dome overhead sparked and shimmered where the enemy missiles, which managed to slip through our countermeasures, impacted it. An army of drones, like a swarm of diamond-shaped bugs—flew a short distance above the dome, zapping as many incoming threats as it could.

Countless trees lining the edge of the forest were charred, some uprooted. Smoke in the distance seemed to hint that our attackers had been forced to retreat under heavy fire. While the people manning the lasers by the crystal poles were still in position, the archers that had been blindly shooting over the wall from the square had moved. Considering the angle with which the missiles that made it past our defenses hit the dome, we were being attacked on at least two more fronts.

While running towards one of the emergency medical stations, I contacted the auxiliaries at the others. To my relief, the coast was still clear with no wounded to report; the Yurus were failing to breach our defenses. So far, the farms we'd been unable to enclose in the wall weren't burning. That didn't mean the Yurus wouldn't lay siege to try and starve us out. But we had enough reserves, smaller farms and greenhouses to let us hold out for a looooong time.

As soon as I reached the station set in an empty hangar, I was stunned to see Emilia and Tanner—the two auxiliaries—busy preparing hyposprays and setting up portable stasis inducers on a few hover stretchers.

"What's going on?" I asked Tanner.

He turned to look at me, his brown eyes filled with worry. "The Zelconians are going out after Vyrax, and a few members of our militia are insisting on tagging along."

"WHAT?!" I exclaimed.

"The Yurus split their forces to attack us on three fronts, hoping to overwhelm us and breach the weakest spot. They even sent some drones to Synsara so that our allies would abandon us to go protect their city. But those Zelconians of yours rocked our defenses," Emilia said, awe laced with disbelief filling her voice.

I pretended not to hear her referring to them as *my* Zelconians. But my head jerked left to look out the window towards the mountain.

"They're fine," Tanner intervened, guessing my concerns. "The drones were just a diversion. That tall, scary Zelconian with the dark red crest told us their upgraded defenses obliterated the drones without problem."

"His name is Skieth," I said distractedly.

Tanner looked sheepish. "Yeah, that's it. And in the past week, your husband had his people hide special cameras in fake branches that Martin and the crafters prepared."

"Fake branches?" I asked, flabbergasted.

Tanner nodded. "Yeah, I worked on a few of them. They're pretty damn cool. You can't even see the camera inside. The branches have a pointy hook, with the direction in which it needs to be stuck into the trunk or onto another branch to look natural. The Zelconians placed them everywhere. The minute the Yurus came out of stealth, we got a very clear view of their headcount and current status."

"Check it out," Emilia said with excitement.

She punched a few instructions on the monitor that would normally display the vitals of a patient, and connected it to the camera feeds of the forest near this station.

"Dakas wanted us to be able to see the battle in our respective sectors so that we could prepare for whatever type of injury we saw happening, or to have rescue sent there," Emilia explained.

She selected one of the feeds on the mosaic display and tapped on it to zoom in. It showed a group of Yurus mostly in disarray. Many were wounded, though nothing grievous. Vyrax was barking orders that we couldn't hear. Judging by the reaction of his men, they were clearly balking.

He's losing his authority over them.

A few were still manning missile launchers but most were busy shooting down our own missiles.

"Wait a minute, how are they not detecting our cameras?" I asked. "Surely they have scanners?"

"They probably are detecting them without realizing what they are," Emilia said smugly. "Your genius husband again—or rather his dad apparently—taught them how to create organic cameras. It's basically like an eyeball organism that responds to certain wavelengths. A scanner would pick up the presence of an inoffensive large bug or small critter."

"Wow," I whispered, genuinely impressed.

"The downside is that it can't be turned or controlled. The angle you see now is all you get," Tanner said.

I nodded distractedly, still analyzing what I was seeing on screen. "Our missiles don't seem to be lethal."

"Right," Emilia said. "They switched not too long ago, right before Graith and the others went out after Vyrax."

"They're already gone?" I exclaimed.

As if in response to my question, a number of Yurus on screen suddenly looked up, a panicked expression on their faces as they raised their weapons towards the sky. Alerted, the other Yurus behind looked up as well, none of them appearing to see anything. At the same time, a few of them fired their blasters blindly. A series of bright lights exploded everywhere, filling the main display and half the feeds from the mosaic with white. Even I blinked.

The lights faded seconds later to reveal at least twenty Zelconians coming out of stealth, descending upon their enemies like dark angels of death. My heart skipped a beat when some Yurus further back—obviously less affected by the flash grenades— started shooting at the Zelconians. But our allies thankfully had their energy shields raised before them. Many Yurus started shouting, their eyes widening in horror as they stared at the Zelconians.

"What the hell is happening?" I whispered, more to myself than the others. I highly doubted they knew any more than I did.

Some of the Yurus turned and fled as if the hounds of hell were in pursuit. Vyrax was shouting orders, while protecting his eyes with his forearm, and shooting blindly at the Zelconians. They had landed and were slowly advancing in the creepiest fashion. Then I saw it.

"Switch to that camera!" I said urgently to Emilia while pointing at it.

"What?"

Despite her confused expression, she complied. The feed popped up, filling two-thirds of the screen. From that angle, I could clearly see the faces of at least four of our allies. But it was their eyes that held my attention. The constellation of stars within were glowing and pulsating. With a bone-deep conviction, I realized that they were not just hypnotizing their prey but also inducing nightmarish visions or thoughts that were causing them to flee.

At the same time, members of our militia came out of stealth. They were flying overhead on their armored zeebises. They threw a couple of concussion grenades at the Yurus in the back before taking aim at them with their blasters.

Graith barked a series of commands. I asked Emilia to switch back to the camera view with the widest angle. The handful of still belligerent Yurus appeared to calm down upon hearing his words. I would have given anything to have sound on this damn thing.

Vyrax seemed taken aback, hesitated, then lowered the arm covering his face, which he'd no doubt hoped would shield him from becoming enthralled by the Zelconians' power.

They exchanged a few words, Graith looking calm yet implacable while Vyrax looked incensed. They appeared to agree on something, and the Yurus backed away, forming a half circle behind their leader while the Zelconians and our militia did the same behind Graith. Vyrax tossed his blaster at one of his grunts and gestured at another who brought him a pair of battleaxes—one of them the ornate one he had held on their first failed attack. Graith retrieved some sort of baton hooked on his weapon's belt and hanging on his hip. He held it in front of him, and it expanded into a proper battle staff.

"They're going to duel," I whispered in disbelief.

"For the outcome of this war?" Tanner asked with a sliver of fear in his voice.

I shook my head. "No," I said with conviction, despite the worry in the back of my head. "Graith wouldn't gamble our future without our consent."

While I believed those words at a visceral level, the Exarch had to have promised Vyrax something juicy enough to make him and his goons pause their hostilities long enough for a duel.

They haven't truly stopped, just this team.

As a matter of fact, missiles were still being fired at our dome by the two teams attacking us on the other fronts.

The only offer I could think of for swaying Vyrax was the promise that if Graith lost, the Zelconians would abandon us to fight this battle against the Yurus on our own. The more I thought about it, the more plausible it became.

Despite the Zelconians' invaluable help in setting up our defenses, that work was now completed. It was only a matter of using them the right way. Our allies had properly trained my father and our militia to do exactly that. And our mastermind and strategist was Dakas, my husband. Even if Graith lost—which I didn't even want to contemplate—our colony would be able to hold its own against the Yurus, at least for now.

Renok released a strange floating sphere, putting an end to my musings. It flew to a height of about three meters between the two males, maybe a bit more—it was hard to see from this angle. A small flash emanated from the sphere, and a wide dome of energy surrounded the two leaders, its shape vaguely reminiscent of a cake dome.

My eyes widened in understanding. "They're leveling the playing field by preventing Graith from flying out of range."

"Shit," Tanner said, discomfited. "I was just thinking that it was going to be an easy win with him flying."

I never saw the signal that started the duel. Vyrax rushed Graith with both battleaxes raised, his mouth wide open, likely with a war cry. Graith stood still, legs slightly parted, his staff at the ready. I'd expected him to dodge at the last minute—and suspected Vyrax thought the same. But the Exarch shoved his staff forward, holding it horizontally with both hands and hooking both battleaxes on it. Graith pulled his staff in while flapping his wings to move backward, yanking Vyrax towards him. He then lifted both of his feet. I thought he was going to kick the Yurus leader in the chest, but he brutally raked his talons down Vyrax's front.

Vyrax tried to jump back, but his axes, still hooked on the staff, prevented him from doing so. He lowered his head, violently swiping it at his opponent's face, likely trying to gouge him with his horns. But Graith let go of the staff with one hand, sliding it sideways as he pivoted out of range of Vyrax's attack. The Yurus leader glanced down at his chest where at least six vertical wounds were bleeding, matting his fur.

For half a second, I'd viciously, shamefully hoped Graith's talons would eviscerate Vyrax, spilling his guts to the ground. From here, I couldn't judge the severity of the wounds. But seeing how the Yurus lunged at Graith again, they probably weren't half as grievous as I'd wished. They launched into a dance of attack and dodge, circling each other, with Vyrax using brute force and savage swings of his axes, while Graith used more tactical—almost opportunistic—attacks, and expended a lot less energy. A part of me wondered if he was doing this to tire his opponent, or to enrage him, or both.

A few times during their clash, they got locked into a hold where Vyrax systematically tried to headbutt his rival, maim him with his horns, or bash his legs with his hooves. But he tried the hardest to tear feathers from his wings, which the Exarch did a wonderful job of keeping out of reach. Vyrax did, however, manage to pluck some of his down feathers, leaving Graith with a couple of bleeding bald patches.

Graith also seized the opportunity to sneak in some vicious hits of his own. The sharp talons of his hands and feet did a number on the already heavily scarred Yurus leader. Since his feet could grab like hands, Graith could effectively destabilize his enemy in close-quarters by holding on to his ankle, yanking or pulling on it, or lacerating it. But the most disturbing blows were inflicted with his beak.

The third time he did it, his beak sank in deep between the joint of Vyrax's right shoulder. By the way that arm went limp and his fancy axe fell out of his hand, Graith had certainly severed or seriously torn Vyrax's shoulder muscles and tendons. The initial cheering of the Yurus crowd for their leader died down as he backed away, swinging his other battleax at his opponent to keep him at a distance. However, with his main weapon hand disabled, Vyrax was now fighting a losing battle.

That seemed to trigger Graith, who lost the restraint he had previously shown. He unleashed his wrath on his rival. Moving at dizzying speed, he twirled his staff around, bringing it down savagely on Vyrax's good arm, legs, and face, forcing him to back away and remain on the defensive. Despite the limited height afforded by the dome arena, Graith used his wings a few times to swoop down on his opponent, the added velocity increasing the strength of his blows.

It quickly dawned on me that Graith could have ended this battle already, but this was punishment. I didn't know if past history or the desire to make an example that would deter further attacks fueled this merciless beating, but the Exarch was pounding Vyrax into the ground. A well-placed blow of his staff right between the horns of the Yurus leader finally ended the battle. His eyes rolled to the back of his head while he crumpled to the ground.

Tanner and Emilia shouted with joy, in sharp contrast to the solemn and stoic demeanor of all the people in the forest. Graith came to stand in front of his vanquished enemy. He spoke a handful of words. Probably asking if any would challenge his victory. As sole response—at least from what I could see from here—the Yurus merely turned around and walked away, leaving their battered leader at Graith's feet. The Yurus who had been manning their portable missile launchers packed them up to leave as well.

A few minutes later, the missiles being launched at us from the two other fronts went silent.

The war was over. The battle was won.

CHAPTER 18
DAKAS

I emerged from the deepest slumber I could ever recall experiencing. My bed felt strange and confined. And the scent of the air was off... way off. Most disturbing, I couldn't feel the soft warmth of my mate's body against mine. My eyes jerked open. Instead of the smoothly carved stone ceiling of my bedroom, I looked up at the white walls and bright lights of the Kastan medical clinic.

"Hey sweetie," Luana's gentle voice said while her delicate hand caressed my forearm in a soothing fashion. "It's okay. You're safe. You've just woken from an induced coma to let you heal. So, it's normal if you're a little disoriented."

Induced coma?

That question no sooner popped into my mind than a flood of memories swept it away: our trip to the woods, my conversation with Martin, the sudden attack by camouflaged enemies, and then pain ... loads of pain.

"The village?" I asked, sitting up so quickly a wave of dizziness crashed into me.

"Slowly, Dakas. You must take it easy," Luana admonished. "The village is fine. We didn't sustain a single casualty, and only a handful of self-inflicted wounds over mishandled weapons or panic. You were our one true source of worry. The Yurus never even came close to breaching the defenses you designed for us."

"The battle is over? How long have I been out? There was poison ..." I turned to sit at the edge of the pod then stiffened, my eyes widening as I looked down at myself. "My legs ... I can feel them again."

"Honey, stay still. You have a lot of questions, and I will answer them all. But first, let me examine you to make sure everything is fine. I will fill you in on everything you missed."

She stepped between my legs, and an odd mixture of emotions flooded into me from my mate. Relief, amusement at my impatience, pride, but also sadness and disappointment.

Why is she ...?

And then it hit me. I'd been grievously injured. I'd felt myself dying. She would have felt it, too. Yet, I felt no pain. I could breathe easily and didn't even see a scar where the blade had penetrated my flesh to puncture my lung. Even with an advanced medical pod, this would have taken many days to heal. Luana had been my last thought when I believed myself dying. But now that I was feeling renewed, I hadn't even spared her a single one.

"Tell me if this hurts," Luana said. She cupped my face, gently bending my neck to one side then the other.

I didn't respond. I just slipped my arms around her waist and drew her to me. Her surprise quickly turned to a timid joy, and another emotion I couldn't define. She melted against me the minute I captured her lips. Luana wrapped her arms around my neck, her embrace soon taking a more desperate edge.

Something was off. I broke the kiss to give Luana a questioning look, but she buried her face in my neck. And then the wall she'd been trying to erect around her emotions crumbled. My mate's sharp intake of breath was undeniably caused by an attempt to hold back tears.

"Oh, my love. It's okay. I'm here," I whispered, caressing her hair.

That opened the floodgates. She clung to me, sobbing and apologizing between more choked sobs.

"I could feel your pain. I felt you say goodbye. When they said you'd gone over the wall, I thought I was going to lose you," Luana said against my neck.

I tightened my embrace and wrapped my wings around her in a comforting gesture. While broadcasting soothing psychic waves to my woman, I softly sang to her, my cheek resting on the top of her head. Had we been in Synsara, I would have brought out pink crystals for their calming effect and yellow ones to enhance their potency as I sang to Luana.

In that instant, I realized that fear of losing me represented only a fraction of what had caused her current breakdown. The stress of the past few weeks, her father's grievous injury, the threat of war, and being thrust into the leadership role she never asked for, then being forced into a marriage of convenience and adapting to her new reality, the actual war, and then my near-death had been one pressure too many. And yet, she had bravely carried them until all danger had passed.

Her breaking down in tears right this instant wasn't a show of weakness, but the confirmation of just how strong she was to have withstood all of this with such strength when others needed her. Added to everything, Luana's growing empathic abilities undoubtedly further messed with her emotional control.

When she finally regained her composure, Luana wiped her face with the back of her sleeves. She gave me a sheepish smile between two sniffles. "Sorry about that. If nothing else, you won't have to shower."

I smiled and wiped the lingering tears from her face with my thumbs. "It is for me to apologize, not you. I should have warned you that I was going out. I got overconfident because our scanners showed nothing, and the Yurus hadn't been pestering us.

Plus, you never have to apologize for needing me to comfort you. We are each other's safe havens."

My heart warmed at the tender emotions my mate projected towards me. It was much too early for us to be in love, but we were certainly treading down that path. Although she allowed me to reclaim her lips in another kiss, guilt quickly pulled her away.

"I should be examining you to make sure you're fine instead of molesting you," Luana said with an embarrassed laugh before putting me through a battery of tests.

The whole time, she updated me about all that had transpired in the nine days I'd been unconscious. I couldn't believe I'd 'slept' through the war. Still, hearing how our defenses had remained impenetrable filled me with pride.

"We're at a bit of a stalemate with Zatruk, Vyrax's former right hand," Luana said while making me bend in all kinds of ways to check my spine. "He's currently their acting leader and demanding that we return Vyrax to them."

"What? Return Vyrax?" I asked, freezing halfway through a motion.

A troubled expression crossed Luana's brown eyes. She gestured for me to follow and headed towards a medical pod in the corner of the room.

"Are you serious?!" I exclaimed upon seeing the Yurus leader's face through the glass dome of the medical chamber.

"Graith didn't kill him during the fight. He just messed him up pretty badly," my mate said with a shudder. "That final blow to his head did a number on him. There was some massive internal bleeding and major swelling in the brain. It has been touch and go from the start with him, and it still is. We know next to nothing about the Yurus anatomy. Even Feylin didn't have much in the Synsara database. I had to keep him in stasis for the first few days just to map out his anatomy and try to comprehend the inner workings of his physiology."

"Why save him at all?" I asked, confused.

Luana gave me a disapproving glance. "You sound just like Graith. We shouldn't let someone die just because they were idiots. My father agrees that we should do everything in our power to mend him and then negotiate a permanent truce between our people. We can't spend the rest of our lives sneaking into the woods with a Zelconian babysitter."

I scratched the down feathers on my chest, wondering how best to word this. "This is a waste of effort, Luana. Vyrax is as good as dead. Assuming you manage to heal him, his clan will not welcome him back with open arms. Humans defeated him twice, and he lost a duel to the death against Graith, forcing his people to retreat. His failed war cost the lives of many of his people, not to mention their countless weapons you say we wrecked during the battle."

"Gosh, you sound exactly like Graith," Luana repeated, her shoulders slumping with discouragement.

"Because we know the Yurus. You're only healing Vyrax so they can execute him," I said with sympathy. "Let him go peacefully. Even if he recovers and chooses to leave Cibbos, where would he go? How would he leave? Since Vyrax has nothing left to offer, I doubt the mercenaries he was dealing with would take him in. Then again, they might try to sell him off as a slave or in some of those sentient species zoos my father said existed on certain planets."

My chest constricted at Luana's distress. Her natural compassion truly amazed me.

"I'm a healer," she said in a dejected voice. "How am I supposed to just let him die when I know I can mend him?"

"Sometimes, you have to let go. You shouldn't force someone to live, knowing you are condemning them to a life of hardship, guaranteed pain, or worse still, a horrible death," I countered gently. "But don't fret over it. I'm sure your father and our Council are having intense discussions about it, especially if Zatruk is pressuring you."

"That he is. He most certainly is."

I smiled at her somber expression and kissed the tip of her nose. "Come on, finish poking and prodding me. I need my doctor to give me a clean bill of health so that I can steal my mate back home and have my way with her."

Luana laughed, gave me a playful tap, and resumed torturing me.

Five days after she discharged me from the clinic, Luana and I stood in the square, her father and his Council standing in the center, and Graith, Skieth and my brother flanking them on the other side. Behind my woman, the unconscious form of Vyrax lay on a hover-stretcher. Even now, after the countless discussions that had eventually led her father and his Council to cave in, Luana continued to hate that it had come to this. And yet, she not only understood our logic, had she been in charge, my mate would have followed the same course of action with just as much reluctance.

As the imposing silhouette of Zatruk—the albino Yurus— cleared the tree line, I mind-spoke with Minkus to confirm our stealthing scouts in the forest had not detected a greater number of troops than agreed upon or any heavy artillery that would spell foul play. So far, nothing to report. I didn't believe Zatruk would try anything foolish. He was without question the smartest Yurus I'd ever encountered.

Riding his krogi, he looked nonchalant as he approached the wall with four bodyguards in tow. It was more for show than anything else. If we intended to kill him, he wouldn't walk out of here alive. Truth be told, I didn't fully understand why he had agreed to this meeting inside Kastan. I had a billion different theories, but none quite added up. Whatever his motives, I had no doubt it included his desire to prove to his people that he didn't fear walking into the enemy's lair and didn't need a full army behind him.

Despite the worry gnawing at him, Mateo—my father-in-law—once more displayed a phenomenally implacable expression as he deactivated a small section of the energy field directly in front of us. Zatruk and his bodyguards rode in. I'd wondered if he would leave one or two of them on the other side of the wall—not that it would have done them any good if we turned on them. The wall went back up as soon as the last Yurus cleared it. While their leader showed mind-boggling self-control, the nervousness and worry emanating from his guards was palpable even to non-empaths. Zatruk stopped about five meters in front of Mateo before dismounting his krogi, his guards imitating him.

He took a few more steps then stopped, striking his chest with his fist in a greeting gesture, once more mimicked by this retinue.

Mateo, my mate, and I slightly bowed our heads while Graith, Skieth, and my brother clicked their beaks.

"Thank you for accepting our invitation, Warrior Zatruk," Mateo said in a respectful tone, "and welcome to Kastan."

"I thank you for the invitation, Colony Leader Mateo, but I'm only here for one thing," he said, his red eyes casting a pointed look at the hover-stretcher behind Luana.

"And you will get what you came for," Mateo said in the same calm and polite voice. "But first, we have a couple of matters to discuss."

Leading a negotiation outside, under the glaring sun, and standing up couldn't be more bizarre. However, it was the Yurus tradition. They believed that comfort made people complacent. Things dragged on too long because no one negotiated in good faith for the first half of the meeting, sometimes even longer. Why would they when they didn't feel rushed or uncomfortable? A cushioned seat, drinks, and maybe even snacks only meant each party would play a game to see whose patience wore out first to try and get the upper hand on them.

"Until Vyrax has been returned to us, there will be nothing to discuss," Zatruk said in a tone that brooked no argument.

"How do we know that you won't simply walk away once we've given you what you want?" asked Counselor Allan, who was also one of the two members of Mateo's Council.

"Aside from my word, you don't. Similar to how I came here with nothing but your word that this wasn't a trap," Zatruk said, his voice growing colder.

To my surprise, he reached inside a small pouch on his weapons belt and retrieved what resembled dried white petals, tossing two into his mouth. The strong reaction that gesture provoked in my mate drew my attention. It hadn't alarmed her, but it seemed to confirm something Luana believed. She narrowed her eyes at him, which further piqued my curiosity.

I hated the nine days we had wasted with me being unconscious. Without that interruption, by now, our bond would be strong enough for us to have basic telepathic conversations without draining Luana. I'd give anything to be able to discreetly ask her. The subtle smile that stretched her lips and the sideways glance she cast my way confirmed Luana felt my emotions.

"You make a fair point," Mateo conceded, to the Counselor's dismay. "Therefore, on the same basis of trust in your good faith, we will give you what you want."

Luana's displeasure surged upon hearing those words. She'd known this would happen but still struggled with it. I resisted the urge to caress her back in a soothing gesture. Instead, I gave her a psychic caress and felt her gratitude in response.

Mateo looked at his daughter, who gave him a stiff nod. Pinching her lips, Luana turned to the hover-stretcher and set it to follow. I didn't like that she was going so close to the Yurus, but I perceived no threat or malice from him. He watched her approach with an unreadable expression in his red eyes. I could, however, sense an odd fascination.

When the stretcher stopped in front of him, Zatruk continued to stare at my female—for a few seconds too long. For the space of an instant, I wondered if he was trying to provoke me—which he was doing a wonderful job of—but was forced to admit that genuine curiosity in Luana had prompted his behavior. He finally turned his attention to Vyrax, and deep contempt took over his emotions.

"You can deactivate the portable stasis device. He no longer needs it," Zatruk said.

Pinching her lips again, Luana complied. As soon as she was done, she turned around and returned to my side.

The Yurus walked up to his leader, pulled out his dagger, and stabbed it straight through the eye of Vyrax, twisting it this way and that to make sure his brain was damaged beyond repair. A violent spasm shook the body before it went still.

Fury blasted through my mate. She made no effort to hide it, although she remained quiet. The same anger emanated from her father, while horror radiated from his Council. Counselor Allan made a retching noise and averted his eyes.

Zatruk pulled the blade out, casually wiped it on the chest fur of his dead leader, then put it back in its sheath on his belt. He then yanked out the largest earring dangling from Vyrax's lobe, tearing the skin in the process. Once more, he wiped the blood on the dead Yurus' fur before attaching the earring to his own earlobe.

As soon as he was done, the four bodyguards shouted in unison in Yurusian something that came down to 'All hail Chieftain Zatruk.' I realized then that this earring acted as the equivalent of a king's crown. Zatruk couldn't fully ascend without his former rival's death and recovering this bauble.

He turned his gaze to my mate. I braced, ready to intervene if he disrespected her.

"Do not waste your anger over feelings compassion for Vyrax," Zatruk told her in a mocking tone. "Had his plans succeeded, I can assure you he would have shown your people—and especially you—no mercy whatsoever. Whatever you may think, I did him a kindness. If *this* upset you, you would *hate* witnessing the fate that awaited him had he returned once more a failure. This was painless to him—not that he deserved such easy passing."

Luana nodded stiffly. Zatruk gave her that intense look again. This time, I shifted my wings and took half a step forward, drawing his attention to me. It wasn't like me to mark my territory, but his interest in my mate was rubbing me the wrong way. His smirk further stretched his lips around his large tusks. Dismissing me, he returned his focus on Mateo.

"Now, I officially have the authority to negotiate with you, Colony Leader Mateo. Speak," Zatruk said.

The shock that coursed through Luana, echoed mine. We had all assumed that, with their leader incapacitated, the second in command automatically had the power to make decisions that would be followed by their people.

"We do not wish to engage in a drawn-out war with the Yurus," Mateo said. "As you can see, we are not helpless. We can withstand your attacks and inflict serious damage in return. We will not be made prisoners inside our own village or have our people unable to go into the forest without risking getting assaulted by yours. We will no longer put up with random raids. Any raider will be killed on sight. If your people want some of our goods, we can open trade discussions. But the time of the Yurus bullying the human colony is over."

"Raiding is part of my people's DNA," Zatruk replied, matter-of-factly. "Whatever my thoughts on your wishes, what makes you think it is even possible? The Yurus Bloodlust isn't some switch one can simply turn off."

"Oh, but I think it is," my mate interjected, drawing every

eye to her. "I've had an interesting insight into Yurusian anatomy while trying to heal—in vain—your former leader. I know why you're eating those petals. A clever move on your part. You *can* control your people's belligerent instincts if you want to. The question is: do you?"

Zatruk snorted and gave Luana a slow once over that pissed me off. She lifted her chin defiantly, which only broadened Zatruk's smile.

"I like you, little human," he said with a hint of amusement in his voice.

"You'll forgive me if I'm unable to reciprocate the sentiment," Luana said in a glacial tone.

Instead of getting offended, Zatruk threw back his head and laughed out loud. His guards also chuckled and looked at my woman with new eyes, an appreciative glimmer sparkling within.

"I really do like you, little female. Too bad the pretty bird already claimed you," Zatruk said nonchalantly, ignoring my huff. "I have heard your requests, Colony Leader Mateo."

"They are not *requests*," Mateo retorted, stopping himself short of spelling out that they were in fact demands.

Zatruk smirked, almost daring him to do so. "Like I said, I've heard your *requests*," the albino Yurus repeated when the silence stretched. "Your people can go about their foraging safely … for now. You will hear from me again."

After casting one last disdainful look at Vyrax's corpse, Zatruk slammed his fist to his chest, walked to his krogi, which stood quietly behind him, and mounted. Counselor Allan opened his mouth to argue, but Mateo discreetly signaled him to let it go. Zatruk's mount was already walking slowly towards the wall while the bodyguards were mounting their own beasts. To my relief, Mateo opened the energy field, letting the Yurus leave without a fuss.

As soon as the wall went back up behind them, Mateo turned

questioning eyes to me, which surprised me. The pureblood were more powerful empaths than I was.

"I perceived no malicious or deceptive intent in him," I said, casting an inquisitive look at Graith.

He confirmed with a nod. "He doesn't want war or to quarrel with humans," Graith added.

"A peaceful Yurus?" Luana said in a dubious tone.

Graith snorted and shook his head. "I don't know that he wants peace. The feeling I gathered from his emotions is that he doesn't deem humans to be worthy opponents."

"Whatever his intentions, he certainly wants to be in control. He eats praxilla leaves because they help numb his aggressive tendencies. The Yurus being this violent and belligerent is not cultural but genetic. They have extremely high levels of testosterone and serotonin, both of which influence aggression."

"Which explains why he's so confident he can rein in his people," I said pensively. "He has a very clear plan in his head that he wants to see through. But I have no clue what it is. We will need to keep a close eye on him."

"But will it be safe for our people to go out again?" Mateo insisted.

"Yes," Graith said with conviction. "For the time being, you have a truce. Let's hope it lasts."

CHAPTER 19
LUANA

Over the couple of weeks that followed that encounter with Zatruk, life returned to a semblance of normal back in Kastan. His silence during that time unnerved me. But he kept his word that our people would be able to forage and venture into the forest unimpeded. While the Zelconians continued to escort them for the first week, we eventually equipped everyone with a personal stealth shield so they could hide and flee if they ever ran into trouble.

This was but the first of many useful technological tools that became the norm. The wind of change was blowing over the colony. The younger generations were finally speaking out and demanding to have a louder voice in the direction of the colony and its future—*their* future. I didn't envy my father having to juggle with everyone's temper and sensitivities, but draining that abscess was long overdue.

The bond forming between our colony and our new allies further fueled that change. I understood better now why our founders had presented the Zelconians like boogeymen to be avoided at all cost. It was never about them being evil or malicious, but their entire society pursued the exact opposite of what my people had come here seeking. And people like Lara and Martin were all too eager to discover more.

Graith had actually authorized humans to visit Synsara in small groups. The elders saw too many of our younger population jumping at the opportunity, and it drove home that, without compromise, they would lose them. Like it had been the case with me, a single tour of Synsara had killed in them any desire to go back to the bland and backward village we grew up in.

The funniest part was all the single women eyeballing the Zelconians, although many had expressed their envy at me snagging the only hybrid around. With his mostly human face and body, his Zelconian features just made him look hot. The pureblood fully covered in feathers, with bird feet and beaks took a bit more getting used to. But many of the ladies were starting to look past that because the Zelconian males had a way of making you feel special and unique—the power of their empathic abilities at work.

And when it came down to looking after me and making me feel special, Dakas went the whole nine yards. Unbeknownst to me, he'd obtained Graith's blessing to upgrade the city's walkways to make them safer for me. Just like with the hover lifts, a one-and-a-half-meter tall protective energy wall automatically activated to prevent my falling into the drop—that I'd taken to calling the chasm—if it detected me to be less than thirty centimeters from an edge of the walkway.

Initially, I'd worried it would inconvenience everyone, even those at the other end of the walkway. But Dakas's clever system was designed to only erect a two-meter-wide wall in my vicinity. This way, only I would be shielded without hindering the Zelconians from freely dropping off the ledges before taking flight. They'd added an app to my armband which allowed me to disable a specific wall manually, but only after it had gone up. I couldn't unilaterally disable that safety measure—not that I would ever want to.

That had moved me deeply when he showed it to me upon our return to Synsara, the day after I'd given him a clean bill of health. Now, with more humans allowed to visit the city, the system had been modified to react like this upon detecting any human DNA.

Soon after it was first modified for all humans, it caused a rather comical moment when poor Dakas lunged straight into the wall that rose in front of him because of his partially human DNA. As he'd been taking flight at that moment, it looked as if he'd been pushed over a railing. He fell head first, swiftly recovering and returning to hover in front of the energy field with the most hilarious 'what the fuck?' expression on his face.

While I continued to fly down to the colony four days a week to perform my doctor duties, Feylin had granted me some office space at the Zelconian clinic to facilitate my study of their medicine, assisting in their treatment, and doing some more advanced medical research in my free time.

I had just finished with my latest patient—a painful ingrown feather at the base of his left wing—when my husband walked in.

"Ready to go?" he asked me telepathically.

I grinned, focused, and responded in a similar fashion. *"Yes, ready."*

Dakas beamed at me. Whenever we were in a safe environment, he made me practice mind-speak to help strengthen my psychic muscles. I loved being able to talk to him in public without anyone being able to hear us. Naturally, that always brought out the naughtier side of me.

"Where are you two going?" Feylin asked teasingly when I went to say goodbye.

"Dakas is taking me on our first flight," I said with a grin. "He's been pestering me about letting him carry me while he flies around. But I didn't want him putting that kind of strain on himself—or putting my sorry ass at risk—until he had fully regained his strength after that shengis poisoning."

Feylin's feathery brow shot up, and she clicked her beak in that way I'd come to associate with a snickering laughter for a Zelconian. My eyes narrowed at her before I cast a surprised look at Dakas whose blue skin had taken a darker hue.

What is he embarrassed about?

"Have fun *flying*," Feylin said with a mischievous expression.

Without waiting for my response, she turned back to her computer, her wings shifting a few times to help regulate her body temperature.

Dakas took my hand and lured me out of the clinic.

"What just happened?" I asked suspiciously.

Dakas merely gave me his signature 'That's for me to know' grin, which he adopted whenever he didn't want to answer something. It made me itch to kick his ass. He led me to the edge of the second level's walkway, the protective wall immediately going up, then pulled me into his embrace. While I hadn't allowed him to fly me around outside, now that I'd mastered the hover lifts, I usually let him carry me like a bride from one level to the next when we were together. His strength never ceased to amaze me as he effortlessly picked me up and took flight.

My arms wrapped around his neck, I let my gaze roam over the inner city. I loved Synsara, its colors, lights, smells, and just being surrounded by flying people, especially the children—when they behaved. And the sounds! I'd come to differentiate the different sounds wings made while the Zelconians flew: fast, slow, hovering, gliding. But also their vocalizations.

Dakas's people often sang or hummed. Half the time, I doubted they even realized it. Someone nearby would just as subconsciously join in, harmonizing with them. Then there was the cooing. I would never get over the sight of big, muscular, badass-looking males cooing like doves. Even though the pitch was deeper, it was still hilarious. The beak clicking and grinding was a lot more complex and nuanced. It could be used as a greeting, a warning, a sign of impatience, of anticipation, or annoyance. Many a fledgling had a parent click their beaks at them. I didn't know why it amused me so much to see the little ones hang their heads in shame, some of them wrapping a fist around the tip of their small beaks in a sign of contrition. It was adorable and completely insincere. The little brats would seize the first opportunity to do it all over again. If I could feel it with my limited empathic powers, what was it like for their parents? What would it be like with our own children?

I turned to look at Dakas. He was eyeing me with his usual tenderness, which always made my toes curl.

"Whatever thoughts just crossed your mind, I love how they make you feel," Dakas said, still soaring towards the dome covering the city.

"I was wondering what it will be like to feel our children's emotions, especially when they are up to no good," I confessed.

Dakas chuckled, the happiness radiating from him wrapped around me, melting me like warm butter. "I guess we should start working on it to find out."

"I thought we had been pretty vigorously doing just that?" I deadpanned, thinking about how insanely active we were.

"Practice makes perfect," he said, his voice dropping down an octave. "Clearly, we need to up our game."

"Is that so?" I asked, opening wide, not-innocent-at-all eyes as he headed towards one of the side openings under the dome which gave access to the outside world.

He nodded with a soft—but highly suggestive—hum. My stomach lurched and my heart skipped a beat as he shot out into the early evening sky. With only a few flaps of his wings, Dakas had taken us away from the mountain. A shiver ran over me, not from fear, but from the cool air against my skin. I completely trusted Dakas to keep me safe.

However, I would lie by saying that finding myself hundreds, if not thousands, of meters above the ground, with nothing but my husband's arms around me as a safety net, didn't give me the heebie-jeebies. It was akin to that 'oh shit' feeling you got on a roller-coaster when it reached the very peak of the rail, right before it goes down that insane drop. It was that moment of clarity when you questioned your life choices while readying to scream your lungs out as you enjoyed the heck out of the ride.

But the chill of the night and my skittish feelings soon vanished as the beauty of Cibbos' landscape at night took my breath away. It was as if an invisible hand had activated a dimmer that gradually lit the flora below. The glowing colors of the trees, plants, and even some rocks, challenged those of the bioluminescent phytoplankton in the river below. It seemed to dance along the shoreline with the gentle movement of the waves washing on the beach.

Dakas began his descent, gliding close enough over the tree-tops for my fingertips to caress their leaves if I reached out. The creatures that woke at night joined their voices to create a melodious soundtrack hailing our brief passage through their territory.

We eventually landed inside a cave, far away from civilization. Considering the long distance we'd traveled, I thought Dakas needed to rest. But as soon as he set me down on my feet, he claimed my lips in a hungry kiss that I was all too eager to return. His hands immediately slipped under the hem of my shirt, lifting it as he caressed his way to my breasts. He paused there, first fondling them over my bra before lifting it to tease and pinch my nipples.

When I moaned against his lips, he broke the kiss only long enough to rid me of both my shirt and bra. That didn't stop his mouth from finding ways to connect with my skin. I loved how Dakas always became almost frantic whenever he undressed me.

Although he enjoyed how flattering clothes looked on me, my husband wished I could go around naked like he did. He wanted to feast his eyes on my body—which he adored, flaws and all— but he also wanted instant access. Seductive stripping did nothing for him. Clothes were just an annoyance to be ripped and discarded.

Thankfully, he didn't rip mine, but worked diligently at getting me out of them. Kissing a path down to my chest, he licked and laved my hardening nipple while unclasping my pants. Dakas didn't like me wearing pants, which he found even more infuriating than skirts. I normally wore dresses for him. However, knowing we were going flying, wearing pants had made more sense to me. From the look my husband gave me, he clearly disapproved.

Still, his lips followed a path down my stomach, pausing long enough for him to lick my outie navel before pursuing their journey south. At the same time, he tugged down my pants and panties. A smug chuckle escaped him as my stomach constricted with anticipation while he nipped at the tender flesh of my pelvis. Resting a hand on the soft feathers of his shoulder for support, I lifted a leg to step out of my pants. As soon as my foot cleared the fabric, Dakas grabbed that leg behind the knee, keeping it up and leaving me open so he could bury his face between my thighs.

Throwing my head back, I cried out and held onto both of his shoulders. Aside from his natural talent when it came to using his tongue, Dakas always masterfully used his empathic abilities to pleasure me exactly the way I wanted. In moments, he had me burning from the fire building within me. As we stood near the entrance of the cave, bathed in moonlight, the cool evening breeze on my feverish skin gave me goosebumps.

As soon as Dakas sensed me starting to crest, he inserted two fingers inside me, crooking them at the right angle to rub on my sweet spot. At the same time, he sucked on my clit with renewed vigor, making me climax with a sharp cry. My nails dug into his shoulders as I struggled to keep my balance, still standing on one leg. Through my haze, I felt his pain over a couple of down feathers I'd damaged close to his nape. The smugness radiating from him quelled any guilt that tried to rear its head.

Every time we had sex, I always managed to accidentally pluck a few of his down feathers. I had panicked at first, but he'd reassured me saying that the only way a Zelconian didn't lose feathers during sex was if his performance sucked. Flaunting a bald patch from making your woman see stars gave you major bragging rights—not that I wanted anyone to know our business.

Dakas finally put my leg back down and kissed his way back up my body and to my lips as he rose to his feet. I gratefully leaned against him to steady my wobbly legs. Still devouring my lips, Dakas lifted me. I instinctively wrapped my legs around his waist and felt him extrude. The warm wetness of his pre-lubricated and fully erect shaft pressed against my stomach. He broke the kiss to stare me in the eyes with an intensity that made me dizzy.

I didn't need him to tell me what he wanted. Without a word, I sneaked a hand between us and closed it around his stiff length. After giving it a good squeeze and a couple of strokes, I aligned it with my opening and carefully impaled myself on his cock. Dakas hissed with pleasure, his face taking on a snarling expression that was sexy as fuck. His sharp claws extruded from the tips of his fingers, stinging my butt cheeks as his grip tightened on me. I loved that sensation and the sliver of fear it elicited in me.

Fuck! He was so big. I would never tire of that wondrous feeling of fullness and the incredible extra sensations provided by the spiraling ridge around his shaft. It always felt like it was undulating inside of me, even though that wasn't the case. Holding me up, Dakas began to thrust upward into me, carefully at first as I adjusted to his non-negligible girth.

The midnight-blue of his constellation-filled eyes suddenly darkened, and the stars within became brighter. Seconds later, through the pleasure of his cock moving in and out of me, the familiar tingling of a psychic connection washed over me, starting from my head and flowing all the way down my body. When it reached my toes, I felt myself falling. My vision blurred, my environment replaced by a sea of stars in a midnight-blue void that matched his eyes.

Dakas had used his hypnotic powers on me before, usually to play pranks like making me think my zeebis Goro had walked into the house and was eating our plants. This was the first time he'd completely blurred my reality. A strangled cry escaped me and my arms tightened around his neck when the flapping sound of his wings reached my ears and the cool night wind caressed my burning skin as he soared.

Fear and exhilaration warred against the pleasure of my husband's cock still pumping into me as he flew us through an environment that I could no longer see. I'd wondered about sex in flight since the first time Phegea had mentioned in passing that some of them still observed the old tradition of the mating flight between newlyweds.

With my sight taken from me, every single one of my senses felt enhanced. I couldn't even see Dakas, only feel his strong body wrapped around me, holding me tightly, his mouth claiming mine as he pounded into me. Each stroke appeared to move in sync with the flapping of his wings, his length pulling out with an upward movement and thrusting back in with a downward movement.

I held onto him for dear life while surrendering to the sensory overload induced by this hypnotic blindness. It enhanced every sound, every touch. His pleasure and emotions flooding my empathic perceptions only increased my own, to the point where I felt on the verge of combusting. Only the cool air of the wind whipping past us kept my skin from bursting into flames.

The scent of water tickled my nose seconds before its cold touch licked my heated back.

I detonated, my body shaken by the violence of my orgasm. For a split second, I feared my spasms of ecstasy would throw Dakas off his flight and make us crash into the water. Yet, no fear emanated from him, only waves upon waves of pleasure, fueled by my own, and he continued to fly with a control that defied logic.

Although he spilled his seed inside of me during that second climax, Dakas kept thrusting until he wrested a third orgasm from me. I cried out his name. This time, he fully yielded to his own release, joining his voice to mine. I was too far gone to panic about his slightly erratic flight pattern. Through the haze of bliss, I eventually felt him land, and wrap his wings around my shivering body. Feeling safe and warm, cocooned in both his embrace and the tenderness of his emotions, I knew that I was falling in love with my husband.

～

Two days after our mating flight, Dakas started acting strangely. Although he assured me everything was fine—and he genuinely meant it—I could feel something was off. My husband was a major cuddler. Yet, whenever I tried to snuggle with him that day, he pulled away from me. It disturbed me all the more that he didn't even seem to realize he was doing it. His skin felt a little warmer than usual, and even his scent smelled a bit different.

None of it was significant enough for me to ask to examine him. I didn't want to look like I was blowing things way out of proportion. Dakas was probably just having one of those random foul mood or under-the-weather days everyone gets from time to time. Maybe it simply manifested in a different way than with humans. I left it alone, although I kept a discreet eye on him.

When he declared himself too tired to make love that night—he who normally woke me at least once if not twice every night for additional rounds—I knew something was wrong. I didn't fear that his growing feelings for me had changed. Dakas was definitely falling in love with me, as I was with him. The same tenderness continued to emanate from him whenever he saw me or talked to me. But something was affecting his mental state and natural propensity for physical displays of affection. He didn't even embrace me or cover me with his wing as he normally did when we slept.

My husband went out like a light. Although he had no trouble sleeping, Dakas usually stayed awake until I dozed off. Looking at him, curled up almost in a fetal position, when he'd specifically gotten a massive bed because he loved sprawling all over it, he made me think of a little boy bracing for the terrible thing he expected to strike him in the not-too-distant future. And yet, I perceived no sense of doom emanating from him.

I felt lost in our huge bed without his warmth against me. For the first time, I didn't enjoy that empathic ability so much. Right now, it confused me far too much. I prayed that whatever was bothering my husband would be gone in the morning. Closing my eyes, I surrendered to a fitful sleep, partly fueled by Dakas's strange emotions.

I woke up with a start. I couldn't say what triggered it, but a powerful wave of distress slammed into me the minute my eyes snapped open. Finding Dakas gone from our bed and far too many fallen feathers scattered on his side of the mattress freaked me out. The first thing that came to mind was that the shengis venom had somehow taken a hold again in Dakas. Only four days ago, I'd removed all of the antidote nanobots from his system since he'd developed enough antibodies of his own. Had that been a mistake?

"Dakas?" I called out as I jumped out of the bed and hurried to the bathroom whence his emotions emanated.

To my shock, his distress gave way to panic and shame …
but I perceived no actual pain. I opened the door to find him
standing in front of the large mirror that occupied the back of the
room, away from the water.

"Oh, my God, Dakas! What happened?!" I rushed towards
him, horrified, my blood turning to ice while trying to imagine
what in the world could have caused this.

"Don't touch me!" Dakas exclaimed, raising both of his
palms in front of him, his eyes widening with worry. I stopped
dead in my tracks, eyeing him with disbelief. "I'm fine."

"What the fuck do you mean you're fine?" I exclaimed, my
innards twisted with fear at his bedraggled appearance. "You've
lost all of your feathers, and your skin looks raw!"

And I wasn't even exaggerating. Most of his feathers lay in a
pool at his feet. A handful still hung onto his body, scattered here
and there. The skin that had once held feathers had taken a
purplish hue. Had his skin not been blue, those areas would have
been red. They were covered in a million tiny bumps that made it
look like only parts of his body had goosebumps. Even the
feathers of his crest and tail had fallen out. To my shock, I
noticed a large bag next him where he'd started stuffing his
fallen feathers.

"I'm just molting," Dakas mumbled, avoiding eye contact.

My jaw dropped, and my gaze slowly roamed over him as I
reevaluated his appearance with this new knowledge.

"But … but I thought birds gradually replaced their feathers
in stages," I argued. "They only lose a couple here and there at a
time. When they're done growing back, they lose a handful more
elsewhere so that they're never grounded."

Dakas's featherless wings shifted in that way I'd come to
recognize as either a shrug or a sign of embarrassment,
depending on the context.

"It is true of most birds, and of Zelconians in general," Dakas
conceded. "There are a few species that lose all of their feathers

pretty much at once or over a few days. As a hybrid, it has always been so in my case. I'll be helpless until they grow back, which generally takes two to three weeks, but sometimes up to four weeks."

I suddenly got flashbacks of some of the chickens in Anita's farm that had been separated from the others after losing most of their feathers. I'd assumed they'd been sick, so she'd isolated them to avoid spreading their illness to the others. Had they been molting?

"Wow, I see," I said, blown away. "I'm not actually feeling pain from you, but a lot of discomfort. Does it hurt?"

Dakas shook his head. "It doesn't exactly hurt, but my skin feels a little raw and is extremely sensitive. Physical contact isn't particularly pleasant."

To my undying shame, that made me feel better. He hadn't been keeping me at arm's length because he no longer wanted to snuggle with me but because it was physically uncomfortable.

He looked at himself with a dejected expression. "I'm sorry for my less-than-appealing appearance. I had hoped it wouldn't happen for a few more weeks. I'm afraid you're stuck with a husband looking like a plucked chicken for a little while."

The shame seeping back into his voice annoyed me.

"You do look like a plucked chicken," I said with a shrug, causing him to recoil in surprise. "But you're *my* plucked chicken, and you're not allowed to be embarrassed because of your appearance. Molting is a natural process for your species. I married a birdman, with all that it entails. Frankly, now that I know you're not dying, I think you rock the bedraggled look rather nicely," I added teasingly to lighten the mood.

Dakas snorted, his embarrassment waning, replaced with a sliver of amusement. "But that means I won't be able to hold you or snuggle with you for a while. I felt how it upset you when I was so distant last night."

I waved a dismissive hand. "You have nothing to apologize

for. I certainly didn't when I got my period two weeks ago and told you to stay away in no uncertain terms."

This time, Dakas chuckled. "You were rather grumpy and definitely not cuddly."

"Exactly. Now, it's your turn. I guess I'll finally get to see just how good you are at controlling those hover lifts," I said, eyeing him mockingly. "You sure made enough fun of me for my clumsiness."

Dakas groaned and took on a mulish expression. "I'm not leaving the house. Graith will not let me hear the end of it. He'll offer to carry me around just to annoy me."

I burst out laughing. The Exarch was the biggest brat I'd ever met. As much as he had intimidated me on our first meeting, I now loved him like both a pesky big brother, and that mischievous uncle or grandfather who you just can't resist helping to cause trouble.

"If it's going to take three to four weeks for your feathers to grow back, you won't be able to hide in here," I said with compassion. "First, you'll start climbing the walls being cooped up this long, and second, people will start wondering what I've done to you. Either way, Graith will find out."

Dakas's shoulders slumped in exaggerated defeat, which only made me chuckle more.

"Stop pouting," I said affectionately. I pointed at the feathers on the floor with my chin. "I'll pick these up, and then I'll apply a soothing cream on your skin. It does wonders for people with eczema or sunburns. I'll be gentle."

Dakas welcomed my offer but insisted on picking up the feathers with me. To my shock—although I should have anticipated it—he had us carefully divide the long feathers from the down ones. The former would go towards making arrows, while the latter would be used for pillows and cushions.

Applying the soothing ointment on my husband turned out to be quite the riot. I had initially feared it would have been too uncomfortable for him, but it was the loudest I ever heard him coo. The blissful expression on his face had me in stitches.

By the time I was done, his every emotion clamored as strong a desire to draw me into his embrace as I felt. I leaned forward and pressed my lips to his. We exchanged a long and tender kiss. His bedraggled appearance didn't affect my desire for him. He sensed the moment my arousal reared its head.

He broke the kiss, locked eyes with me. "You are so amazing, my Luana. Do you know how much I love you?"

My heart leapt in my chest, and I barely refrained from throwing myself at him and cuddling against him.

"I don't quite know," I said teasingly, although my voice quivered with emotion. "But you will have many years to show me and to find out how much I love you right back."

He beamed at me, his starry eyes even more arresting with his bare crest no longer commanding all the attention.

"I will enjoy every minute of it," he said before reclaiming my lips.

EPILOGUE
LUANA

During the first five days of his molting, Dakas remained quite sensitive and stubbornly refused to leave the house. He spent quite a bit of time on the terrace. However, the few times we got strong winds, he came right back inside, as even that bothered his skin. By the sixth day, the little fluff feathers that had been growing on his chest, shoulders, nape, and groin— similar to a baby bird's natal down—had become plush and fluffy, taking the tenderness away with it. Being able to cuddle with him against that insane softness was wonderful.

On the seventh day, during our first venture out into the inner city, Dakas received plenty of teasing. Thankfully, all of it was affectionate. He also got petted A LOT. Everyone and their brother, males, females, and especially children, wanted to caress his ridiculously soft fluff feathers. Despite mumbling and grumbling about charging a petting zoo fee, Dakas enjoyed the loving attention his people gave him.

During that time, I realized that every other Zelconian was also molting, but with a stark difference for the males—more specifically for the non-mated males. They, too, ended up with a somewhat strange appearance over those weeks as they molted into their breeding plumage. I'd thought their chest and crests had been beautifully colorful. But now, they were taking on much brighter hues than the duller feathers they'd previously had, which helped with camouflage during the non-breeding season. The patches of bright new feathers sprinkled amidst the dull ones had my OCD kicking into overdrive.

With the next migration looming closer, these males would be looking their finest with the vibrant colors of their chests and crests drawing the attention of the potential partners they would meet at the other Zelconian cities. While both genders could migrate, most of the travelers were males. They would split into four flocks, each heading towards a different Zelconian city.

Aside from allowing the single members of the tribe to find a mate, migration also lessened the burden on food requirements during winter. The Zelconians still largely relied on foraging and hunting for their supplies. This year, because of the exceptional situation, a majority of migrants would come to Synsara to keep the warrior numbers up in case things got heated again with the Yurus. With their granaries all but overflowing and the support our colony would provide, there would be no problem keeping everyone well-fed throughout winter.

But the Yurus didn't become a problem.

Zatruk kept his word. Kastan returned to a new normal where the energy wall remained down throughout the day, only going back up at night. People regained their freedom of movement, traipsing around the forest without fear. In fact, the Yurus leader opened discussions with my father about trade opportunities, mainly for grain and meat. They were tentative talks for now, but when Kayog showed up again, strongly encouraging such talks, I realized the UPO was up to something. My gut told me they were trying to bring the Yurus into the fold, but only time would tell.

To my surprise, I found out that chasing rogue fledglings around the city had actually inspired the Zelconians' national sport Lazgar, named after the most notorious little brat of all times. A special arena with looping obstacles that would shift over time had been set up near one of the outer plateaus of the city. There, groups of twelve to twenty individuals would chase after Lazgar—a drone—and attempt to capture it before time ran out. The more quickly you caught it, the greater your score.

Dakas was quite miserable about missing a few of those tournaments while waiting for his feathers to grow back. The minute they did, he went out of his way to show off just how badass he was at rocking this game. It was a good thing, too, because I had no intention whatsoever of learning how to use a jetpack to chase after our future little hellions. And God knows we didn't miss a chance to work on conceiving them.

In the meantime, Dakas and my father grew closer. My husband wasn't just a brilliant strategist, he was also an engineer. With the younger population demanding more and more changes, a great deal of revamping was happening, especially updating some of our most obsolete systems and materials with the high-end ones that the Zelconians possessed. Lara, the colony's engineer, was over the moon.

It also turned out to be a sneaky way for humans and Zelconians to exchange technology. Although the colony theoretically had full access to the public knowledge base shared by the members of the UPO, in practice, we faced a number of restrictions, especially when it came to advanced stuff like spaceships and weapons.

With the strong bond forming between our 'protectors' and us, the UPO had to make sure we didn't pass on too much expertise that would unduly accelerate the natives' access to interstellar travel and to technological evolution as a whole. It wasn't that they didn't want the Zelconians to achieve it, but they needed to be allowed to acquire the proper maturity that came with this type of revolution. You couldn't learn responsible development and use of technology unless you went through the painstaking process of creating it yourself, with all the moral dilemmas it entailed.

To my shock, I also discovered that my father was grooming Dakas to take on a leadership role in the colony. Like me, Dakas had mixed feelings about it. We both felt it was important that humans lead the colony. But Dad seemed to have something different in mind, not so much for Dakas to be the actual colony leader, but his or her right hand and Council member. I could see that. Anyway, it wasn't for anytime soon, and we were fine with that.

The other news that knocked me on my rear was Martin getting all googly eyed over a young Zelconian female named Shaya. Like him, she was a woodworker and one of the most talented sculptors of Synsara. She'd carved the stunning organic archways in our house. I didn't pry about whether she'd recognized him as her soulmate, and just wished them the best of luck.

I discovered that I was pregnant on the morning of our second human wedding in which my father would finally give me away.

Finding out how much Dakas had hated the public aspect of our first expedited marriage had left me speechless. He'd done such a wonderful job of not only hiding it but also of reassuring me. Renewing our vows so that we could have a proper wedding, with the dress, the flowers, and the maids of honor didn't make his toes curl. Still, he played along to make me happy and because he could see that it meant a lot to both my father and our people as a whole.

Learning that he was going to be a father made that day magical for him.

It was the most magnificent wedding of Kastan, with ornate

flower pots adorned with glowing crystals, more such light blue crystals woven into my dress, train, and veil, my stunning party of human and Zelconian bridesmaids and groomsmen, and Renok standing as his brother's best man.

The ceremony went by in a dream. Dakas and I answered Counselor Allan's questions and spoke our vows aloud. But the vows that truly mattered to me were the ones my husband and I exchanged telepathically, reaffirmed by our empathic bond that wrapped us in our mutual love.

"When I came to you all these months ago to beg for your assistance, I never thought it would so completely change my world," I said through mind-speak. *"Thank you for recognizing me as yours, for saving my people, for loving me more than I ever could have hoped for, and for lending me your wings so that I, too, could soar. I love you more than words can say and hope my emotions convey the depth of what you mean to me."*

A wave of love exploded out of him, crashing over me with such force my knees wavered.

"No, my love, it is I who must thank you," Dakas responded telepathically. *"After countless migrations, I had lost all hope of finding my soulmate, and then there you were. I was so different and imposed on you under difficult circumstances while your father fought for his life. You could have shut me down, maybe even resented us and our bond. But through all of these hardships, where most would have crumbled, you stood fast for your people, gave our union a chance, and embraced the future that we could have. You are steel and silk all wrapped into one. I only helped save your people. But YOU saved my life. You are my wife, my heart, and the other half of my soul. I love you, Luana."*

Dakas leaned forward and pressed his lips to mine.

I vaguely heard Counselor Allan gasp before speaking in a hesitant voice. "Err… we weren't quite there yet. But … uh … I guess you can kiss the bride."

As laughter and chuckles rose through the temple, I pressed myself against Dakas. He wrapped his wings around me, hiding us from prying eyes. Sheltered in the cocoon of his wings, I kissed my husband, my best friend, the love of my life.

THE END

VYRAX

ZEEBIS

ALSO BY REGINE ABEL

THE VEREDIAN CHRONICLES
Escaping Fate
Blind Fate
Raising Amalia
Twist of Fate
Hands of Fate
Defying Fate

BRAXIANS
Anton's Grace
Ravik's Mercy
Krygor's Hope

XIAN WARRIORS
Doom
Legion
Raven
Bane
Chaos
Varnog
Reaper
Wrath
Xenon

THE MIST
The Mistwalker
The Nightmare

BLOOD MAIDENS OF KARTHIA
Claiming Thalia

VALOS OF SONHADRA
Unfrozen
Iced

PRIME MATING AGENCY
I Married A Lizardman
I Married A Naga
I Married A Birdman
I Married A Merman

EMPATHS OF LYRIA
An Alien For Christmas

THE SHADOW REALMS
Dark Swan

OTHER
True As Steel
Bluebeard's Curse
Alien Awakening
Heart of Stone
The Hunchback

ABOUT REGINE

USA Today bestselling author Regine Abel is a fantasy, paranormal and sci-fi junky. Anything with a bit of magic, a touch of the unusual, and a lot of romance will have her jumping for joy. She loves creating hot alien warriors and no-nonsense, kick-ass heroines that evolve in fantastic new worlds while embarking on action-packed adventures filled with mystery and the twists you never saw coming.

Before devoting herself as a full-time writer, Regine had surrendered to her other passions: music and video games! After a decade working as a Sound Engineer in movie dubbing and live concerts, Regine became a professional Game Designer and Creative Director, a career that has led her from her home in Canada to the US and various countries in Europe and Asia.

Facebook
https://www.facebook.com/regine.abel.author/

Website
https://regineabel.com

Regine's Rebels Reader Group

https://www.facebook.com/groups/ReginesRebels/

Newsletter

http://smarturl.it/RA_Newsletter

Goodreads

http://smarturl.it/RA_Goodreads

Bookbub

https://www.bookbub.com/profile/regine-abel

Amazon

http://smarturl.it/AuthorAMS